"The truth is that you upset me when you said there is a connection between the two dead girls. I had not considered that. So I have been reading the files for two years back. I found these." Encino tapped the stack of folders. "I can't permit you to read them. But"—he sighed eloquently—"I must leave the office for a short time. How can I know what happens behind my back? Please use my desk."

Five seconds later, he was gone, and I was alone with his files. There were seven folders. Carol Christie's was on the top, and I took it first. By the time I finished, I was dripping sweat on his blotter. My shirt was soaked and sticking to my back, along with most of my jacket. I didn't ask Encino's permission to use his phone—I just grabbed it and dialed Ginny as well as I could with my hands shaking like cowards.

"Brew," she started, "what's wrong?"

I brushed past her anxiety. "I'm at Missing Persons. You've got to get down here."

"Why? What's happened?"

"There are seven of them," I said. "I don't care what the cops say, this is no accident."

"Make sense, Brew! Seven what?"

"Seven thirteen-year-olds. No, five. Two of them were twelve." I knew I wasn't getting through to her, but I couldn't help myself. I was too upset to pull it together.

"What the bloody hell are you talking about?"

I pushed the phone against the side of my head as hard as I could, trying to make that damn inanimate plastic steady me. I wanted to howl, but I couldn't get enough air into my lungs. "Carol Christie didn't drown because she couldn't swim. She drowned because she OD'ed on heroin. And that's not all. Before she drowned, she—" But I couldn't say it over the phone. Carol was only thirteen. There are some things you can hardly say out loud at all.

"I'm on my way," Ginny told me. "I'll be there in fifteen minutes." Then the line went dead, leaving me with nothing but an empty phone to hang on to.

THE MAN
WHO KILLED
HIS BROTHER

Stephen R. Donaldson

TOR®

A TOM DOHERTY ASSOCIATES BOOK
NEW YORK

This is a work of fiction. All the characters and events portrayed in this book are either products of the author's imagination or are used fictitiously.

THE MAN WHO KILLED HIS BROTHER

Copyright © 1980, 2002 by Stephen R. Donaldson

All rights reserved, including the right to reproduce this book, or portions thereof, in any form.

Edited by Patrick Nielsen Hayden

A Tor Book
Published by Tom Doherty Associates, LLC
175 Fifth Avenue
New York, NY 10010

www.tor.com

Tor® is a registered trademark of Tom Doherty Associates, LLC.

ISBN: 0-765-34125-5

First edition: November 2002
First mass market edition: October 2003

Printed in the United States of America

0 9 8 7 6 5 4 3 2 1

—to *Barbara, Jim,* and *Debbie,*
the best siblings I could wish for

PART ONE

Tuesday Night/Wednesday

I was sitting at the bar of the Hegira that night when Ginny came in. The barkeep, an ancient sad-eyed patriarch named José, had just poured me another drink, and I was having one of those rare moments any serious drunk can tell you about. A piece of real quiet. José's cheeks bristled because he didn't shave very often, and his apron was dingy because it didn't get washed very often, and his fingernails had little crescents of grime under them. The glass he poured for me wasn't all that clean. But the stuff he poured was golden-amber and beautiful, like distilled sunlight, and it made the whole place soothing as sleep—which drunks know how to value because they don't get much of it.

It made the dull old fly-brown *santos* against the wall behind the bottles look like the saints knew what they were doing and it made the drinkers at the tables look peaceful and happy. It made the men playing pool in the back of the room look like they were moving in slow motion, flowing through the air as if it were syrup. It made José look wise and patient behind his stubble and his groggy eyes. It was one of those rare moments when everything is in the right place, and there's a soft gold light shining on it, and you feel like you're being healed. It never lasts—but you always think it will, if you just stay where you are and don't stop drinking.

By the curious logic of the drunk, I felt I'd earned it. After all, I'd been drinking most of the time for several days now, just trying to create that amber glow for myself. So when Ginny walked in the door—when every head in the bar turned to stare at her—I didn't know which to feel first, surprise or resentment. There wasn't any doubt she was looking for me.

I had the right to be surprised. For one thing, she had no business walking into the Hegira like that—especially at night. The Hegira is down in the old part of Puerta del Sol, on Eighth Street between Oak and Maple. Cities are like that: The old parts—where the descendants and countrymen of the founders live—have street names like "Eighth" and "Oak." The rich suburbs—half of them built in the last ten years—have flashier names like "Tenochtitlán" and "Montezuma." And in the old part of town women don't go into bars at all. When the Chicano and Mestizo and Indian women want their men to come out, they stand on the sidewalk and send in their children.

As Ginny pushed her way through the door, scanned the room, and came striding over toward me, the quiet buzz of voices stopped. José's eyes went blank and empty—you could tell if she spoke to him he was going to say he didn't speak English. The men with the pool cues stood very still, as if they were waiting to start a different kind of game.

But I also had another reason to be surprised. This wasn't the way Ginny was supposed to come looking for me. She came looking for me often enough—I would've probably drunk myself to death by now if she hadn't been so faithful about it—but this wasn't the way. We had a system worked out, and she was breaking it.

What the system did was let me get ready. She didn't bother me in the morning, when I was taking those first stiff drinks, trying to push the sickness back down my throat where it belonged. She didn't bother me during the day, when I was drinking slow and steady to control the shakes. She didn't bother me in the afternoon, when I started to hit the bottle harder because the stuff didn't seem to be having any effect. She didn't bother me in the evening, when I went to places like the Hegira looking for amber and comfort. She didn't bother me when I left whatever bar it was and bought a bottle and wandered away into the night to pay the price.

No, we had a system.

When I was ready for her, I knew where to go at night with my bottle. One of the benches in a cheap little park down on Tin Street. It was still in the old part of town, which meant the city didn't water the grass and the cops didn't roust drunks who spent the night there. And when the sun came up I'd be sitting on that bench, waiting—just waiting because I was too sick to hope. And then I'd see her walking over to me. She always came from the east—the sun was always behind her, so I couldn't see her face. She always said, "Brew." (My name is Mick Axbrewder, but not even my enemies call me Mick.) I always said, "Ginny." And then she always said, "I need you."

That's when I knew I was going to get sober and go back to work.

Sometimes I said, "What do you need me for? I'm a drunk." But that was just a variation. She never gave me a straight answer. I wouldn't have known what to do with a straight answer.

So I was surprised when she walked into the Hegira looking for me. But I resented it, too. I was having one of those rare moments, and she took it away from me. And I wasn't ready.

But Ginny Fistoulari isn't the kind of woman who lets things like that stand in her way. She's tall—about the only time she doesn't look tall is when I'm standing beside her—and five years younger than I am, with the kind of lean and ready look about her you see in a good racehorse. Her eyes are the same color gray as the .357 Smith & Wesson she carries in her purse, but other than that you wouldn't know she's tough as rivets unless you look at her up close. From a few feet away she's just an attractive blonde with a nice mouth, delicate nostrils, and a perfect chin.

Up close you can see her nose was broken once—broken the way a nose gets broken when somebody clips it with a crowbar. The clown who did it didn't live to regret it. She shot him three times in the face. For that the commission almost took away her license. She's tough the way you have to be tough in order to spend your time getting involved in the messy side of other people's problems. As a result, she's reasonably successful. Fistoulari Investigations can afford to refuse surveillance cases and domestic problems, even if it isn't making her rich.

Maybe she would've made more money if she hadn't insisted on dragging me back to work every time one of her cases got hard. Maybe in the long run she could've had pricier clients if that big goon working for her (me) wasn't always in trouble with the cops for carrying out investigations without a license. I don't know. When I was sober, I never asked her why she put up with me. I just did the work. She didn't have any use for my gratitude.

But this time I wasn't grateful. I wasn't ready. When I saw her striding straight at me as if the Hegira and all its patrons didn't exist, I wanted to tell her to go to hell. I could see from the way the men watched her that I was never going to be welcome in the Hegira again. And I resented that—a bar where you can get amber and quiet is hard to find. The words were right there in my mind. *Go to hell, Ginny Fistoulari.*

If I'd said that, she probably would've turned around and walked away and never come back. So it was a good thing I kept my mouth shut.

But I had to do something. I swung away from her and went back to my drink. The stuff was there waiting for me. It was the right color, even if the feeling was gone. I wrapped my fist around the glass and raised it in the direction of my face.

Ginny's hand came down hard on my wrist, slapped the glass back to the counter so hard the stuff spilled all over my fingers. Which isn't easy to do to me, even when I'm not expecting it.

If anyone else had done it—anyone at all—I would've taken their hand off. At the wrist. People don't do that kind of thing to me—just like they don't call me Mick.

Only this wasn't anyone else. It was Ginny Fistoulari. I couldn't even try to get her hand off of me. I was doing everything I was capable of when I worked up enough energy to be mad.

"God damn it, Ginny—"

She came right back at me. "God damn it, Brew"—she

had one of those voices that can do anything, melt in your mouth or tear your skin off your bones—"you're going to come with me, or I swear to God I'll let you have it right here." At the moment she sounded like being pistol whipped. She didn't shout—she didn't have to. When she used that tone on me, there was no question about which one of us was in charge.

So much for my being mad. I've never been able to be mad at her at the same time she was mad at me. Which is probably a good thing. But this time I didn't have the vaguest idea *why* she was mad at me.

I didn't want to have any ideas. I wanted to drink. Without looking at her, I said, "I'm not ready."

Her voice practically jumped at me. "I don't give a flying fuck at the moon whether you're ready or not. You're going to come with me."

That reached me. Ginny doesn't talk that way very often. Only when she's furious. I turned, met her eyes.

She didn't look furious. The anger was just in her voice, not in her face. Instead, she was worried. Her nostrils were flaring and pale, and there were lines at the corners of her eyes that showed only when she's worried. And her eyes were wet. They looked like they might overflow any second now.

I couldn't remember the last time I'd seen her look so concerned. Concerned about me. All of a sudden my throat was dry, and I could barely scrape the words out. "What's the matter?"

Anybody else, and the tears would've been running down her cheeks. But not her. She was Ginny Fistoulari, private investigator. Licensed by the state to work on other people's misery. Human trouble and pain did a lot of different things to her, but they didn't make her cry. She just looked straight at me through the wet and said with all the anger gone out of her voice, "Your niece is missing."

I heard her, but something about it didn't penetrate. "Alathea?" Of course I had a niece, my dead brother's daughter. Her mother hated me. Alathea was another one of those people I was responsible for without being able to do anything about it. And on top of that I liked her. But I couldn't seem to remember what she looked like. "Missing?"

I couldn't call up an image. All I got was her name—and a blank wall of dread. "What're you talking about?"

Ginny didn't flinch. "Lona called me today. I've been looking for you ever since. Alathea has been missing for a week."

I went on staring at her. Then it got through to me. Alathea was missing. Her mother had called Ginny. Ginny had come looking for me. We had work to do.

There were things about it that didn't make sense. But right then they didn't matter. Not with Alathea missing, and Ginny looking at me like that. I fumbled some money onto the bar, got off my stool and started for the door. I didn't know how much I owed because I didn't know how much I had to drink, but José didn't even blink at me so I must've paid him enough—or else he was just glad to get a woman out of his bar without trouble. I stumbled once, then Ginny took my arm. I didn't say good-bye to the Hegira. Together we went out into the night.

2

Ginny took me back to my apartment to get me sobered up. I didn't have a car, and she'd left hers at my apartment, so we had to walk.

I live in one of those run-down apartment houses on the edge of the old part of town. The place was just far enough from the center to have been named La Cienga Apartments, but still close enough to be in danger of being torn down for urban renewal every time the city fathers felt like they had to make some kind of choice between "modern" and "quaint." In Puerta del Sol those words are really two different names for "*profitable*"—the city is growing, and people like to come for a visit, so it's just a question of whether money is going to be made from redeveloping real estate or from tourism.

Right then I didn't give a damn. They could blow up the place or sell tickets to my bedroom for all I cared. I was in one of those horrible "between" places any drunk can tell you about—too drunk to cope, not drunk enough to be anesthetized. I was half blind with dread and my mind kept repeating, *Alathea Alathea, Alathea.* I wanted Ginny to talk to me, tell me what was going on. But she just hung on to my arm and dragged me along and didn't say a thing.

The walk must've done me some good. She didn't have to carry me upstairs.

At least I was spared the embarrassment of a messy apartment. I'm tidy enough when I'm sober, and I hardly ever visit my apartment when I'm drinking. The place smelled musty and it needed dusting, but it wasn't a mess.

I was a mess. Getting sober is something I usually do for myself. It's not a pretty business, and you don't like having people watch. With Ginny there I kept noticing things that didn't usually bother me—like the fact that I couldn't put one foot in front of the other. Or that I stank. How many days had I been wearing these clothes? I had no idea. I needed a drink, and I didn't like having Ginny see it.

She didn't give me any choice. Before I could get past Alathea's name to try do something for myself, she had me undressed, God knows how. When you're six foot five and two hundred forty pounds, other people usually can't just take your clothes away from you. Then she pried me into the shower. She slammed on the water and left me there as if she wanted me to drown. But after a while she came back, scrubbed me, got me out of the shower and into an old bathrobe. Then she began pouring coffee down me.

That lasted for a while. Then the coffee and the other stuff started to do a little dance inside me, and I threw up for a while. After that I felt better. I was about to tell Ginny about Alathea when I fell asleep.

It was dawn before she woke me up and began treating me again. Orange juice, coffee, toast, vitamin pills of all kinds. She's a vitamin freak—carries whole bottles in her purse, along with her .357. She even got me shaved. But it was close to nine before I was in any condition to go anywhere. All that time she didn't say a word. And I didn't ask any questions. I was too sick.

I was going to be sicker. Already I wanted a drink so bad it brought tears to my eyes—and this was just the beginning. Shame is an awkward thing to live with, and having Ginny there, having her see me like this, made me ashamed on top of all the other remorse and responsibility. And there aren't many cures for it. Sometimes work is one of them. But the only one you can actually count on is alcohol.

But Alathea was missing. When Ginny asked me if I was ready to go, I didn't answer right away. I went over to the dresser in the bedroom half of the apartment and got out my gun, a .45 automatic, which is about the only gun I've ever found that doesn't feel like a toy in my hand. I checked it over, made sure it was loaded, then strapped on the shoulder holster and put the .45 under my left arm. Then I looked Ginny in the eye as steadily as I could and said, "Alathea is my niece. My brother's daughter. She's thirteen years old, and beside the fact she's one of those cute kids that makes you happy just to look at her, she also happens to like me. For some reason, Lona has never told her exactly what happened to her father. She thinks I'm just her nice old Uncle Brew. And besides that, she's solid as a rock. Half the time these days when things get too much for Lona, Alathea carries her—which is one hell of a job for a thirteen-year-old—and she does it beautifully. It doesn't matter whether I'm ready or not. Let's go."

For a second there, Ginny almost smiled. The lines of worry around her eyes faded. She seemed to shake herself, and then it was as if she hadn't been up most of the night taking care of me. She didn't look tired anymore. "That's more like it," she said, mostly to herself. She handed me a jacket, and a minute later I was walking down the stairs.

Talk is cheap. I wasn't ready, and it showed. I almost didn't make it down the stairs. My knees felt like mush, and the stairwell kept trying to stand on edge. There was a little voice in the back on my head saying, *You need a drink you need a drink you need a drink*. It wasn't easy to ignore, even with Ginny watching me.

But I didn't figure out why she was acting so much like she was worried about me until she took my arm to steer me toward her car. Of course she knew all about the connection between me and Alathea. Now she thought something serious had happened to my niece. She was afraid of what knowing that would do to me. She knew killing Richard had pushed me right to the edge. She was afraid whatever happened to Alathea would push me over.

I wanted to ask her about that. Ask, hell! I wanted to drag it out of her. But I put it off. Just climbing into her Olds left me weak as an old man. And I'd forgotten my sunglasses. Already the sun was beating down on the streets like bricks out of the dry thin blue sky. Made my eyes hurt. If it hadn't been for the tinted glass in the Olds, I might not have survived as far as Lona's house.

*   *   *

Lona Axbrewder, my brother's widow. I wasn't exactly her favorite person. There was one question I had to ask. When we parked in front of the house, I stayed where I was for a minute, trying not to hold my head in my hands. Then I said, "Why did she call you? You know how she feels about me."

"Ask her yourself," Ginny said. "I'm not a mind reader." But her voice was stiff, and I'd heard that stiffness before. It meant she knew the answer and didn't want to tell me.

"Maybe," I muttered to myself. Maybe I would ask her. I was in no condition to know what I was going to do. I had enough problems just getting the door open and climbing out onto the sidewalk.

Lona lives down on Mission Street in a neighborhood that's only about two levels up from my apartment building. None of the houses for blocks in all directions are new, none of them look big enough to have more than two bedrooms, and none of them are out of spitting range from the house next door. But it's a nice enough neighborhood, and people don't spit. Lona's house is adobe, but that squat brown shape is softened by rose trellises that frame the top and sides of the front door. She must've watered those roses twice a day to make them look so nice.

I spent a minute standing on the sidewalk, looking around. Trees along the walk cut out a lot of the sun, and after the glare of the roads and traffic it was restful in a way to just stand there, looking. The whole place was restful—shade, trees, grass, tidy brown houses. It looked like the kind of place where nothing ever happens. I didn't want to move—didn't want to find out any different.

But Ginny took my arm again, and before I knew it we were standing in front of the door, and the door was opening, and Lona was telling us to come in. Then the door shut behind us, and my retreat was cut off. I felt like I'd made a fatal mistake. The voice in my head started to shout, *You need a drink*! It sounded desperate.

Dumbly, I let Ginny steer me. We followed Lona into the living room and sat down.

I couldn't see very clearly. The room was too dark—she

had all the shades pulled down and didn't turn on any lights. That made the air dim and cool and comforting, which was nice. It almost seemed like she did it for my benefit, as if she had any reason in the world to give a good goddamn how I felt. But it didn't let me read her face. I wanted to know how hard she was taking this thing. That would tell me a lot.

The outlines I could do from memory. She was small and vague and somehow brittle, like most wives of cops I've ever met. They don't start out that way. It just happens to them because they're afraid of losing their husbands, and they can't share the danger—or even the strain—and they can't feel good about it because nobody loves a cop. It's like living with a man who has some kind of terminal disease. She had medium-length brown hair and a habit of pushing both hands through it, pulling it away from her temples as if she were trying to drag some horrible grimace off her face. Even before she lost her husband she used to make me nervous. Now she could've made me scream with no trouble at all.

She sat Ginny and me down on the Naugahyde couch across from the TV, then asked us if we wanted any coffee. Ginny said, "Yes, thanks," before I could even think about the question. Lona pushed her hands through her hair, then left us alone.

I suppose I should have been thinking about Alathea—as a way of fighting off the need—but I was too strung out to have any control over my thoughts. I was sitting exactly where I used to sit when Richard and I watched football together. I knew from memory that there was a picture of him sitting on top of the TV, staring at me with that lopsided grin of his. Richard Axbrewder, my younger brother. Rick and Mick. It was when he died that people stopped calling me Mick.

Died, hell. I killed him, and half the city knows it. The papers didn't exactly play it down. One of them had it right there on the front page,

PRIVATE INVESTIGATOR KILLS COP. BROTHER

SHOOTS BROTHER. There's no way I can pretend I didn't do it.

It happened five years ago, when Ginny and I were partners. I remember everything about it. I was sitting at a table by the window in Norman's, which is one of those downtown bars that caters to the business-man-getting-off-work trade. It just happened to be right across from the First Puerta del Sol National Bank. I was having a few drinks— exactly six, according to the testimony of the barkeep—and trying to make up my mind about whether I wanted or had the nerve to ask Ginny to marry me. Not an unpleasant kind of indecision, and I had enough stuff in me to glow while I thought about it. It was almost dark outside, but the street-lights hadn't come on yet so I couldn't see very well, and the air was dim and relaxed.

Then I heard gunfire. I snapped a look out the window and saw a man running away from the bank in my direction. He was carrying a bag of some kind and waving a gun over his shoulder, shooting at something behind him. There was a cop chasing him. I jumped to the conclusion he'd just robbed the bank.

I was out the door and on the sidewalk in no time. I had the .45 in my hand. I shouted at the man to stop. When he pointed his gun at me, I fired a couple of times. He kept running, but the cop chasing him went down.

It turned out the man was a purse snatcher. Richard had already been chasing him for three blocks. If the snatcher hadn't had a gun, I would've been indicted for manslaughter. As it was, the commission read the results of my blood-alcohol test, charged me with "negligence," and took away my license. For good.

The cops were not amused. For a while, a bunch of them used to roust me every time we ran across each other. I spent a lot of time in the drunk tank in those days while bruises I couldn't remember getting turned black-and-blue on my ribs and face. Probably that was where I got in the habit of not letting anybody touch me. But after a couple of years they let it ride. Then I got into trouble only when some cop got the bright idea I was working for Ginny without a license. But that's pretty hard to prove, because I was careful and I never got caught doing the kinds of things you're not allowed to do without a license. So far I've been able to get away with it.

So what? So now I don't drink in bars like Norman's anymore. I go down to the old part of town, where they don't care what I look like or smell like as long as my money's green and my Spanish doesn't sound like it came out of a textbook in some Anglo school. When I'm not working on a case for Ginny, I'm drunk. When I am working on a case, I'm sober. She's the one friend I've got, and everybody who remembers Richard hates me. Except Alathea. She doesn't know I shot her father.

Or at least she *didn't* know. Maybe she was missing because she ran away when she found out the truth—the truth her mother hadn't told her.

I was trembling deep down inside my gut. When Lona brought the coffee, I had to hold the cup with both hands to keep from spilling it. While I drank it down, she stood right in front of me as if she was waiting until I finished to start screaming at me. But she just refilled my cup, then put the pot down where Ginny could reach it, and went to sit in the armchair beside the TV. Her hands she knotted in her lap, as if she were trying to keep them out of trouble.

When she spoke, her face was aimed at me, and her voice was brittle. "Will you take the case?"

"Of course," Ginny said smoothly. Her tone was sympathetic-neutral. Gentle but businesslike. The kind of tone she uses when she doesn't want a client to break down. "But I have to ask you a lot of questions."

"Yes." Lona sounded small and far away. The light was so dim I couldn't even see her lips move—her voice could've come from anywhere in the room. All of a sudden, I knew for a fact it was serious. Lona wouldn't have me sitting in front of her like this if it wasn't serious. She kept the room dark so I couldn't see the need in her face.

The trembling climbed up through my bones. I had to clamp my forearms between my knees to keep from shivering.

"How long has she been gone?" Ginny asked.

"Eight days." Her voice was as brittle as it could get. Brittleness was the only defense she had left. "Last week Tuesday she went to school and didn't come home."

"Did you call the school?"

"Yes. That evening. First I called some of her friends, but they didn't know where she was. They said they hadn't seen her since PE. So then I called the school. She goes to Mountain Junior High. It's just five blocks up the street. They said after fifth period she wasn't in any of her classes. Fifth period was PE. They thought she must've gotten sick and gone home. But she didn't come home. She didn't." Lona was insistent. "I don't have anywhere to go on Tuesdays and I was here all the time."

"I understand," Ginny said. As smooth as Vaseline. "What did you do after you called the school?"

"I waited—I waited a while." Her hands were starting to twist in her lap. One of them went up to push at her hair, but she jerked it back down again. "As long as I could stand. Then I called the police."

"You called the police." Ginny was good at neutral sympathy. I wasn't. Alcohol is a jealous comforter, and it doesn't like to let go. Right then my nerves had all the abstinence they could stand, and now they were going to get even with me. I was going into withdrawal. I was shaking all over. My head was shivering on my neck—my brains rattled in my skull. The need was using a vise to squeeze sweat out of my forehead. My jaws hurt because I was grinding my teeth, but I had to do something to keep from groaning out loud. I had to have something to hang on to, and the only thing in reach was Lona's voice.

"Yes," she said, in the same small brittle voice. "I talked to Missing Persons. Sergeant Encino. I've talked to him half a dozen times, but he doesn't help. He says he wants to help, but he doesn't. The first"—for a second her voice shuddered as if she was about to lose control, but she didn't—"the first time I talked to him, he said she'd probably be home in a couple of days. He said kids are like that, they run away, and then they come home. He gets cases like that all the time. He said—he said it's department policy that they don't even start looking for runaways for three days. It's about impossible to find runaways because most of them are trying hard not to be found, and anyway most of them come home in three days. That's what he said.

"If I wanted the police to start looking for her right away, he said, I'd have to go down and swear out a complaint against her. File charges against her! He advised me not to do that. If I did, he said, the police would start looking for her right away, but if they found her they wouldn't bring her home. It's not against the law to run away and they couldn't bring her home against her will. They'd put her in some kind of juvenile shelter—he called it a JINS facility—where she could run away again whenever she wanted, and I wouldn't get her back until a judge in juvenile court ruled on my complaint.

"I said, What if she hasn't run away? What if something happened to her? But he just told me to try not to worry, and to call him when she came home."

She dug out a handkerchief and blew her nose. Then she went on. "So I did what he told me. I tried to wait. He's a police officer, isn't he? He works for Missing Persons, doesn't he? He knows what he's talking about, doesn't he?" She was talking to Ginny now, asking Ginny to tell her she'd done the right thing.

But after a minute, she aimed herself at me again. "I tried to wait. But I couldn't. I called him again Wednesday, and Wednesday night. I asked him to check the hospitals. Maybe she was hurt. Maybe she was in a hospital, and the doctors couldn't call me because they didn't know who she was and she was hurt too bad to tell them.

"He told me I didn't have to worry about that. He said the hospitals always call the police when they have a patient they can't identify and they hadn't had any calls like that recently.

"I wanted to call the hospitals myself, but I didn't. I waited. I used to do a lot of waiting when Richard was alive."

I was dripping sweat, and my head almost split open when she said his name.

"I tried to do it again, but it wasn't the same. He was a grown man. He was doing what he wanted to do. She's a child. A child!"

"What happened then?" Ginny asked. She might as well have been living in another world. Lona was talking to me. She and I were tied together in that dim room by fear and need. Ginny's questions were just cues, promptings.

"Thursday in the mail I got a letter from her." She didn't offer to show it to us. "It said, 'Dear Mom, I'm not going to be coming home for a while. I've got something to work out. It might take a long time. Don't worry. I'll be all right. Love Al—Al—'" But she couldn't say the name. For a long minute she didn't go on. I could feel her eyes on me, but I wasn't looking at her. I was looking at the place where the sweat was dropping from my face onto my pants and sinking in, making a dark patch in the material—just watching the sweat fall and hanging on to her voice.

"What did you do after you got the note?"

With an effort, Lona got started again. "I—I called Sergeant Encino. What else could I do? I asked him to help me. He told me I'd have to file a complaint. Even though she's just a child." She didn't shout, but the protest in her voice was so strong it almost made me lose my grip.

Ginny asked softly, "Did you do it?"

"No."

"You don't believe the note." It was just a statement of fact.

"No!" She was so vehement I looked up at her. "She wouldn't run away from me. Never!"

"I appreciate that, Mrs. Axbrewder, but it doesn't prove anything. Can you tell me why you're so sure?"

The question didn't faze her. She'd thought about it a lot since Missing Persons had asked her the same thing. "Because she wasn't the kind of girl who runs away from problems. If she had something bothering her, something she hadn't told me—which I don't believe—she wouldn't have to run away from it. Her father taught her"—then she faltered, but only for a second—"her father taught her to stand her ground."

I believed her. I was in pain from head to foot—I wanted to pound my hands on my knees, just to distract myself from the hurting inside—but I believed her. If Alathea had run away because she found out about me and her father, found out her mother had never told her the truth, then the note didn't fit. She would have been angry, and it wasn't an angry note. And I couldn't think of anything else in the world she would run away from. She wasn't the kind of kid who gets herself into trouble she can't handle. She had too much common sense.

Lona was right, the note didn't fit at all. There had to be something wrong with it. Something. But I was in no condition to figure out what. I wanted more coffee—wanted to try to trick my nerves into thinking the stuff was on its way—but I couldn't control my shakes enough to even pick up the cup. Something inside me was at the breaking point. If this withdrawal went on much longer, I was going to be a basket case.

Ginny must've been thinking along the same lines, because she asked, "What about the handwriting? Do you recognize it?"

"It's hers," Lona said carefully, "but it's different than usual. She has such neat writing, she's always gotten A's in penmanship, and this is so messy. It looks like she wrote it while she was riding in a car over a rough road."

"How about a postmark?"

"Sergeant Encino asked me about that. It was mailed right here in town."

Suddenly I passed over the crest and the crisis began to recede. You never know if the first one is going to be the worst or the easiest, but this one was beginning to let go of me. The pain ran out of me like dirty dishwater. It left me feeling like I'd been bedridden half my life, but at least I was able to get my voice back. Without looking at Lona, or unclenching myself at all for fear the need might turn around and come back at me before I had the chance to recover, I asked her, "How was the note signed?"

She didn't answer. I could feel the air of the living room pleading with me, raging at me, hating me, but she didn't answer.

My voice grated in my throat. "How did she sign her name?"

A long time passed. Finally Lona pulled herself together enough to say faintly, "Alathea."

Alathea. That was it. Proof this whole thing was serious—that there was trouble worse than just a runaway thirteen-year-old. It was a minute or two before I realized I hadn't said what I was thinking out loud. From somewhere inside I mustered up the strength to say, "She never called herself Alathea. Everyone else did, but she didn't. She called herself 'Thea.' That's what her father called her, and she never called herself anything else."

"That's right," Lona said. Just echoing what she heard in my voice. She knew it was true. It just hadn't occurred to her.

"All right." Ginny said. "I can accept that." Back-to-business Ginny Fistoulari. "We'll take the case on that basis. I don't know what all I'll need from you, but I'd like to start with a list of her friends. Names, addresses, phone numbers for everyone you can think of."

"Sergeant Encino asked that. I thought you'd want a copy." She got up and handed Ginny a sheet of paper, then went back to her chair. She never turned her face away from me the whole time. We weren't finished with each other yet.

But Ginny wasn't finished either. Maybe she didn't like being left out of the silence. She stood it for half a minute, then said, "I've just got one more question, Mrs. Axbrewder. Alathea disappeared last week Tuesday. Why did you wait more than a week to call me?"

"Sergeant Encino told me to wait and try not to worry. He told me she'd come back when she was ready. I thought I was doing what Richard—what Richard would want me to do. But then I read, in yesterday's paper—I read about that Christie girl." She was under too much strain. Her brittleness was starting to crack. "Since she didn't come home, I've been reading the paper every day. Every word. I've been looking for some kind of news that would tell me what happened.

"Yesterday I read about that poor Christie girl. Carol Christie. The paper said"—she was right on the edge—"she ran away from home three months ago, and Monday they found her body in the river. She was just thirteen, the same age as my Alathea." Her hands were jammed into her hair, pulling at the sides of her head as if that was the only way she could keep herself from crying. "The same age."

I didn't have anything else to offer, so I gave her something to get mad about, hoping it would help her hang onto herself. "But why us, Lona? Why me? If you have to have a detective, you could've called some of Richard's friends on the force. They would've referred you to someone you could trust."

"Because you owe me!" Her sudden vehemence was as physical as a fist. "You took my husband away from me! You owe me my daughter back!"

"We'll do our best." Ginny came between Lona and me as if she were afraid we were about to start hitting each other. "There are no guarantees in this business, but we'll do everything we can. Which is more than the police are doing.

"Now." Ginny was on her feet, and I joined her. Force of habit. I didn't actually feel strong enough to stand. And I sure didn't want to tower over Lona like that. It was a cheap advantage, and with her I didn't want any cheap advantages. But I've been following Ginny so long now, taking orders from her, I hardly ever think about it anymore. "There's one thing we have to settle before we can get started. My fee."

"There doesn't have to be any fee," I said, ashamed money had ever been mentioned.

"Mrs. Axbrewder has to pay something," Ginny snapped. "If she doesn't, I can't call her my client. And if she isn't my client, I don't have any legal standing. Anybody who wants to can tell me to stuff it."

There was no help for it. Lona was looking at me, and I had to say, "She's right, Lona."

She didn't say anything for a long minute. When she found her voice again, she wasn't angry any more, just weak and helpless, and at the end of her rope. "I don't have much," she said. "Richard's pension is so small. And my job—I work as much as I can, cleaning house for some of the neighbors. It's hardly enough to pay for clothes." Then she said, "I have a hundred dollars."

Ginny said, "Fifty will be plenty." Fifty bucks would just about pay two days' rent on her office. "If I get in trouble with the commission I can always tell them it was only an advance."

The commission frowns on private investigators who work cheap. The same kind of argument doctors and lawyers use—people who work cheap are presumed to be shoddy and unscrupulous. Unprofessional. If I still had a license, I'd be in danger of losing it twice a day.

Lona shuffled out of the room and came back a minute later with the money. Ginny took it without counting it and gave her a receipt. Before I could think of anything else to say, Ginny and I were out on the walk again and Lona had closed the door behind us. In the whole time I hadn't had one good look at her face.

Ginny made straight for the car, but I dawdled along for a moment. Though the sun was getting hotter, in the shade of the trees it was still bearable. I wasn't eager to sear my butt on the vinyl of the Olds. And I wasn't satisfied, either. There were things I needed to know.

"All right," I said at Ginny's back. "Spill it."

She stopped, then turned around, looking blank. "Spill what?"

But she couldn't fool me with that. Her face has more than one kind of blank, and this wasn't the right kind. Besides, she'd turned around too quickly—like she was expecting me to say something.

"You know what I'm talking about."

She came back toward me a couple of steps. "When you've been drinking I never know what you're talking about."

That was a cheap shot, and she knew it. As soon as she

said it, she winced in regret. But I sloughed it off. It just confirmed she knew something she wasn't telling. So I said, "The hell you don't. You're scared of this case, Fistoulari. You're scared of it because of me. You're afraid something about it is going to get to me. I want to know why."

"You heard her." Ginny nodded at the house. "She didn't tell me any secrets."

"Yeah," I growled. "First you're worried about me, and then you won't tell me why. If you've got so goddamn little confidence in me, why didn't you just leave me out of it? You don't need me to find a runaway."

Now she came close and looked right up at me. "She's your niece. You've got a right to be involved. Besides, I thought you'd want—"

"Don't say it. Of course I want to help find her." For a minute I glanced around the neighborhood, looking for suggestions. Then I locked on to her again. Something about that broken nose of hers did funny things to my insides. Sometimes I wanted to kiss it so bad I had to grit my teeth. Now I wanted to hit it. "Maybe I'm asking the wrong question. Let's be professional about it. It's just a case. Like any other case. There's just one thing wrong with it. You don't do missing persons. Why start now?"

"She's your—"

I didn't let her finish. "Don't do me any favors."

That got through to her. All of a sudden, her eyes went cold and narrow, and her nostrils flared. Just for a second, her voice had the soft hot sound of an acetylene torch. "That's cute, Axbrewder. All right, you want it? You got it. I read the papers, too. I read about Carol Christie. There's one little fact your sister-in-law neglected to mention. According to her parents, Carol Christie was an excellent swimmer."

An excellent swimmer. Oh, hell. You don't have to be an excellent swimmer to be safe in the Flat River. If you're half as tall as I am, you don't have to know how to swim at all.

"When a reporter asked the cops if they had any reason

to think she might've been killed," she went on, "they didn't deny it."

I scanned the neighborhood one more time. It still looked like the kind of place where nothing ever happened. It was too tidy, and there was too much sunshine.

I turned my back on it and followed Ginny to the Olds.

3

While she started the engine, I pulled down the sunshade to give my aching head a little protection. Then, more to let her know I was still with her than to satisfy my curiosity, I asked, "Where do we go from here?"

She glanced over at me. "How long has it been since you had a full meal?"

That was the kind of question she usually asked me. I shrugged. She didn't need an answer.

As we pulled away from the curb, she muttered, "You ought to be more careful. If you don't get regular meals, it'll stunt your growth."

I suppose I should've at least grinned. She was just trying to clear the air. But I didn't have the energy for it. The little strength I had I was using to think about thirteen-year-old girls who end up dead in the river for no good reason. As far as I knew, there was zero connection between Carol Christie and Alathea, but just knowing something like that could happen to my niece gave me a cold pain in the stomach.

And maybe there was a connection. In this business, things like that happen all the time. Accidents happen by themselves—crimes have a way of tying themselves together. I was in no mood to grin at bad jokes, even when I knew why Ginny was making them.

We didn't have to go far to find food. In a few blocks, we were in one of those small business sections that looks like someone just dropped a bunch of white concrete bricks out of the sky and ran away before anybody could catch him and make him clean it up. Pawnshops, grocery stores, insurance offices, and gas stations stood facing every which way. With all that sun on them, they were blinding—I could hardly tell them apart. But Ginny's eyes handle brightness better than mine, and after a couple of minutes she pulled into a Muchoburger that was just opening up. We went inside, ordered cheeseburgers and about a gallon of coffee, then sat down at one of the tables.

We didn't talk while we waited for the food, and after that I was too busy eating half-raw hamburger and the vitamin pills that Ginny handed out like my life depended on them. When she'd had enough to eat, she got down to business.

"We need to talk to this Sergeant Encino. But he probably doesn't come on duty until midafternoon, so we've got five or six hours to do our homework. I suppose we could start with this list of Alathea's friends, but I'd rather wait until they get home from school, so they can't check what they're saying with each other—just in case there's something going on that they want to keep secret."

I nodded. My stomach didn't much like what I was putting in it. But I liked it better than the dread.

"Any suggestions?"

She was just being polite. She knew what our choices were as well as I did. But she was usually polite when we were just starting a case. That was generally the only time when she wasn't way ahead of me. As soon as she had a handle on what was happening, she wouldn't waste time being polite.

Anyway, I owed her some politeness myself. And if she was giving me a choice, I wanted to use it. There were some things I wasn't ready for yet, so I said, "We might as well go to the school while we're out this way. It's closer than your office."

That must have been what she wanted to do herself. She said, "Good enough," and went to pay the check. I finished up, drank down as much of that coffee as I could stand. Then we got in the car and drove to Mountain Junior High over on the corner of Mission and Natividad.

It wasn't the best junior high in the city—the best ones are called middle schools—but it was far enough from the old part of town to be better than the worst. It didn't look

like a converted warehouse, and it wasn't cramped into a
plot of ground too small to hold that many kids, and it didn't
have a chain-link fence around it. In fact, it had several
buildings built around one another, and there was a small
gymnasium and a ragged playing field. It was the sort of
place where some kids would be perfectly happy—and some
would get started on drugs.

We went in and found our way to the main office, where
Ginny showed her ID to a secretary and asked to see the
principal. The secretary informed us the principal was "out."
But when she heard why we were here, she told us the vice-
principal was really the person we ought to talk to. Vice-
principal Rumsfeld was "in."

She was a taut little woman with a severe hairstyle and
an air of terminal fatigue, worn out by burdens. You could
tell by the tension compressing her lips that she was responsible for "discipline" and had long since used up whatever tolerance she was born with.

Her office suited her. It was stark and forbidding, and the
chairs were uncomfortable. Probably in her career she'd
seen thousand of kids squirming on those chairs. Probably
Ginny and I didn't look much different to her than those
kids.

"You want to know about Alathea Axbrewder." She
sounded like a blunt instrument. "There's nothing I can tell
you. She came to school last week Tuesday, but didn't attend any of her classes after fifth period. That was physical
education. She hasn't been here since. In the old days, we
had truant officers who tracked down runaways, but now
the police are supposed to handle it. They do a poor job."

"What about Alathea herself?" At times like this, Ginny
was a model of diplomacy. She could be firm, even insistent,
without sounding pushy or irritating people.

"What do you want to know about her? She was a good
student, bright and pleasant. Her teachers liked her, and she
didn't get into trouble. She seemed more grown up than
most girls her age. That happens quite often when a child
loses a parent. The added pressure forces them to mature
more rapidly."

"She doesn't sound like the kind of girl who runs away."

Vice-principal Rumsfeld's lips got tighter, and her hairdo suddenly seemed even more severe. "What kind of girl is that, Ms. Fistoulari? All kinds of children run away."

"At thirteen?"

"They run away because they are in pain. No one is immune to pain—not even children."

The stiffness in her voice made me revise my opinion of her. She wasn't the Wicked Witch of the West. She was tired because she was the school's disciplinarian, and she didn't like her job. I said softly, "That bothers you."

"It *concerns* me, Mr. Axbrewder. A society that can't care for its children is in very serious trouble. I do what is in my power here, but I'm a poor substitute for a healthy family or a constructive sense of life. When a child like Alathea runs away, she places herself entirely beyond my reach."

"Ms. Rumsfeld," I said, "Alathea didn't run away."

She looked at me sharply. "Do you have some reason to believe that?"

"She's my niece. I know her pretty well."

"Your confidence is misplaced. Alathea isn't the first young girl to run away, and won't be the last. I admit that in the past most runaways were boys. Perhaps as boys they believed they were expected to be adventuresome. But in recent years, more and more girls have done the same. Twelve- and thirteen-year-olds, Mr. Axbrewder."

"How recently is that?" Ginny asked.

"I can't say—I've only been aware of it for the last year or so. Fortunately, Alathea is the first from our school, but other junior high and middle schools have had more than their share."

"Can you give us any details?" Ginny was groping—but that's normal. At the beginning of a case, you have to look under every rock you find.

"I don't have any," Ms. Rumsfeld said. "I don't see what possible use they could be to you, but if you feel compelled to look for them, the school board may be willing to help you." She was dismissing us. "In a case as serious as a runaway, the board receives copies of all reports as a matter of course. In fact, they have copies of all our files on every student."

Ginny and I stood up. Ginny thanked her for her time and turned to open the door. I said, "When we find out what happened to her, we'll let you know."

"Don't find out what happened to her," the vice-principal snapped. "Find her. Bring her back."

"We'll try," Ginny said. She ushered me out of the door, and we went back to the Olds.

Sitting in the car, she said, "Maybe she did run away."

"Maybe none of them ran away," I countered.

After a minute she said, "Right." She put the Olds in gear, and we headed in the direction of her office.

Fistoulari Investigations is in the Murchison Building, one of the three buildings in Puerta del Sol that stands more than five stories tall. It's on the other side of the city from Mountain Junior High, but the new freeway makes it fairly easy to get to. We had the Olds parked in the basement garage and were on our way up in the elevator before noon.

We hadn't been working on it very long, but so far I had the distinct impression that we weren't getting anywhere. If something had happened to Alathea, it was a secret, and we didn't know who could tell us what it was. So we had to start trying to eliminate the obvious.

The Murchison Building isn't cheap, but it isn't as expensive as it looks. It sits in what used to be the business center of Puerta del Sol, a good three miles down Paseo Grande from the ritzy real estate where the banks live these days. The owners have always had trouble attracting tenants, and the place is never more than two-thirds occupied. Which is why Ginny can afford to operate there, along with a handful of half-reputable lawyers, some chancy doctors, and a few insurance companies that may or may not have any assets. The elevator and the halls are carpeted, but the lighting is bad so you can't see that they don't clean very often. Too many of the walls have the kind of smudges you would expect to find in places where people get arrested regularly—the kind sweaty palms make while the rest of the body is being frisked.

But Ginny's office is in good condition. FISTOULARI IN-VESTIGATIONS is neatly lettered on the door, and inside the air-conditioning works. The waiting room has a plastic potted plant, a side table covered with old magazines, and only three chairs. But three chairs is about all it needs—most people won't even bother to wait in a private investigator's office if someone else is already there. And the office itself is at least comfortable. It holds Ginny's desk and files, a large sofa, a couple of roomy chairs, two phones, and a picture window looking out toward the valley of the Flat River. The carpet is clean because I keep it that way. The walls are bare except for a couple of framed diplomas and the display copy of Ginny's license—all part of making the place look "professional."

Fortunately, there was no one in the waiting room, so she didn't have to juggle clients. We went into the office, and I started up the electric coffeepot while she went through her mail. After she'd read it all—and thrown most of it into the wastebasket—we went to work.

On the phones.

Ginny called the school board and set up an appointment to see the chairman the following afternoon. Then she went down the list of Alathea's friends, asking their parents' permission to visit their homes and talk to their kids. Calling for permission is a nice touch, when you can afford it—forestalls a certain number of complaints to the commission. I used the other phone to eliminate at least some of the obvious.

Didn't take either of us very long. I'd never worked on a runaway before, but I knew a place that was in the business of telling people like me where to look. Tel-a-Help. Basically, it's a referral agency for all the social services in San Reno County, including state and federal bureaus. They gave me five different numbers—The State Bureau of Children's Services, the National Runaway Hotline, the National Drug Abuse Hotline, the San Reno County Crisis Hotline, and the police. I thanked them politely before crossing the police off my list.

I wanted to cross off the National Drug Abuse number,

too—but I didn't. Couldn't afford to. It was one of the obvious possibilities I had to check, and I had a sick feeling about it. So I did that number first. It's one of those toll-free 800 numbers. The way my head felt, you'd have thought I was about to pass out from anoxia—but I gave them my spiel and listened to their answer. "We're a confidential information service, Mr. Axbrewder. We can't give out the names of the young people who call us. But we always urge runaways to call their parents, and no reputable drug treatment facility or social service agency in the country would accept a thirteen-year-old girl without making some effort to contact her parents." When I hung up, I was practically gasping for breath.

The Bureau of Children's Services and the Crisis Hotline gave me variations on the same answer—confidentiality, always urging the runaways to get in touch with their parents, etc. In five minutes I was starting to understand Lona's outrage at the new laws and the public machinery that exist for the "benefit" of runaways—which seems to mean, "protect them from their parents."

But the National Runaway Hotline—another 800 number—was an improvement. Part of their business was to pass messages back and forth between kids and parents. And whenever possible they got the name of any runaway who called so that they could at least assure the parents their child was safe. All the names and messages were fed into a computer so that they could be retrieved instantly.

No one named Alathea—or Thea—Axbrewder had ever called the National Runaway Hotline.

I almost hung up—but snatched back the receiver and asked, "Did you ever get a call from a girl named Carol Christie?"

That was the wrong thing to say. All at once the voice at the other end of the line turned distant and suspicious. "Why do you ask, Mr. Axbrewder? Is she a relative of yours?"

I didn't have any other way out, so I said, "She's dead. I'm worried about Alathea, and I'm trying to find some kind of pattern."

The voice was silent for a minute. Then it said carefully, "There's no Carol Christie in the computer."

"All right," I said. "It was a dumb question. Tell me this. Out of all the kids who run away, how many call you? What percentage?"

"We don't have any reliable figures, but our best estimate is only about twenty percent. We're not as well known as we need to be."

"Thanks."

I hung up the phone, looked at Ginny. In spite of the AC I was sweating. But I wasn't due for another crisis yet—and if one was coming there wasn't anything I could do about it anyway, so I just tried to shove it out of my mind. When Ginny put down her phone, I asked, "What've you got?"

She pushed her list away from her. "We're going to be busy this evening. How about you?"

"Nothing." I sounded disgusted to myself.

"Relax," she said. "If you found her this fast, you wouldn't know what to do with yourself for the rest of the day." She was jollying me—but her eyes had that worried look in them again. She gave me the impression that she was asking herself how long I could hold out without a drink.

I got up, went and faced her across the desk, and said, "I don't like it when you look at me like that. Let's go talk to Carol Christie's parents."

I was half hoping she had something better in mind. I wasn't feeling any readier to visit them than when the idea first occurred to me. It was like calling the Drug Abuse Hotline—something in me was afraid of it. But we had to do it. We were looking for some kind of pattern, and we wouldn't know if there was any connection between Carol Christie and Alathea unless we checked it out.

Ginny knew that as well as I did. She said, "Good idea," and pushed herself out of her chair. She looked in Tuesday's paper for the names of the Christies, then got their address out of the phone book. Five minutes later, we were back in the Olds.

The Christies lived quite a ways out, in what they call the North Valley. Puerta del Sol lays down its inhabitants horizontally instead of stacking them vertically, so it's a sprawling place. And the way the population's growing these days, there are suburbs and even industries sitting on ground that was neglected dirt ten years ago. The city spreads in all directions, but mostly north and south along the valley of the Flat River, where water is a little easier to come by.

Mr. and Mrs. Christie lived all the way out at the northern tip of the sprawl. Where the cowboy money lives. Half the people out there wear old Stetsons and plaid shirts and faded jeans and dusty boots, and if you met them on the street you wouldn't know they're solid gold on the hoof. Most of them probably get their money from things like real estate, but the way they dress you would think they get rich just by looking so by-God Western. Before we were within five miles of the Christies, every house we passed was an ersatz ranch, with a split-rail fence, three acres of ground, and two horses.

When we got to where we were going, we found that the Christies ran a stable, complete with riding lessons, trails, and about thirty of the mangiest-looking horses I'd ever seen. They used a converted horse trailer for an office. When we went inside, we found Mary Christie there, working on a set of books.

She looked up as we came in and said, "Howdy, folks. What can we do fer y'all?" Her cowboy twang was stretched pretty thin over an accent that sounded like it probably came from Boston. But she was dressed right in not-too-new, not-too-clean, let's-go-muck-out-the-stalls clothes, with a red bandanna knotted around her neck.

Ginny said, "Mrs. Christie?" Her professional voice made it sound like she had every right in the world to be standing there asking personal questions. "I'm Ginny Fistoulari." She flipped her ID out of her purse and showed Mrs. Christie the photocopy of her license. "This is Mr. Axbrewder. We'd like to ask you and your husband a few questions."

It didn't take much to make Mary Christie forget about horses. Ginny's ID was enough. She practically jumped to her feet, went to a window behind her, and jerked out, "John!" There was an edge in her voice that sounded like panic at first, but I put it down to strain. It was only two days ago that her daughter had turned up dead. Then she came and stood in front of us with her arms clutched across her stomach as if she wanted to hide it. "Questions about what? What do you want?" Her twang had deserted her.

Ginny said evenly, "We'd like to talk to you about your daughter, Carol."

"Why?" She was as jumpy as a hophead. "What has it got to do with you?" Then she was at the window again. "John!"

Now I knew it wasn't just strain. Mrs. Christie was afraid of something.

From outside, a man's voice—real cowboy, this time—answered, "Ah'm comin'." Ten seconds later he was in the trailer with us.

He was tall and rangy, like a cowboy is supposed to be, with a grizzled, weather-bitten face and a cigarette stuck in his teeth. His battered old hat was pulled down tight on his head, probably so it wouldn't fall off when he was riding. He scanned Ginny and me, then asked slowly, "Now, what's all this-here ruckus about?"

"They want to know about Carol," Mary Christie said quickly—too quickly. "They want to ask questions about her."

At that, her husband's eyes narrowed until he was practically squinting at us. Deliberately he took the cigarette out of his mouth, threw it through the doorway. Then he said, "Naw, they don't want to ask no questions. They was just leavin'." If he was worried about the fact I was three inches taller and seventy pounds heavier than he was, he didn't show it.

But I didn't need Ginny to tell me this was no time for muscle. I just stood my ground and let her handle it.

She said, "We have good reason for asking." If it came down to a bluff, she could match John Christie any day. "We don't want to pry into anything that doesn't concern us, but we're working on a case that's remarkably similar

to Carol's." Remarkably similar, hell. Both girls were thirteen—period. "If you help us, we might be able to prevent
the same thing from happening again."

She made it sound practically inevitable. But Mr. Christie
wasn't having any. "You said one thing right," he drawled.
"You ain't gonna pry. There ain't no case on Carol. She
was a good li'l girl, and you ain't gonna dig up no dirt on
her. If other folks want to let their young'uns screw around,
it ain't no concern of mine."

Ginny faced him squarely. "Nobody said anything about
dirt. That was your idea." Then she asked harshly, "If Carol
was such a good swimmer, how did she happen to drown?"

Christie felt that. For a second, his eyes went out of focus.
His hands twitched as if he were getting ready to swing at
Ginny. I shifted into position to block him. But instead of
moving, he just said in a dead voice, "Get the hell outta
here."

Ginny considered him for a moment, then turned to Mary
Christie. The woman was staring back at her with something
like nausea in her face. Sharply Ginny said, "All right. Let
it happen to other girls. Why should you care? There's just
one thing I have to know." She knew how to be tough. "Did
she write to you at all after she ran away? Was there a
note?"

John Christie barked, "Mary!" For a minute she just stood
there, squirming with indecision and grief. Then, abruptly,
she jerked open one of the desk drawers, fumbled for a sheet
of paper, and handed it to Ginny.

Ginny gave it to me without looking at it. If John Christie
wanted it back, it was safer with me. I put it in my pocket.

"Thank you, Mrs. Christie," Ginny said softly. "I hope
you won't regret helping us." Then she went to the door.
"Come on, Brew. Mr. Christie thinks we should leave."

I followed her out, half expecting Christie to jump me as
I went past him. But he didn't. He slammed the door behind
us, and a second later we heard him yelling, "God damn it,
woman! You want the whole fuckin' world to know?" We
could hear him until we got into the Olds and shut the doors.

I didn't say anything. I just took out the note, and we looked at it together.

It said, "Dear Mom and Dad, I have to go away for a while. I have a problem, and I have to take care of it myself. It might take a long time. Don't worry about me. Love, Carol."

It was written on half a sheet of good twenty-pound bond, but the handwriting was a mess.

4

We didn't say anything. We didn't have to. We both knew what to do next. Ginny started up the Olds, and we headed back into the city. Hurrying. We wanted to get to Lona.

It was after four o'clock when we reached her house, so we didn't waste any time. Ginny was better at this kind of thing than I was. I waited in the car while she went to talk to Lona.

Even that way, it took a while. Lona didn't want to let go of her note. It was the last tangible thing she had from Alathea. But we needed the original—a copy wouldn't do us any good. I was relieved to see it in Ginny's hand when she came back to the Olds.

With her sitting beside me, we compared the notes. The similarity of the wording made my stomach ache, but Ginny was looking at other things. She compared the writing quickly, pointed out that the ink and scripts were different, then started to examine the paper.

Lona's note was written on half a sheet of twenty-pound bond.

Both sheets had been neatly torn—not cut—along one edge.

When Ginny held them up to the sun, we could see that they both had the same watermark.

I said, "Sonofabitch." Something deep in my chest was trembling. I was overdue for another withdrawal crisis.

"This doesn't prove anything," Ginny said stiffly. "There's a lot of this kind of paper around. It's a big company. It doesn't prove anything unless these notes came from the same sheet." She put the notes up against the sun again, then said, "No chance. Look what happens when I put the torn edges together."

I looked. The watermarks were facing in opposite directions. The top third of the mark on Lona's note was cut off—and it wasn't completed anywhere on the other sheet.

"Terrific." I could taste bile in my mouth. The lining of my stomach wanted alcohol. Wanted to be numb. "Two thirteen-year-olds run away from home and write notes that say almost exactly the same thing on the same kind of paper, with the same kind of bad handwriting. Of course it's just a coincidence. Why didn't I think of that?"

"I didn't say it was a coincidence," she replied with elaborate patience. Just letting Axbrewder know she wasn't senile yet. "I said it wasn't proof." Then she grinned—a shark's grin, eager and dangerous. "That's the difference between us and the police. We don't need proof." She threw the Olds into gear. "Let's go talk to Encino."

We were on the trail now—I could see it in her eyes.

I left it to her. I was thinking about the Christies. They were scared about something—and anything that could worry John Christie would probably frighten Lona to death.

We went down Mission, then crossed over on Gypsum until we hit Paseo Grande and turned right. A couple of miles down Paseo Grande we came to the new Municipal Building—the pride of the mayor, the joy of half a dozen construction companies, the flower of a couple architects, and the treasure of the bank that floated the loan. I didn't know anyone else who liked it.

From the outside, it looks like a country club for millionaires. An ordinary citizen can no more walk in there and feel comfortable than fly to the moon. All those fountains and flower beds might've been a good idea, but unfortunately the main part of the building hangs over the fountains and flowers and walkways. A square mountain of white concrete leans on the back of your neck—from some angles you can't even see what holds it up—so by the time you get to the doors and start climbing to wherever you have to go, you already feel intimidated. And of course there's no parking. Official cars have a private garage—ordinary citizens have to scramble for what they can get.

We were lucky—we only had to walk a couple of blocks.

Inside, there isn't a scrap of carpet or one warm soft color in the whole place. It looks like a brand-new abattoir. Since there aren't any windows, and the blank fluorescent lighting is always the same, you can't tell whether it's day or night.

I suppose I should've been used to it. I'd been in the city jail, up on the top floor of the police department wing, at least a couple of times. But I was always at a disadvantage here. I could never remember the names of the cops who rousted me when I was drunk. I couldn't remember anything about them, except they always looked short. But they knew who I was. The whole situation gave me a definite paranoid feeling.

But I figured I should be pretty safe in Missing Persons. They didn't have any reason to know me. So I just kept my coat buttoned and my hands at my sides, hiding the .45 under my left arm, and followed Ginny, trying to ignore the fact I could feel another withdrawal attack coming on.

The sergeant at the front desk issued us passes and told us where to go in the dull mumble of a man who'd spent too many years repressing a secret yen to *really* tell people where to go. We did what he told us, and a couple of corridors later we were at a glass door. The glass was safety plate with steel mesh sandwiched into it, and it said MISSING PERSONS across the top. We went in.

A Formica counter stood so close to the entrance that the door almost hit it when it opened. Behind the counter, there were four desks and a row of file cabinets. That was all. Missing Persons wasn't a very big item in the police budget.

Three cops sat at the desks, two women and a man. The man was a sergeant, so he out-ranked the women. Of course, they made us wait. Cops always make you wait as long as they can. It's in the Officer's Handbook. Eventually, however, one of the women, Policewoman Rand, asked us what we wanted. Ginny asked for Sergeant Encino, using her I'm-an-important-citizen-don't-mess-with-me voice. The man found himself off his butt and standing in front of us faster than he wanted to.

He was short, barely tall enough to stare at Ginny's clavicles. He had dark olive skin that complemented his dark blue uniform, and his close-cut black hair was so tidy that you would think he trained it with a whip. His mustache was assertive but not aggressive. And he had Chicano eyes—sad, world-weary, and arrogant. Sure enough, both the name tag pinned over his left shirt pocket and the ID clipped to his right shirt pocket said, "Sgt. Raul Encino, Missing Persons."

Ginny introduced herself, flashed her license, mentioned my name. Encino looked back at her with his face blank. That's also in the Handbook—treat everyone like two of them and a sandwich would be just about right for lunch. "What can I do for you?" He had just enough accent to make what he said sound more interesting than it really was.

"Information," Ginny said crisply. "We're trying to find a young girl named Alathea Axbrewder. Her mother reported her missing eight days ago."

Encino's expression was perfect, as noncommittal as a rock. "Mrs. Axbrewder chose to make no complaint. We look for her daughter, of course. Each patrol officer has a description. But without a complaint—" He gave us a delicate Chicano shrug. "You understand, it is not against the law to run away from home. The girl is a minor, so we have our eyes open for her. But in a city so big as Puerta del Sol, we are unlikely to find her. Also she has possibly left the city. The sheriff's office has been informed. What more do you want?"

With just a hint of sarcasm, Ginny said, "You assume she ran away."

"Why not? As I have said, the city is big. Girls disappear each week. Do you think she has been kidnapped? That is doubtful. For what purpose? There has been no demand for ransom."

That was true enough. Any hint of kidnapping, any hint at all, and this whole situation would've been different. For one thing, Lona would've had the FBI camped in her living room. But that didn't faze Ginny. In the same light-acid tone, she said, "I don't know whether I'm talking about kidnapping or not. I haven't gotten that far yet. What I'm interested in right now is thirteen-year-old girls who disappear and then turn up dead." She was trying to irritate Encino, nag him into defending himself. Maybe spring loose some spontaneous information.

I could see the muscles along his jaw tighten, but he didn't change his ground. "Is Alathea Axbrewder dead?"

"Carol Christie is."

He blinked. As far as the rest of his face was concerned, he was sound asleep. "Of what interest is Carol Christie to you?"

"There's a connection between her and Alathea."

"Are the parents of Carol Christie your clients?"

Ginny could've refused to answer that. She had a right to protect her client. But I guess she didn't see any point to it. She said, "I've been retained by Lona Axbrewder."

"Then the death of Carol Christie is of no concern to you."

"I said there's a connection." Ginny let herself start to sound angry. She took out the notes and put them down on the counter in front of Encino. "Both Alathea and Carol wrote to their parents after disappearing. If you look at them, you'll see that they were written on the same kind of paper. The sheets were torn in half the same way. What they say is almost identical, and the handwriting is similar."

"That's most ingenious." Encino didn't even glance at the notes. "Unfortunately the truth remains. Carol Christie's death can be of no concern to you. The rights of your client do not include her. Mr. Christie and his wife desire privacy."

"Says who?"

"Their wishes were made known to the investigating officer, Detective-Lieutenant Acton."

Investigating officer, huh? Ginny was getting somewhere. Now we knew there was enough wrong with Carol Christie's death to interest the cops.

But she didn't stop to chew it over. She had Encino backing up, and she kept at him.

"That's wonderful. The Christies don't want people to know what really happened to their daughter, so the cops clamp a lid on it. Having money is good for something after all. I just wonder what you and Acton are getting out of it."

Encino's composure split for a second. *"Hija de la puta."* Before he could get it back, I reached for him. I was going to knot my fist in the front of his nice blue uniform and shake him up good. But Ginny stopped me with an elbow that almost caved in my ribs. I could feel blood pounding in my face.

The sergeant had his blankness back in place, but he couldn't keep the rasp out of his voice. "Go away. You Anglos, you're all the same. A girl runs away and is later found dead. There's an investigation, and everything is kept with great propriety, even from the papers, to avoid distress for the family. But someone hires private investigators, and because they can't do their jobs they accuse the police. It's like that everywhere. And why? Because the girl is white. Anglo. If a Chicano girl runs away, and the mother asks for help, you Anglos say, 'What do you expect? Look for her in the brothels.' And if that Chicano girl is found dead, then the papers print every rumor they hear about her, true or false." His sneer twisted his whole face. "Go away. You interfere with my work."

My pulse was still racing, but I heard him. I picked up the notes, pulled open the door, said to Ginny, "Come on." But she was really mad now. Leaning over the counter, she thrust her face at Encino. "I work for whoever asks me," she said very softly. "I don't have any control over who asks. I just take whatever they ask and give it my best shot. That's *my* work."

Encino jerked his head contemptuously. *"Muy bravo."*

I took Ginny's arm, dragged her out into the corridor, and shut the door behind us. She threw off my hand. Stalked along for a minute in silence. Then she said, "That sono-fabitch."

I said, "He has a point."

"He has orders. Somebody told him to put a lid on Carol Christie. It's not my fault he doesn't like it." Then she asked, "How come you're so sympathetic all of a sudden? Two minutes ago you wanted to take his head off for him."

I didn't have a good answer to that, so I just said, "I spend a lot of time in the old part of town. Probably he's a good cop."

"A good cop," she snorted. She didn't say anything more until we got into the elevator. Then she muttered, "You big ape, you've got to learn to keep your temper."

"Dear God," I said. "Did I lose my temper? I'm pitifully sorry. It's never happened to me before."

She said, "Aw, shut up." But she didn't sound so angry anymore. After a minute, she asked, "What was that he called me?"

" *'Hija de la puta.'* Daughter of a whore."

She considered that briefly, then grinned. "It sounds nastier in Spanish." When the elevator doors opened, she led the way out.

Following her toward the exit, I had a wild urge to put my arms around her and kiss the back of her neck. But when we walked out into the late afternoon, the sun hit me in the eyes like a hammer. Suddenly my head was reeling for a drink. It was coming, and there was nothing I could do about it. Except get a drink. My nerves pleaded for the stuff. *Get a drink get a drink get a drink.* Feel the alcohol flow like bliss through the sore lining of my stomach straight into my blood.

Usually when I go sober, I have three big withdrawal crises—along with half a dozen or so smaller ones—before my body gives up on pain and starts looking for other arguments. So far this time I'd only had one. One coming on, and after that at least one more to go. With the sun in my eyes, and my brain aching, I didn't think I was going to make it.

I didn't realize I was just standing there with my fingers clamped over my face until Ginny came back for me. She put her hands on my arm. "It's that bad?"

"All of a sudden. Doesn't usually come on this fast."

She said, "Is there anything I can do?" But she knew there

wasn't. She'd done everything anybody could do when she came looking for me in the first place.

I said, "Take me home."

She shook my arm. "No chance. We've got all those friends of Alathea's to go see, remember? We're late already."

I said it again. "Take me home."

"Brew," she whispered, "I don't want to leave you alone."

With an effort, I pulled my hands off my face. I must've looked pretty fierce, because she winced. "I want to be alone. It's bad enough when I'm alone. This morning was easy. It's going to get worse. Do you think I like having you watch me fall apart?"

That reached her. It didn't ease the tight worry in her face, but it got me what I wanted. She took me home.

By the time she got me up to my apartment, the pressure in my skull was squeezing sweat out of my face like beads of thirst. I shook like a cripple. It was all I could do to get across the room and sit down on the convertible couch I use for a bed.

This one was going to be a sonofabitch.

Had it ever been this bad before? I couldn't remember. Probably not. Every time is always the worst.

Ginny sat down beside me for a while. She looked like she wanted to hold my hand. "Are you going to be all right?"

From somewhere, I dredged up the energy to say, "There's nothing here. I never keep the stuff in my apartment."

"That isn't what I asked. I asked you if you're going to be all right."

I said, "You go on." If she didn't leave soon I was going to scream. "Talk to Alathea's friends. I'm going to sit here. As long as I have to. Then I'll get something to eat. Then I'll go to bed. Pick me up in the morning."

"All right." She didn't like it, but she swallowed it. "I'll make sure the answering service knows where I am." A minute later she was gone.

A minute after that, I wanted to cry out, *Ginny*!

But this mess was one I'd made for myself, and I was going to have to live with it. So I just sat where I was and watched the sunlight in the room get dimmer.

Soon there were red-hot bugs crawling along my nerves, ticks and chiggers and cockroaches of need, and at one point I thought I could hear high-pitched mewling sounds coming from somewhere in the vicinity of my face. But I just sat where I was and waited. Waited for the sun to set. Waited for night. There was a cure for this, and I was going to go get it. Never mind what I'd told Ginny. I was going to go as soon as it was dark. As soon as I recovered enough control over myself to move.

I hung on for the sake of the dark. After a while there was no more light in the room, and the pressure eased a bit. Not much—this was going to be a long one—but enough so that I could tell my arms and legs what to do with some hope of having them listen to me.

I lurched into the kitchen and drank what felt like about a gallon of water. Then I left my apartment, struggled down the long stairs to the street, and went shambling in the direction of the old part of town.

Looking for that cure.

5

The cure I had in mind was an old Mestizo named Manolo.
Somewhere in the old part of town, he would be sitting alone in the corner of a bar, sipping a glass of anisette, and looking for all the world like the last remains of some long-dead grandee's noble family. He'd be sitting there like a sleepwalker, and if you saw him you'd be afraid to wake him up for fear the shock might fuddle what was left of his wits. But all the time he'd be as alert as a cat, soaking up little bits and hints of rumors, facts, information, as if he took them in through his pores. He knew a world of secrets. And if you asked him the right questions—or if you asked them the right way, or maybe if he trusted you for some reason—he'd tell you one or two of them.

There was a good chance he'd be able to tell me the secret of Carol Christie, and I knew how to ask.

I had an idea in my head that made my nerves crawl as bad as the DT's, and this was the only way I knew of to check it out.

I'm not like Ginny—I'm not a puzzle solver. For instance, it might never have occurred to me to compare the watermarks of those two notes. My brain doesn't work that way. I get where I'm going—wherever that is—by intuition and information. In a city like Puerta del Sol, there are a lot of information dealers, and I know at least half of them. And I'm not talking about stool pigeons, punks who shill for the cops.

Like most independent businessmen, old Manolo was a specialist. Next to el Señor himself, Manolo knew more than anybody in the city about who's doing what to whom and how in the grubby world of drugs. The cops could put away most of the pushers in the state if they just knew what old Manolo knew.

I was doing my best not to think too much about Alathea. I didn't dare. I was already too jittery—if I stopped to consider what I was thinking, I might not be able to control myself until I ended up at the bottom of a bottle somewhere. No, all I wanted to know was how a good swimmer ends up drowning in the Flat River.

It was the kind of question you had to ask at night. People like old Manolo don't exist during the day. When the sun comes up, they evaporate, and all you can find of them is what they leave behind—a rank, sodden body snoring away like a ruin on a pallet full of fleas somewhere, as empty of answers as an old beer can.

But I didn't get the chance to ask. I wasn't more than five blocks away from my apartment, just turning onto Eighth Street on my way toward the Hegira and all the other bars where Manolo might be drinking his anisette, when things started to get out of hand.

Down from the corner of Eighth and Sycamore, there are a couple of abandoned buildings with a long dirty alley between them. They're close enough to the old part of town so even the cops don't walk into an alley like that unless they have backup on the way. I was just about to cross in front of that alley when the screaming started.

A woman screaming, terror and pain. Somewhere back in the semidarkness of the alley.

My body is faster than my brain, and by the time the woman screamed again, before I'd even thought about it, I was headed toward the sound as fast as I could run.

Probably I should've pulled the .45 out where I could use it, but when you're as big as I am, you get in the habit of thinking you don't need a weapon. Anyway, I had good reason not to trust the way I handle a gun.

This time—for once—it turned out I'd done the right thing. The only reason the woman didn't get hurt worse was that I got there so fast. The man had already torn off most of her clothes, and he had her on her back in the dirt. She fought like fury, but he was much too strong for her.

He should've heard me coming—I'm not exactly light on my feet—but he must've been too far gone. Holding her down, he sprawled himself between her legs and started to thrust at her.

I was moving too fast to land on him without hurting her, so instead I caught hold of the back of his shirt with both hands as I went past and used his weight to pivot me to a stop. I was ecstatic with rage—the pressure inside me was exploding. Frustration and dread and all the long pain of trying to fight my way off the stuff came to a head in a second, and I went happily crazy.

The man wasn't small, but for all the good his size did him he might as well have been. My momentum lifted him bodily into the air, and as I pivoted I swung him around and slammed him against the wall of the building. When he bounced back at me, I saw he had a switchblade, but even that didn't slow me down. I blocked it aside, grabbed him again, wheeled, and threw him face first into the other wall as if I were trying to demolish the building.

Before he could turn, bring his knife around, I got him. With a long swing that came all the way up from my shoes, I hit him in the small of the back, just on the left side of his spine.

A gasp of pain broke out of him. His knife skittered away into the dark somewhere. He spun around and flipped forward, fell on his face, then jerked onto his side, arching his back as if he were trying to get away from the pain. His legs went rigid, and he kept pushing with them, slowly skidding his body in a circle.

There was a high keening noise in my ears, like the sound of blood rushing through my head, and I had a terrible urge to haul off and kick him. I wanted to do it. I could already feel the jolt of my toe hitting his back. But I didn't. He'd had enough.

Instead I turned away and went to see about the woman.

She huddled, sobbing, against one of the walls. She had her knees pulled up tight in front of her, and she clutched the remains of her clothes about her desperately, as if those scraps were all that was left of her. Her face was pressed against her knees. She didn't look up when I spoke to her.

I hunkered down in front of her. Not knowing what else to do, I put one hand on her arm.

She flinched away so violently that I had to draw back. But at least the movement made her lift her head. I saw she was Chicano. It's hard to tell the age of young Chicano women—when they first stop being kids they look too old for their years, and later on they look too young—but I didn't think she was more than seventeen. Not pretty, but beautiful. Either the bad light or the tears made her eyes look dark as bruises.

"Hush child," I said to her gently in Spanish. "The harm is past. I am Señor Axbrewder. My name is known in many places. Are you injured?"

She didn't say anything. But she made an effort and finally managed to swallow her sobs. In answer to my question, she shook her head.

The man on the ground behind me groaned.

Her eyes jumped fearfully toward him, but I said, "Do not fear. He is hurt, and will not harm you now." This time when I touched her arm she looked back at me and didn't flinch.

"That is well," she said in English. Strength was starting to come back into her face. There was a dignity in her tone, perhaps in the way she spoke English, that touched me more than any amount of crying. "He is a pig, and I spit on him."

I liked her English so much I switched to it myself. "We'll do better than spit on him. The rape laws around here are pretty tough." That's one advantage of living in a state where some of the old Spanish traditions and values still carry weight. "We'll put him in jail. He won't get out until he's too old to even think about doing something like this again."

She nodded her head once, sharply. "Yes."

"Good."

I got up to check on the man. He was groaning louder and moving around a bit now, but he wasn't going anywhere. He was a white dude—an Anglo all dolled up in the kind of cowboy-tourist finery no self-respecting Westerner would wear. That made him a hit-and-run rapist, the kind that never gets caught because by the time the cops go looking for them they're already in some other part of the country, bragging about how those "Mex chicks" couldn't get enough of them. "Not this time, ace," I muttered at him. Then I went back to the woman and asked her name.

She said, "Teresa Sanguillán."

"Well, Teresa Sanguillán." All of a sudden, I was trembling—reaction, I guess—and I had to fake a hearty tone to keep my voice from quavering. "I'm afraid you've got a long night ahead of you. We'd better get on with it."

She didn't respond. The brief look she cast down at her clothes said more than enough.

I groped mentally for a second, then shrugged off my jacket and handed it to her.

Her eyes snagged momentarily on the butt of the .45 under my left arm, but then she took the jacket. I turned my back and went to look for the knife. I found it a few feet away, snapped it closed and dropped it into my pocket. Then I started to rouse the dude.

While I was shaking him to his feet and she was getting herself covered as best she could, I asked her how she'd happened to run into this clown.

I liked her—she had spunk. Now that her fear was over, she was just mad. But it was a controlled mad, cold and vehement. I was glad about that, because it meant she wasn't going to back out on me, refuse to press charges. In a tight, even voice, she told me she worked as a domestic out in the Heights, where a lot of professional people live. She was on her way home to her mother and two younger sisters, but the bus she had to take didn't go into the old part of town, so every evening she had to walk this way home in the dark. The Anglo had been on the bus with her, and when she got off he followed her, giving her some sort of speech about how girls weren't safe on the streets alone at night. It only took him three blocks to start treating her like a hooker, and when she gave it to him to understand that he was mistaken, he turned nasty.

The whole thing made me want to hit him again. While

I was getting him up, I saw his penis still hanging out of his open fly. I was tempted to leave him that way. But on second thought, for the sake of Teresa Sanguillán's dignity, I tucked him in and zipped him up. Then I lifted him to his feet and dragged him along. The three of us went out to the street.

In that part of town, you can't find a unit at night if you go looking for it with a bloodhound. I didn't feel much like lugging the dude all the way back to Cuevero Road in hopes of spotting a cop or a working phone booth, so we went on down Eighth Street and turned in at the first bar we came to. The few lethargic drinkers in the place looked at us with only momentary interest despite our far-from-tidy appearance. The barkeep knew me and let us use his phone. First I called the cops. Then Teresa called a friend who had a phone, so the friend could take a message to her mother. Then we went back outside to wait. It would've been nice to sit down in the bar for a rest, but considering the shape I was in, I didn't want to stay in such close proximity to all those bottles.

It was an easier decision than it should've been, almost twenty-four hours since my last drink. I was wearing my white armor—knight rescues maiden—which helped. But that was only part of it. Vanity is no match for alcohol. If it were, half the distilleries in the country would go out of business. No, the main thing was that I was working, doing something I believed in. While we stood out there on the sidewalk I almost didn't regret that I wasn't back in the bar having a drink.

I passed the time by shaking the dude every time he started to fade or shutting him up whenever he started to groan, and by asking Teresa questions—simple questions, the kind she could answer without having to forget that she was mad. After about five minutes the cops arrived. There were two of them in the unit, and they drove up quietly, trying not to attract attention.

Once they heard what had happened they didn't seem very eager to make an arrest. They inspected Teresa and the dude and me, and shuffled their feet, and asked us a bunch of questions without writing any of the answers down, generally making it clear that they wanted us to forget the whole thing. I suppose I could understand their situation—in this city, Anglo versus Chicano was every cop's nightmare. But I wasn't having any. Teresa Sanguillán and I were citizens, the dude had committed a crime, and we had a right to have him arrested. I handed over the knife, and finally the cops gave in. They piled us into the back of their unit and took us over to the Municipal Building.

The building is just as bad at night as it is during the day. It's always disorienting. During the day you have the impression that the sun set hours ago, and at night you end up thinking it's noon outside. But this time I didn't let it bother me. As long as Teresa had her chin up, I didn't intend to let anything get in my way. I knew it could turn out to be messy, but I didn't care.

The so-called arresting officers took us to the duty room, where all the detectives had their desks. The person who designed the room was either a drunk or a real joker—the place looked like the embalming room of a mortuary. For a while we were ground along by the usual routine of police work. The arresting officers made a statement to one of the detectives. He tried to ask the dude a few questions, but the dude was hurting too bad to make sense, so the detective put him in the tank to wait for a doctor. Then a couple of detectives took Teresa and me to opposite sides of the room—so we couldn't check our answers with each other—and made us tell our stories a few times. After that, we were given the opportunity to sit around and wait.

The cops do stuff like that on purpose. They try to put pressure on the people filing the charges. Most of them don't actually want the people to back out, but from a cop's point of view, if a victim is going to back out, the sooner the better. Saves wasted effort and frustration later on. So they give you a chance to reconsider. A long chance.

While we were waiting, we saw the doctor come in. He examined the dude, then went away muttering to himself. A few minutes later, two paramedics arrived with a stretcher and carted the dude off on it. Teresa watched them go, but the anger in her eyes stayed.

After another half hour or so, a different detective came over and introduced himself as Captain Cason. He was a short, fleshy man with hands like shovels and eyes so flat and pale that from the side they looked like the eyes of a blind man. His voice had a particular rasp with which I was all too familiar—the hoarseness of a man who does a lot of interrogating. He took Teresa across the duty room into his office and shut the door.

They were in there a long time. When they came out, she looked shell-shocked, like she was about to faint away right there on the floor. I had a sick taste in my mouth as I hurried toward her.

Cason tried to stop me. He put himself between us, steered her over to a nearby desk and told the detective there to arrange a ride home for her. Then he took my arm and tugged me in the direction of his office.

I slapped his hand off and stepped around him. For one second Teresa looked straight at me. Her face was as pale as if she were bleeding internally, but there was a hot red spot of color on each cheekbone, and her lips were tight. Her dark intense eyes didn't flinch. Half her anger was aimed at me.

Cason barked, "Axbrewder!" But I ignored him long enough to tell her in Spanish, "I will put him in prison by myself if you do not speak against him." Then I turned away. Cason was getting ready to muscle me, and I didn't want that to happen. I said to him, "Tell your detective I want my jacket back." Then I strode straight into his office and dropped myself into one of the chairs.

He followed me in, shut the door, and sat down. He put his hands on the desk and kept them there as if they were too heavy to carry around. Or maybe he just didn't want me to forget how strong they were. With that harsh rasp of his, he demanded, "What did you say to her?"

The bad taste in my mouth was getting worse, but I made an effort to keep my vocabulary polite. "The opposite of what you said."

"Huh?"

"You told her I wasn't going to testify for her." That was what I'd seen in her eyes. I didn't need her to explain it. "You tried to scare her off by telling her she'd have to carry this alone in court. You must've had a fine old time describing how ugly a rape trial can get."

"Is that so?" Cason growled. For a second there, he didn't sound quite so sure of himself. Then he rallied. "Well, I've got news for you, smartass. You aren't going to testify."

"How do you figure that?" I said, hoping there wasn't something important about all this that he knew and I didn't.

"You're a known alcoholic. You were in the part of town where you do your drinking. The arresting officers found you outside a bar. Who's going to believe a thing you say?"

"That's cute." The taste in my mouth made me sound like him. "The only problem is that I'm sober."

"Is that a fact?" he drawled. "How do you propose to convince a jury?"

I almost laughed at him. "You're wasting my time. I'll call you as a character witness. Even you won't be able to explain why you didn't give me a blood-alcohol test." He blinked at that a couple of times, but didn't say anything. "Come on, Captain," I went on. "You're playing games with me. Why don't you cut out the bullshit and tell me what's really going on?"

His fingertips began to touch each other lightly. "The man's name is Charles Saunders, and he's from Cleveland. We're trying to get in touch with his wife. The doctor says he may have a ruptured kidney." Then his hands jumped into fists. "Goddamn it, Axbrewder! Haven't you ever heard of minimum force?"

" 'Minimum force?' " I countered. "What's that?"

"He could sue you for every penny you ever had!"

"Is that a fact?" Deliberately I imitated Cason's tone.

"We can probably get you off the hook if you let this thing drop."

I felt like it was my turn to get angry, but I held back. "So let him sue me. That's my problem. I don't give a shit what he does as long as he does it in jail."

"Smart-ass!" Cason barked. "I wish you still had a license, so I could get it pulled for this."

"Yeah, well, I appreciate your consideration. But I'm just a private citizen. I saw a crime being committed, and I intervened. I went in hard because there wasn't time for anything else. He had a knife. I didn't have a chance to ask him if he was going to use it." I tried not to sound too angry, but I couldn't swallow all of it. "What the hell's the matter with you, anyway? You like rape? You want clowns like this Saunders running around loose?"

"Shut up, Axbrewder," he said softly, "or I'll stuff it down your throat."

"Just what we need around here," I shot back. "More police brutality."

"All right." He was furious. "That's enough. You want to be cute? I'll give it to you straight. This Sanguillán"—he made her name into an insult—"is just another Mex chippy who tried to back out when she didn't get enough money. It happens all the time. That's why she was out on the street alone at night. Saunders just got sucked in. He's a tourist here, and he deserves an even break. A ruptured kidney is a hell of a price to pay for not having enough cash on him. This won't go any farther. You're not going to testify."

"Because he's Anglo," I said carefully.

"If that's the way you want to put it." His hands were flat on the desk, as if everything was settled.

I got to my feet. "Teresa Sanguillán has a perfectly respectable job as a domestic in the Heights. That'll be easy to prove. She was on the street at night alone because that's the only way she can get home. But even if she *is* 'just another Mex chippy,' it doesn't make any difference. She was being *raped*!" I couldn't stop myself. I hammered my fist onto the top of his desk so hard that a couple of files fell off onto the floor. "If you try to sit on this, I'll go to the DA." District Attorney Martínez was notoriously unsympathetic toward racist cops. "He might like to find out how many rape investigations you've quashed since you got your promotion."

Captain Cason was standing behind his desk, and his

hands were twitching, and he was saying, "You sonofabitch, you—!" But I wasn't listening. I'd had enough of him. I threw open the door and went out into the duty room.

I'd been in there longer than I thought. Teresa was gone, and my jacket waited for me on the corner of a desk. Everybody in the duty room stared at me, but I ignored them. I shoved my arms into my coat, moving fast to hide the way I was shaking. Then I stalked out of the room.

I was in no mood to be interfered with, so when a woman in the corridor behind me called my name, I didn't pay any attention. No, thanks—not interested. I've had enough. But she was determined. "Mr. Axbrewder!" I could hear her hurrying to catch up with me. Oh, hell. I gritted my teeth, shoved my hands into the pockets of my jacket so that she wouldn't see them tremble, and turned to face her.

Policewoman Rand, from Missing Persons.

"Mr. Axbrewder," she repeated, "Sergeant Encino wants to see you."

Encino. Just what I needed. Another racist, like Cason only on the opposite side of the fence. I didn't feel like putting up with him. I had my mouth open to tell Policewoman Rand where Sergeant Encino could stuff it when my right hand found a piece of paper in my jacket pocket. I shut up long enough to take it out and look at it.

It was just a scrap of paper. On one side there was something in Spanish that looked like a grocery list. On the other side, in awkward childlike handwriting, it said, "I am indebted to you. Teresa María Sanguillán y García."

That made a difference, somehow. All of a sudden, Cason didn't seem to be worth the emotion I was spending on him. I folded the note neatly, put it back in my pocket. Then I asked Policewoman Rand, "Where is he?"

She nodded back down the corridor. "In the office."

"All right," I said. "I'll go see him."

She didn't come with me, but continued on the way I'd been going. Maybe it was time for her coffee break. I went back to Missing Persons alone.

Encino was the only one there. As soon as he saw me come in, he got up from his desk and came to stand at the counter, facing me. We stared at each over for a moment across the Formica. Then he said, "I hear that you have stopped a rape tonight."

That took me by surprise. I nodded stupidly.

His sad eyes didn't waver. "I hear that the woman is Chicano."

I didn't say anything to that either. Something was going on here, I couldn't even guess what it was. As a way of answering him, I took out my scrap of paper and let him see it.

"Ah." He read it, then looked back up at me. He was too good at hiding his emotions—I couldn't find anything in his face. After a moment, he said, "So you have spoken with Captain Cason."

For the sake of not acting like an idiot, I mustered up enough voice to growl, "Yeah."

Carefully Encino asked, "What have you said to him?"

It was none of his business, but I was glad to tell him anyway. "I told him to blow it out his ass."

Suddenly Encino's whole face smiled. He was so happy that even his hair looked like it was grinning. He turned serious again a few seconds later, but by then everything between us was different.

"Señor Axbrewder," he said formally, "I've been unjust. Men such as Cason"—he said the name bitterly—"blind me. Accept my apologies."

Before I could respond, he went back to his desk, picked up a stack of manila folders, and brought them over to the counter.

"The truth is that you upset me when you said there is a connection between Alathea Axbrewder and Carol Christie. I had not considered that. So I have been reading the files for two years back. I found these." He tapped the stack of folders. Then he shrugged. "They were investigated. There is no apparent connection."

He didn't let me interrupt him. "I can't permit you to read these. But"—he sighed eloquently—"I must leave the office for a short time. How can I know what happens behind my back? Please use my desk."

Five seconds later, he was gone, and I was alone with his files.

Now I was more than just surprised. But I didn't have time for it. I wanted to read those files, and I didn't know how long the office would be empty. I grabbed up the stack, straightened it in front of me, and got started.

There were seven folders. Carol Christie's was on the top, and I took it first.

Before I finished it, I felt so weak that I feared I was going to fall down. I couldn't help myself—I had to go sit in Encino's chair.

After Carol Christie's, I read the other six files straight through. Then I went back to the beginning and started over again. This time I took notes. Halfway through, Sergeant Encino came back. But he was alone, and I didn't stop.

By the time I finished, I was dripping sweat on his blotter. My shirt was soaked and sticking to my back, along with most of my jacket. I didn't ask Encino's permission to use his phone—I just grabbed it and dialed as well as I could with my hands shaking like cowards. I held on while Ginny's answering service tracked her down. When she answered, they patched me through.

"Brew," she started, "what's wrong?"

I brushed past her anxiety. "I'm at Missing Persons. You've got to get down here."

"Why? What's happened?"

"There are seven of them," I said. "Not counting Alathea. I don't care what the cops say, this is no accident."

"Make sense, Brew! Seven what?"

"Seven thirteen-year-olds. No, five. Two of them were twelve." I knew I wasn't getting through to her, but I couldn't help myself. I was too upset to pull it together.

"What the bloody hell are you talking about?"

I pushed the phone against the side of my head as hard as I could, trying to make that damn inanimate plastic steady me. I wanted to howl, but I couldn't get enough air into my lungs. "Carol Christie didn't drown because she couldn't swim. She drowned because she OD'ed on heroin. And that's not all. Before she drowned, she—" But I couldn't say it over the phone. Carol Christie was only thirteen. Just like Alathea. There are some things you can hardly say out loud at all.

"I'm on my way," Ginny told me. "I'll be there in fifteen minutes." Then the line went dead, leaving me with nothing but an empty phone to hang on to.

PART TWO

Wednesday Night/Thursday

6

Ginny made good time, but it was long enough for me to get a grip on myself. I couldn't afford to fall apart just because this case had turned messy all of a sudden. Alathea needed help in the worst way. So I muttered curses at myself for a while, and finally managed to give Sergeant Encino his desk back. By the time Ginny arrived, I was standing at the counter where I belonged.

She came in so fast that she almost hit me with the door. Her eyes jumped back and forth between Encino and me, trying to figure out what was going on. She was on the alert, ready to explode. But I didn't say anything for a moment or two. I was so glad to see her that I wanted to hug her. Just having her there made me feel steadier. She'd know what to do, know how to cope.

"All right," she panted, out of breath from hurry and anxiety. "What's going on?"

It was still a tough question, but I could handle it now. "After we talked this afternoon, Sergeant Encino went through his files for the past couple years. He found six more young white girls like Carol Christie who ran away from home and later turned up dead. All seven of them were heroin addicts. In one way or another, they all died as a result of overdoses." I faltered for a second, groping for courage, then went on.

"According to the medical examiner, they all showed signs of 'intensive sexual activity.' "

That's how the coroner put it in all seven reports. In each case, he'd concluded that these twelve- and thirteen-year-old girls supported their addictions by prostitution.

Ginny took it in like a sponge. Whenever she's listening really hard, she doesn't react to what she hears—she just concentrates on absorbing it. When I stopped, she asked in a flat voice, "Have you got the details?"

I showed her my sheaf of notes.

She nodded sharply, then turned to Encino. "Were these cases investigated?"

"Of course. Yes."

"And?"

He shrugged. "No connection was found."

"No connection?" she snapped. "They're identical!"

If he resented her attitude, he didn't show it. "Drugs, yes. Prostitution, running away from home. But drugs are available everywhere. For a young girl to get drugs, she needs money. Especially for heroin. It's common. What connection is there?"

I said, "He's right." I didn't agree with him, but he had a good point. "These seven girls lived in different parts of town. They went to five different schools. According to their friends, none of them knew each other. Their parents don't have anything in common." When I thought about it, the individual investigations looked pretty thorough. "None of them went to the same church or belonged to the same club or had the same family doctor."

Ginny didn't even glance at me. "Who did the investigations?"

"Detective-Lieutenant Acton," Encino said.

"All of them?" she demanded.

He nodded.

"Is he a good cop?" I asked.

Encino thought for a moment. "He's Anglo—but not like Captain Cason. He's hard on drugs. It's said he searches for the pushers who supplied these children."

Ginny started to ask another question, but I stopped her with a nudge. Policewoman Rand was coming through the door behind us. I didn't know which racial or political faction she belonged to, but I didn't want to risk getting Encino in trouble for helping us. In Puerta del Sol, the police department is like the city—so fragmented, broken up into groups that can't stand one another, it's a wonder they get any work done at all. About the only time I've ever seen the cops stick together is when one of them gets killed.

Maybe Rand was on the wrong side. Encino's tone changed suddenly as he said, "No, it's impossible. I've done everything I can. No more."

Two hints were more than enough for Ginny. "If that's the way you want it," she sighed in her aggrieved-citizen voice. "We'll get a subpoena if we have to." That was a nice touch. It kept Encino in the clear as far as Policewoman Rand was concerned. I liked it so much that I almost made the mistake of grinning. "Come on, Brew. Let's get out of here."

We turned to go, but the door was already in use. A short dried-up little man practically ran into the office. He had thin gray-and-black hair sticking up in all directions, a stiff mustache covering his mouth, and a face that looked like it'd been redesigned by a pair of cleats long ago. His eyes bulged as if they were about to fall out. He didn't react to us—I don't think he even saw us—but I knew who he was. One of Ginny's less-successful competitors, a private investigator named Ted Hangst. Mostly because he didn't have any choice about it, he worked in the grubby world of "domestic relations," spying for people who were jealous, greedy, or malicious enough to pay him. I seemed to remember hearing somewhere that his wife had run off and left him a few years back.

He almost jumped the counter to confront Sergeant Encino as he thrust half a sheet of paper onto the counter. His hands shook. "See! I told you she didn't run away."

Ginny and I froze.

There was no triumph in his voice—just urgency and fear. "Read it!"

Encino scanned the paper, then turned his sad eyes back to Ted. "It says that she has run away, Mr. Hangst."

"She didn't run away!" he insisted. "This proves it. Listen." He held the note trembling in front of his face.

" 'Dear Dad, I won't be coming home for a while—maybe for a long time. Don't worry about me. There's something I have to work out. Love, Mittie.' " He slapped the paper down on the counter. "See?"

Without inflection, Encino repeated, "It says that she has run away."

"No!" His whole body twitched with frustration. "Mittie didn't write this. It says, 'Dear Dad.' She never called me Dad. She always called me Pop. That proves she didn't write this. She didn't run away. She was kidnapped!"

"For what purpose?" the sergeant asked. "Not for ransom. So why?"

"I don't know." He was close to crying. "It doesn't make sense." Then he recovered his determination. "You've got to help me. I can't get anywhere alone. There are too many things that could've happened. I can't do it alone."

Encino leaned closer to Ted. "Mr. Hangst, I sympathize. We will look for your daughter. We understand the importance. But truthfully there is little we can do." He stopped Ted's response with a short gesture. "For now, you should perhaps speak to Mr. Axbrewder."

"Axbrewder?" Ted turned, saw Ginny and me. "Oh." He nodded at us, swallowing hard. "Brew. Ginny."

At once Ginny said, "We're working on a case that sounds a lot like what happened to your daughter. We'd like to talk to you about it."

Ted said, "Oh," again, weakly. He looked back at Encino. But before he could add anything, Ginny took his arm and started him toward the door. "Sergeant Encino understands the situation," she said reassuringly. "I'm sure he'll do everything he can."

Policewoman Rand was taking in all of this, so I didn't try to thank Encino. I just followed Ginny and Ted out into the corridor and closed the door behind me.

"Where shall we go?" she asked me over the top of his head.

"Somewhere we can eat." I hadn't had any food for close to fourteen hours, and I was feeling it.

Ted didn't resist. He looked like he'd used up all his energy or resolution just going to see Encino. Now he mumbled along beside Ginny like an empty shell. We took him out of the Municipal Building into the night.

The streetlights are bright in that part of town, and you

don't see many stars. But streetlights don't fool anybody. They just make the shadows look more dangerous. The people on the streets—there're always a few—moved as if they had secrets they were trying to hide. The cars that went by were going either too slow or too fast.

Night is the only time when I feel like I understand the city.

We went to a twenty-four-hour diner. After we'd ordered a good-sized pile of food, Ginny asked Ted to show us his note. He took it out without even a question—he looked like he was numb with shock. She scanned it, held it up to the light, then handed it to me.

It was a half sheet of good twenty-pound bond, neatly torn along one edge. The handwriting scrawled every which way. I held the paper up to the light and looked through it. It had part of the same watermark that was on the two notes in my pocket. I dug them out and gave them to Ginny.

She compared them from several angles, studied all three of them against the light, then handed Lona's and Ted's notes back to me.

With the torn edges together, they matched perfectly. Ted's note held the top third of the watermark missing from Lona's. There couldn't be any doubt about it—both these notes came from the same sheet of paper.

Sonofabitch! It was all I could do to contain myself. Fortunately the food began to arrive. I shut myself up by shoveling things into my mouth while Ginny told Ted about Alathea.

Just to look at him, you wouldn't have thought he heard a word she said. But when she asked him, "How long ago did Mittie disappear?" he blinked suddenly, and tears started running down his cheeks. It was hard to watch. His eyes were gushing, but he didn't let out a whimper. A couple minutes passed before he finally answered faintly, "Three days."

Five—no, six—days after Alathea turned up missing.

For no reason in the world that I was aware of, I found myself thinking, *The bastard's getting greedy*. More time had passed between the disappearances of the other seven girls.

Then Ginny asked, "How old was she?"

He had to struggle to make himself audible. "Thirteen." Then he covered his face with both hands. "She's all I have."

When Ginny looked over at me, her eyes were glittering the way they'd glittered after she'd shot the punk who broke her nose. "I'm ready to hear the details now," she said flatly. I glanced at Ted, but she answered, "He has a right to hear this."

He must've been paying attention despite his grief. He pulled out a dirty handkerchief, blew his nose hard. Then he fixed his watery eyes on me and didn't let go.

I put my notes on the table beside my plate and started to recite.

The basic facts were simple enough.

Two years ago, Marisa Lutt, a seventh-grader at Ensenada Middle School up in the Heights, failed to return home from school. Her parents filed a complaint almost immediately. Five days later, they reported receiving a letter from her, asking them not to worry. Her description—"very attractive"—was given to all police units. A detective spoke to her friends, her parents, and their friends, but failed to trace her. Three months later, she was killed by a truck while walking in the middle of the southbound interstate. The M.E. found evidence of massive heroin addiction, which he described as being of recent origin. He also found evidence of intensive sexual activity. The coroner concluded that she'd turned to prostitution to earn money for heroin. Death accidental as a consequence of an overdose. Investigation in progress to determine where she obtained her drugs. She was thirteen years old.

Twenty-two months ago, Esther Hannibal, a seventh-grader at Matthew Pilgrim Junior High down in the southeast part of town, failed to return home from school. Her parents reported her missing, but refused to file a complaint and didn't call again. Her description—"good-looking"—was given to all patrol units. Five months later, she fell off the roof of an abandoned building in the old part of town and died a few hours later of internal injuries. The M.E. found evidence of massive heroin addiction, which he described as being of recent origin. He also found evidence of intensive sexual activity. The coroner concluded that she'd turned to prostitution to earn money for heroin. Death accidental as a consequence of an overdose. Investigation in progress to determine where she obtained her drugs. She was thirteen.

Eighteen months ago, Ruth Ann Larsen, a sixth-grader at North Valley Middle School, failed to return home from school. Her parents were frantic initially and didn't hesitate to file a complaint. Four days later, however, they withdrew the complaint. Her description—"mature for her age"—was given to all patrol units. Three months later, she was found dead in the bottom of a construction pit out on the east side of the city. The M.E. was getting in a rut. Ditto the coroner. And the investigation. She was twelve.

Sixteen months ago, May-Belle Podhorentz, a seventh-grader at South Valley Junior High, failed to return home from school. Her parents reported her missing but were unwilling to file a complaint at first. However, three days later they received a letter from her, asking them not to worry. They asserted that the letter didn't fit their daughter and must have been written under duress. They then filed a complaint. Her description—"lovely"—was given to all patrol units. A detective spoke to friends and so forth and so on. Six months later, she crashed in a hang glider at night and was killed instantly. M.E. and coroner as usual. Investigation as usual. She was thirteen.

Eleven months ago, Rosalynn Swift, a sixth-grader at Matthew Pilgrim Junior High, failed to attend school after missing half her classes the previous day. The school reported her to the police. When questioned, her mother said that she hadn't come home the previous day. Her mother reported her as "a no-good chippy who's only interested in boys" and refused to file a complaint. The school filed instead. Her description—"cute and well-developed"—was given to all patrol units. Investigation went nowhere. Six months later her body was uncovered by a plow in the city dump while sanitation workers were redistributing garbage. The M.E. reported death by suffocation about a month previously. The rest of the report was as usual. She was twelve.

Seven months ago, Dottie Ann Consciewitz, a seventh-grader at Alsatia Junior High, failed to return home from school. Her parents filed a complaint immediately, claiming that she'd been kidnapped by her uncle in Detroit. Three days later, they received a letter asking them not to worry. This they showed to the police as evidence that her uncle had kidnapped her. They claimed she couldn't have written such a letter without his help. She was described as "beautiful." The Detroit police were unable to locate either her or her uncle. Five months later she was found in an empty apartment on the south side of the city. Death by electrocution—bad wiring on an electric hot plate. The M.E. and the coroner had nothing new to say. The investigation went nowhere. She was thirteen.

Three months ago, Carol Christie, a seventh-grader at North Valley Middle School, failed to return home from school. Her parents reported her missing. They appeared distressed, and her father filed a complaint without her mother's approval. Her description—"healthy and pretty"—was given to all patrol units. A detective and so on, without success. Her father called the police frequently to complain. Several times he made vague threats. Three months later—Monday this week—her body was found floating in the Flat River, drowned after a heavy overdose of heroin. The rest of his report was the same as the other six. Likewise the coroner's findings. Investigation still in progress. She was thirteen.

Ginny didn't react to any of it. She was just absorbing data. But a change came over Ted while he listened. Gradually he went rigid. Before I was finished, he'd turned so pale that I was afraid he'd have a coronary. He looked like a man whose whole life was falling apart. So he surprised me when he said in a tight flat voice, "You tell it as if all those girls were tied together—as if this is some kind of sick conspiracy. I don't know about that. What does it have to do with Mittie? She isn't a junkie. And she isn't a wh—" for a second, he couldn't get the word out—"a whore."

"Neither is Alathea," I growled.

"We don't know for sure that there *is* any connection," Ginny said. Her voice was abstract, and she didn't look at either of us. She was just thinking out loud. "All we know for sure is that both Mittie's and Alathea's notes came from the same sheet of paper—which happens to be the same kind of paper Carol Christie's note was on. Those three notes say almost exactly the same thing. If there were anything more solid than that, the cops would've found it by now. Obviously there're a lot of differences. But there're a lot of similarities, too. They were all in the same kind of trouble before they died. They all overlap by about a month—each one died a month after the next one disappeared."

Except for Alathea and Mittie, I said to myself. But I didn't interrupt her.

"And they all disappeared from school. None of them ran away at night, or after school, or over the weekend, or during the summer. Also none of them seem to have been on the stuff for very long."

"Three to six months," I agreed.

"I didn't know it was that easy to get," she muttered. "I didn't know a kid could buy enough of it to actually kill herself in three months—or even six." Suddenly she was angry. "Who the bloody hell supplies children like that?"

I was about to say that was what Acton reportedly wanted to find out, but Ted distracted me. He didn't look like he'd heard what Ginny just said. He was fumbling for his wallet. He got out a picture, showed it to Ginny and me. "And they were all cute."

He was right about that. I could vouch for Alathea. And Mittie looked very nice in her picture. It was hard to believe she was actually Ted's daughter.

For a while none of us said anything. Ginny was staring at a burnt-out light bulb in the ceiling, and I concentrated on eating. Judging from past experience, this would probably be the last food I could hold down until after the next withdrawal crisis. I didn't know when it was going to come—but it sure as hell was going to come. After that maybe being sober would get a little easier for a while.

Ted didn't eat anything. He was fidgeting under the silence. Finally he asked in a thin voice, "What're you going to do?"

Ginny's thoughts came down off the ceiling with a jerk. "The first thing we're going to do is try to get a look at some more notes."

Ted nodded. For a moment his lips trembled. Then he said, "I want to help."

"I'm counting on it." The glitter was back in her eyes. "If Mittie and Alathea really are tied in to Carol Christie and the rest of these girls, we need to move fast. Where did Mittie go to school?"

"Alsatia Junior High."

"All right. You take the Consciewitz girl. Give him the address, Brew." I got out a pen and wrote down the address on one of the napkins. When Ginny starts to give orders, she doesn't kid around. "The report on her mentioned a letter. I want that letter—the letter itself, not a copy. I want to know when they got it. I want to know where it was postmarked. I want to know why they think Dottie Ann didn't write it.

"Then go to the school. I'm not sure what I'm looking for there, so ask them about everything you can think of. Try to find out exactly where and when Dottie and Mittie left school. When you've got all that, call my answering service. We'll figure out where to go from there."

Watching him, you'd have thought that she'd just given him a transfusion. A little blood came back into his face, and some of the rigid way he held himself relaxed. It was just what he needed—somebody to give him orders, make him feel like he was doing something to help Mittie. But he had something else going on, too. There was something distant in his eyes that didn't match the rest of him. Just for a second he gave me the distinct impression that he had ideas he wasn't telling us. Then he left the table to pay his bill.

A minute later he hurried out of the diner. The impression faded as soon as he was gone.

I turned back to Ginny. "You found out something from Alathea's friends."

"Maybe." She started getting money out of her purse. "I'm not sure. I want to take another look at her school. She disappeared after fifth period, PE, right?"

"Right."

"Well, her sixth-period class was Home Ec. Apparently she was the only kid in that PE class who had Home Ec. afterward. So she always went from one to the other alone. The gym and the Home Ec. classroom are on opposite sides of the school, and she didn't have much time to get from one to the other, so she took a shortcut outside the buildings. As far as her friends know, she's the only one who took that shortcut between fifth and sixth periods."

"So whatever happened to her happened on that shortcut."

Ginny nodded. "Seems that way. We'll check it out tomorrow." Then she got to her feet. "Right now I'm going to take you home. You need sleep. If your eyes sink any farther back in your head, you might swallow them."

I couldn't argue with that. I'd been running on nothing but nervous tension for hours now—I did need sleep. And I always have an easier time relaxing when Ginny is in one of her take-charge moods. Spares me having to make decisions for myself. I waited for her to pay the bill, then followed her out to the Olds.

By then it was after midnight, and the night was darker than ever. But that suited me, too. It's hard to work on cases like this during the day. Sunlight makes everything about them seem unreal. At night there's always somebody somewhere who knows the secret. It's just a question of finding the right person and asking the right questions.

And something else kept me from feeling quite so scared for Alathea. The other girls on that list took at least three months to end up dead. Alathea had only been missing for nine days.

On the drive back to my apartment, I told Ginny how Encino had happened to change his mind about letting us see his files. That must've made a difference to her, because when she said good night she didn't look anywhere near as worried as she had earlier. She looked like a woman who knew she was on the right track.

7

The next morning, the phone pounded me awake around eight. It took me a long time to get to it. As soon as I sat up in bed, I had a blinding headache and every muscle in my body hurt as if I'd just gone fifteen rounds with a brick wall. That told me something, but for a while I couldn't remember what it was. All I could remember was the fine sharp taste of whiskey. Remember it—hell—I *wanted* it. For a while there it was worth more to me than love or money.

That explained why I hurt so bad. I'd slept through the first half of a crisis. My muscles ached from clenching, and my poor sodden brain was yowling, prompted by thirst. I was drenched in sweat.

The phone went on hammering at me, but I ignored it. I lumbered into the kitchen, thanking all the gods who watch over slobs like me that I'd had enough foresight to make up a jug of frozen orange juice before I went to bed. I drank about a quart of that while the phone went on ringing. Then I answered it.

"Brew?" It was Ginny. "Are you—no, forget that. Did I wake you up?"

That was an old question, and I answered it by force of habit. "No, I had to get up to answer the phone anyway." I didn't have enough brains with me to think of anything original.

She didn't even pretend to laugh. "How soon can you get ready to go? We've got work to do."

"Come pick me up," I said. "I'll be ready by then."

"We don't have time for that. We've got six sets of parents, five schools, and a school board to talk to. You'll have to rent a car."

"All right." Her tone was infectious. Just listening to her made me feel like she and I actually lived in the same world. "What do you want me to do?"

"There's no point in you going to any of the schools. If they have any sense, they won't talk to anybody until they see a license. Why don't you start with John and Mary Christie?"

"They'll never forgive me."

"I don't give a good goddamn. I want to know more about that note. I want to know what makes them so edgy."

I said, "They'll tell me." People generally tell me what I want to know—one way or another.

"They'd better," she said. Then she went on giving me orders. "When you're through there, go see that other family up in the North Valley, the Larsens. If you finish early, call my service. Otherwise I'll meet you at the school board at one. We have an appointment to talk to the chairman."

"Right." It sounded simple enough. It even sounded good to have her give me things to do alone. A big improvement over having her worried about me. "Anything else?"

"Yes. I need the addresses of those two girls who went to Matthew Pilgrim Junior High. I'll concentrate on the southeast—try to see the parents and talk to the school before I meet you."

I left the phone to dig out my notes, then gave her the addresses for the Hannibals and Mrs. Swift. A moment later, she said, "That leaves two."

"Marisa Lutt and May-Belle Podhorentz."

"Maybe we can check them out this afternoon."

She made sure I knew where the school board was. Then she hung up.

Work. I had work to do. I spent a minute trying to stretch some of the soreness out of my muscles. Then I got dressed.

Breakfast and the rest of the orange juice did a lot to soak the worst of the pain out of my head. By a quarter of nine I was practically functional. More out of duty than conviction, I strapped on my shoulder holster and checked over the .45. Then I made sure I had all the right papers with me—my notes and *the* notes—grabbed up my sunglasses, and went out to start batting my head against the morning.

As it happens, there's a cheap rent-a-relic agency about ten blocks from my apartment. By the time I walked the distance, I felt steadier physically, and they were open for business. I ended up with a middle-aged Torino. I wasn't very comfortable—some cars just aren't designed to fit the human body, no matter what size it is. But it had four wheels and an engine, which was all I needed. Before long I was on my way out toward the North Valley again.

I avoided what was left of rush hour traffic by taking old roads up along the river, but still it took me quite a while to reach the horsy area where the Christies lived. By then I was sweating in the heat. And the sun beat down on me in an almost insulting way—which didn't do anything for my mood, either. When the Torino bounced into the parking lot of the Christies' riding stables, I was ready to be as tough as necessary.

I went through the office door fast, aiming to take John and Mary by surprise. But the only one I surprised was Mrs. Christie. Her husband wasn't there.

When she saw me, she almost jumped out of her shirt. But she didn't yell for John. Instead she asked, "What do you want?" and her voice trembled. Which told me that Mr. Christie was somewhere out of range—maybe on one of the trails or doing business in town. In a way, that was unfortunate. I was primed to throw my weight around, and it wouldn't take any weight at all to make Mrs. Christie talk. Nerves or fear or whatever already put enough pressure on her.

So I sat down in a chair by the desk, crossed my legs, and said in the least threatening voice I could muster on such short notice, "I want to ask you a few questions about Carol."

"Go away." She had to hug herself to keep from shouting. "I can't talk to you. John doesn't want me to talk to you. He'll be back any minute. I'll call the police."

The way her eyes groped around the room as if she were praying for some kind of miracle told me that she was lying about her husband coming back. I countered with a lie of my own. "The cops know I'm here. They know we're working on this case."

"I don't want to talk to you." Somewhere she found the determination to sound defiant. "I don't have to talk to you."

I said, "That's true, Mrs. Christie." Calm, unthreatening. "But if you'll listen to me for a minute, I think you'll find you want to talk. You're afraid of something, and it isn't going to go away until this case is solved. This may be hard for you to believe, but I'm trying to help you.

"You see, I know what happened to Carol. I know she died from an overdose of heroin. I know how she earned the money for her drugs." Abruptly Mary Christie dropped into a chair and put her hands over her face. "There's no reason why you shouldn't answer my questions."

I gave her a minute to absorb that. Then I went on.

"Carol isn't the only one, Mrs. Christie. For two years now, the same thing has been happening to twelve- and thirteen-year-old girls everywhere in the city. Right now it's happening to my niece. That's why I need to talk to you."

She didn't look up, but slowly she took her hands away from her face. I could tell by the way her shoulders sagged that she was giving in. She was under too much strain to fight me and her fear at the same time.

Very gently, I eased her into it. "How long after Carol disappeared did you get her note?"

She took a deep, shuddering breath. "It was three days. We were worried sick."

"I can believe it. Did you happen to notice the postmark?"

"John did. It surprised him. It was mailed here in town."

"Why did that surprise him?"

"He—we both thought Carol had gone somewhere else. She has a lot of friends living in other parts of the state. We thought she must have gone to visit one of them."

"I understand. Mrs. Christie, did anything about the note bother you? Was there anything that didn't sound like her?"

"No," she said. Then, a moment later, "Yes—sort of. Carol didn't write letters. We used to send her to camp every summer, and she never wrote to us. And when she got back she didn't write to her friends. She didn't like to write. She liked to use the phone—she liked to call people. But she wouldn't write. One year she got in trouble at camp because the counselors wanted her to write a letter home like the rest of the girls, and she wouldn't." Finally she looked up at me. Her face was full of distress. "She loved us, that wasn't it. She didn't write to anybody. She didn't like to write."

I wanted to tell her that I understood, that I believed her. But the way she was looking at me gave me an opening I couldn't afford to miss. "Mrs. Christie," I said softly, "what're you so afraid of?"

"I—we—" For a moment she choked on it. But by now it was too late. She couldn't stop herself. "John says we might lose our business. He says if people find out what happened to Carol, they'll think we had something to do with it and stop coming here. They won't want their children to associate with us. But he's just saying that. He doesn't care about it. Carol was a *good* girl. He wants people to remember her the way she was, before—before she ran away."

I waited a moment, then said, "But that isn't it, either."

"No. No. We're both so—so ashamed. We don't want anybody to know. We failed her somehow. There must've been some way we could've been better parents. So she wouldn't have had to run away. That hurts. I keep wanting it to go away, and it doesn't.

"And that—that policeman. Detective Acton?" She looked at me, expecting me to recognize the name. "He th–threatened us. He said somebody is supplying drugs to young girls—all through the city—and the parents are the first suspects. He said he wanted to believe we were innocent, but he needed to keep what happened quiet, out of the papers and everything so nobody would know about it, and if we told anybody, talked to anybody, he would know we were deliberately interfering with his investigation. He was—awful. He looked like he liked hurting us.

"I haven't been able to sleep for nights. I keep having this nightmare that Carol is drowning and screaming for help, and I'm running frantically to try to get to her, but before I can get there Detective Acton comes out of the water and pushes her head down, and all the time he has the most terrible grin." Again she covered her face. "Oh, my baby!"

I didn't say anything. There was nothing I could say. The world is full of pains no stranger can comfort. The only thing I could do for her was find out the truth about Carol.

And keep my eyes open for a chance to give Detective-Lieutenant Acton what he had coming.

I left the trailer, closed the door quietly behind me, and went back to my rented Torino.

When I eased myself into the seat, I almost scalded my back on the vinyl upholstery. The sun had made it hot enough to fry eggs. I spat a few curses, but that didn't accomplish anything. The heat was just another item on a long list of things I couldn't do anything about. I started the engine, then tramped down on the accelerator and slewed out of the parking lot onto the road. For a few minutes I concentrated on speed, trying to build up enough wind to ventilate the car. Then I settled back, got a better grip on myself, and began to look for the Larsens' address.

It shouldn't have been hard to find, but I didn't know the North Valley very well, and for some reason Lujan Street didn't seem to be where I thought it was. Finally I had to stop at a small corner grocery store—the kind of glittering artificial place you find in moneyed neighborhoods, the kind that stocks more caviar than macaroni—to ask directions. Sure enough, Lujan Street turned out to be just about where I thought it was. However, *I* wasn't where I thought I was.

It was late in the morning when I finally parked in front of the Larsen mansion. It wasn't new. In fact, it had the Victorian look of a converted funeral home. But it sure as hell was big. I had to trek half a dozen blocks to reach the porch and ring the doorbell. Along the way, I passed five or six kids' bikes standing to one side.

About that time, the name Bjorn Larsen began to sound vaguely familiar.

A solid matronly woman—who turned out to be Magda Larsen answered the doorbell and invited me into the house.

The front hall was only twice the size of my apartment, and it was decorated, if that's the right word, with four massive iron sculptures as tall as I am. Two flanked the door, one stood beside the staircase, and one guarded the entrance to the living room. That explained it. Ruth Ann Larsen's father was Bjorn Larsen, the famous sculptor—one of Puerta del Sol's few certifiable claims to being an "art center."

Magda Larsen steered me into the living room, and a few moments later we were joined by her husband. He was as thickly built as she was, and as brawny as a steeplejack. He had a pair of welding goggles pushed back on his head and wore an asbestos apron over his T-shirt and jeans. The contrast between his clean hands and grimy forearms showed that he'd just taken off his work gloves.

"This is Mr. Axbrewder," Mrs. Larsen said. "He wants to talk to us about our daughter." Virtually a repeat of what I'd told her at the door. Her tone was noncommittal, almost distant, but her husband stuck out his hand as if he were prepared to welcome anybody she let into the house. "Pleased to meet you, Mr. Axbrewder. Have a seat?" He waved me toward an overstuffed sofa that looked like it ate people for lunch. All the furniture in the room was like that—deep, sturdy, and made to last.

I sat down at one end of the sofa. Magda joined me at the other, and Bjorn took a chair near her, unself-consciously courteous about placing himself so I could talk to both of them at once. "Which daughter did you have in mind?" he asked directly, "Risa or Natalie?"

Their openness made me hesitate. Neither of them had the vaguest notion what I had to say—and neither of them was the least bit afraid of it. I had a sudden desire to just tell them that I'd made a mistake and walk away. Somehow the complete frankness in their eyes made me feel like a child molester—me with all my grim, guilty secrets. I had to make an effort to say "Ruth Ann."

In a way, that announcement didn't make any difference. Mrs. Larsen gave a faint gasp and went pale. Blood flushed through her husband's face. But neither of them tried to hide their reactions—or to attack me with them. When Larsen spoke, he didn't sound either embarrassed or hostile.

"Ruth Ann died a miserable and senseless death. Magda and I will never understand it. What is your interest in her?"

Now that I was started, it was easier to go on. "I'm a private investigator. My niece has disappeared, and I'm trying to find her. It's possible she's going through the same thing that happened to your daughter. If you'd answer some questions for me, it might help me find her."

Bjorn Larsen looked at his wife. She was shaking her head. He turned back to me. "Ruth Ann has been dead for more than a year. Fifteen months now. What do you think our daughter and your niece have in common?"

That was tough to answer. His politeness gave me more trouble than almost any amount of hostility. After groping for a minute, I said, "It works better if I don't tell you. If I told you what I'm looking for, I'd be putting ideas into your head, and anything you said after that might not be completely candid. Naturally you'll react to whatever I say."

"I see." He folded his arms across his chest and considered me gravely.

"That policeman"—Magda Larsen was talking to her husband—"that Lieutenant Acton. He told us not to speak to anybody."

Bjorn nodded. "You see our problem, Mr. Axbrewder."

"Yeah." I saw it, all right—and I didn't much like what I was seeing. "But that was fifteen months ago. We know things now that Acton didn't know then. Look." My voice was rougher than I intended, but I had to appeal to them somehow. "I didn't find out about this from the papers. I know exactly how miserable and senseless Ruth Ann's death was. What I'm trying to do is prevent the same thing from happening again to another vulnerable little girl."

Again Larsen looked at his wife. She'd produced a Kleenex from somewhere and was using it to wipe her eyes. "Ah, Bjorn," she sighed, "tell him. Of all people we should be willing to do whatever we can to prevent such things."

Larsen accepted that without argument. "Very well, Mr. Axbrewder. Ask your questions."

"Thanks. I won't take much of your time." But then I had

to pause for a few seconds, pull my scattered brains together. The living room was starting to get hot, but neither of the Larsens looked like they felt it. Both of them watched me, curious to see what sort of questions I'd produce. I took a deep breath.

"When Ruth Ann didn't come home from school that day, you were very concerned."

"That's true," Larsen said. "She was always a very responsible child. If she were going to a friend's home after school, if she were to be late for any reason, she was very faithful about letting us know."

"So when you realized she was missing, you called the police and filed a complaint."

"Yes. We were reluctant to file the complaint. But we were very concerned, and the police didn't appear to take the situation seriously enough. We filed the complaint in an effort to produce action."

"Then four days later you withdrew the complaint."

"Why, yes." He seemed momentarily confused. "Yes, we did."

"Why was that?"

"Well, you see—" He faltered. "As I say, she was a very responsible girl. We knew that she wouldn't run away without very good reasons. Four days after she disappeared, we received a letter from her. Really, it was just a short note. She assured us that she was all right, and said that she would come home as soon as she had dealt with some problem bothering her. Under the circumstances, we felt it would be a violation of her privacy if the police were to bring her home against her will. We withdrew the complaint." He said this with such dignity that I couldn't argue with him. It was on the tip of my tongue to say that twelve-year-old girls have more important needs than privacy. But I didn't.

He must have seen some of what I was thinking on my face, because he added, "Children have the same rights as any other person. So many children grow up to be spoiled, irresponsible, or unproductive because they are treated 'like children,' which means that their parents are more interested in their own desires for power than in their children's autonomy."

That shook me up. Ruth Ann Larsen had turned to prostitution to support her drug habit, and her parents hadn't even tried to look for her. But my expression didn't make a dent on her father. He believed in his own integrity.

For some reason, so did I. Instead of shouting at him, I just said, "All right. There's only one thing that really matters. Do you still have her note?"

"I will get it," Mrs. Larsen said. She rose out of the sofa, left her husband and me staring at each other. I didn't much care for the view, so I spent my time looking around the room until she came back.

She handed me an envelope. It had a clear Puerta del Sol postmark. Inside I found a half sheet of good twenty-pound bond, neatly torn along one edge. The handwriting scrawled all over the place.

It said, "Dear Mom and Dad, I have to be away for a while, but there's nothing to worry about. I'll be fine. I have a problem to work on. I'll be back when I'm done. Love, Ruth Ann."

Sure enough, the paper had the same watermark as the other notes.

All of a sudden, my throat was so dry that I could hardly swallow. I needed a *drink*. It took me a moment to work enough moisture into my mouth to ask, "Is—is there anything about this that—seems unusual to you? Out of place? Does it sound like her?"

Larsen said immediately, "Of course. It's her writing."

But his wife didn't hesitate either. "No. It isn't like her. It says, 'Dear Mom and Dad.' Our children don't call us by those names. Since she was a little girl she has called us 'Bjorn' and 'Magda.' "

I was cold and shivering inside. Whoever had dictated those notes hadn't even bothered to get them right.

I didn't ask the Larsens if I could have their note. I just took it and left. What else can you do with parents who trust their children too much to protect them?

8

I still needed a drink. Sometimes being sober is like drowning. After a certain point, you know you're going to have to breathe, no matter what. But you don't—not until you pass out. I didn't go to a bar, I went to meet Ginny.

It was a long drive back to the middle of town, but when I got near Central High, where the school board has its offices, I was still a bit early so I stopped to grab a quick lunch. That made it twelve forty-five when I pulled into the Central High parking lot.

Central isn't the newest high school in the city, but it is sure as hell the biggest and most bewildering. You could hide a football field in there and never find it again because the school was built in huge square sections that interlock and form a maze. They had to make it a high school because nobody younger than a freshman could find their way around in it. I was lucky I hadn't gone to school there. I've never been very good at mazes.

A couple of minutes later, Ginny wheeled her Olds into the lot and parked it a few spaces down from my rented Torino. I was glad to see her. The sun on all those parked cars gave the day a glare of futility. Everybody in the whole city could go crazy, rape each other, and drop dead, and it wouldn't make one damn bit of difference to the sun. Ginny was a good antidote for that kind of thinking.

I walked over to join her. Maybe it was just wishful thinking, but I thought she looked glad to see me, too. I caught her making a sneaky effort to check my breath. Then her face relaxed into a smile. For a second there, I almost hugged her. Sometimes her smile does funny things to me.

Then she said, "What've you got?" and we were back to business.

I showed her the Larsens' note and told her about my morning. I didn't leave anything out. Talking about good old Detective-Lieutenant Acton didn't do my blood pressure any favors, but I've never worried much about my arteries anyway.

She absorbed what I had to say, considered it briefly. Then she told me what she'd come up with.

"Mrs. Swift is a real charmer. I must've gotten her out of bed. She came to the door looking like the wrath of God, wearing one of those polyester bathrobes, turquoise and pink paisley. Gave me a headache just to look at her. She acted like she'd invented bitchiness all by herself. All she could say about her daughter was that she was 'no good.' Ungrateful little slut, running off and leaving her poor mother all alone like that. I had to lean on her to get anything else."

I grinned. "Wish I'd seen that."

"It wasn't fun. And hardly worth the effort. She finally admitted getting a letter, though, sometime after her daughter ran away. She doesn't remember when, and she doesn't remember what it said. She tore it up as soon as she read it. She does remember the cops coming to see her, especially after Rosalynn turned up dead. But she claims she doesn't remember who they were or what they wanted."

She paused, then said, "I don't know, Brew. Maybe Rosalynn Swift doesn't fit the pattern. If I were her, I'd run away from that woman seven days a week."

"Yeah, but don't cross her off the list yet. She went the same route as the others."

Ginny thought a minute before she said, "Right."

"What about the Hannibals?"

"Better." She made the transition with a jerk. "*Much* better. I caught them both at home. He works the evening shift down at the paper mill, so he was just having breakfast when I got there. He's a feisty little man who likes to fly off the handle, but his heart's in the right place. Mrs. Hannibal is as steady as a rock, so she keeps him in line. At first they didn't want to talk. Some cop told them not to, they don't remember his name. After all, it was a year and a half ago.

But after I explained what we were trying to do, they changed their minds.

"Judging from what they told me, I'd say that when Esther disappeared they were nearly paralyzed with anger and fear. Furious at her for running away, and at the same time terrified that something had happened to her. It was all they could do to report her missing. They just couldn't bring themselves to swear out a complaint. Mr. Hannibal probably spent half his time shouting and the other half in a cold sweat. Then they got a letter from her telling them not to worry, she was all right. That gave them an out, an excuse to do nothing.

"Looking back on it, they're pretty bitter about themselves. Esther's death gave them a real shock, which probably explains why they were willing to help me in the end. They say they've changed their whole attitude toward their other children. To prove it, they gave me Esther's letter."

Ginny handed it to me, envelope and all.

It had a local postmark. The handwriting was barely legible. The note was on a half sheet of good twenty-pound bond, neatly torn along one edge. It said, "Dear Mom and Dad, I'm not going to be coming home for a while. Maybe for a long time. I've got something to work out. Don't worry, I'll be all right. Love, Esther." The watermark matched the others.

While I studied it, Ginny went on, "I asked them if there was anything about this that bothered them. At first they couldn't think of anything, but then they said there was one thing. One of the many things that made them ashamed of themselves. Esther always came home from school for lunch, which she always complained about because her friends ate in the school cafeteria. But the Hannibals only live three blocks from the school, and anyway they couldn't afford school lunches.

"The day she disappeared, she didn't come home for lunch. The Hannibals didn't think much about it. They assumed a friend gave her lunch, or she bought her own out of her allowance. Now they feel like they failed her by not realizing something was wrong. As if there was anything they could've done." Abruptly Ginny's voice went stiff with anger. "Heaven help the bastard who's responsible for this when I get my hands on him."

I knew how she felt. But we have a reciprocal relationship—when one of us gets mad, the other tries to stay calm. I said, "If Ted doesn't get to him first." Which wasn't much of a contribution, but it was all I had. "How's he doing, anyway? Has he called in?"

She calmed down again so fast it was almost scary. "He called while I was at the Hannibals. He didn't want to talk about it over the phone, he just wanted me to give him more to do. I told him to check out May-Belle Podhorentz and South Valley Junior High. He's supposed to meet us back at the office in a couple of hours."

It was one o'clock when we headed into Central High's monster building and began hunting for the school board wing. The kids must've all been in class, because we saw only one or two. As we walked along the hollow corridors, I asked Ginny if she'd learned anything at Matthew Pilgrim Junior High.

"It probably doesn't mean anything," she said, "but both Rosalynn Swift and Esther Hannibal disappeared at times when they were routinely alone. Esther was there for her last period before lunch, and gone afterward. As for Rosalynn, apparently she had a tendency to get in trouble. Nothing serious. Just trying to get attention. So as a form of punishment she was assigned to clean up the math classroom every day right after lunch, while the other kids were free. Alone. She'd been doing it for about a month—and doing a good job of it, according to the math teacher—when she disappeared. Just didn't show up for her next class. Nobody saw her leave, which isn't surprising since the math room is in the corner of the building farthest away from the playground and the cafeteria.

"The people I talked to were fairly helpful, but they made it clear that I ought to be talking to the school board instead of bothering them. They kept assuring me the board had all the information I needed. I got the impression they want the board to decide for them whether or not we have any legal right to pry into all this."

"Sounds familiar," I muttered. At Alathea's school, Vice-principal Rumsfeld had given me pretty much the same impression.

Then we found what we were looking for, a frosted-glass door in the middle of a blank wall. The lettering on the glass said,

PUERTA DEL SOL BOARD OF EDUCATION
PAUL M. STRETTO, CHAIRMAN
JULIAN Z. KIRKE, SECRETARY

Ginny pulled open the door, and I followed her in.

The rooms inside reminded me of the Municipal Building—no windows, no comfortable colors, everything artificial. Beyond the counter in front of us was a room that looked too small for the ten or twelve desks and thirty or so filing cabinets squeezed into it. At the desks, women in various stages of energy or desperation hacked away at typewriters, scrawled on files, answered phones. Two or three of them in particular had a frightened air, as if someone I couldn't see stood over them with a cat-o'-nine-tails.

We found out why. Before we had time to introduce ourselves to the secretary who did double duty as receptionist, a man came out of an office at the back of the room. He had light blond hair, sleepy eyes, and a mouth so sharp and strong that it looked like he ate steel for breakfast every morning. He wasn't in a hurry, but somehow he gave the impression that he was pouncing.

He said, "Sondra." Although he didn't raise his voice, it cut through the work noise in the room, and a woman two desks away from him flinched. She was young and pretty. After I'd noticed that, I realized that all the secretaries who looked particularly miserable were young and pretty.

The man went over and held a sheet of paper in front of her. He handled the paper gently enough, but in some strange way his manner made the movement look like an act of violence. "Type it again," he said. "This time, get it right." His tone held enough sarcasm to draw blood.

He'd started back to his office when he noticed Ginny and me standing at the counter. He turned toward us. "It looks like Sally is asleep on the job again." The secretary-receptionist flushed and bit her lip. "What can I do for you?" the man asked.

"I'm Ginny Fistoulari," Ginny said. "This is Mr. Axbrewder." If you didn't know her, you would've thought that she hadn't felt a thing. But I could hear the underlying bite in her voice. "We have an appointment with Mr. Stretto."

"He's expecting you," the man said. "This way." We passed around the counter and followed him toward a door in the opposite corner. As we crossed the room, I caught a look at the nameplate on the door of the man's office. It said, "JULIAN Z. KIRKE, SECRETARY."

Then we were in a corridor that ran between more offices and ended up in a big place that looked like a corporate boardroom. Long dark wood table, heavy matching armchairs. Soft indirect lighting. Picture window along one wall overlooking the glare of the parking lot. It was a far cry from the sweatshop where those harried secretaries worked. Kirke guided us into the room and introduced us to Chairman Paul Stretto.

He looked like the kind of man the Republicans run for president—strong lines in his face, a mane of silver hair, resonant baritone voice, just a hint of well-earned fat on his tall frame. He sat at the head of the table as if he'd been born there. At first I couldn't figure out what he was doing in a lowly job like board of education chairman when he could've been elected mayor tomorrow—with a little help from TV. But as we shook hands I got a closer look at him. He was younger than he seemed, and the fine silver of his hair came out of a jar. Probably he was saving mayor for later. After which he'd take a crack at governor.

He gestured Ginny and me toward chairs as if he were offering to knight us. He asked Kirke to stay. "Things always run better around here," he explained, "when Julian knows what's going on."

No doubt. I was already sure that Paul M. Stretto was just

office-sitting on his way to better things. Kirke was the man who actually ran the school board.

When we were all seated around the head of the table, Stretto said, "Now, what can we do for you?" He sounded full to the gills with professional bonhomie.

"Mr. Stretto," Ginny began, "we're private investigators." She showed him the photocopy of her license. "We've been retained to find two young girls who ran away from home early last week. In the process, we've learned that quite a few girls of junior high age have run away recently—in the past two years, to be more exact. Some of those cases bear a striking resemblance to the ones we're working on. It might help us find these girls if we could see some of your files."

"I see." She'd taken him by surprise—most people don't expect visits from private investigators—and he made a great show of thinking hard about it. Which led him to the unsurprising conclusion that he was out of his depth. "What do you think, Julian?"

Before Kirke could answer, however, Stretto said to us, "Julian is the expert on our files. We're in the process of a major overhaul of our record system. Our goal is to computerize the files completely so that Puerta del Sol's entire school system will share a network linked to a central server here. Everything will be available by computer anywhere in the system.

"But"—he smiled warmly—"that's a few years in the future. Right now, Julian is busy getting our files ready for computerization. It's a huge job. First he had to get copies of everything from each individual school. And now he has to put all that data in a usable form. Fortunately he's an expert at it. That's why the board hired him."

Kirke listened to all this without any particular show of respect, but at least he didn't interrupt. On the other hand, he didn't waste time when the chairman finally finished his little speech. Right away, he asked Ginny, "Do you have consent from the parents?"

"Not in writing," she said evenly. "We've spoken to them, that's all."

"We'd be violating the confidentiality of our students if we opened our files without some kind of written permission."

"That's right," Stretto said. Nobody even looked at him.

"In any case," Kirke went on, "I don't think it would be worth your trouble." His voice held just a hint of a sneer. "What could you possibly find? From our point of view, all runaways are the same. They're all having trouble of some kind. They all miss school for a while. Eventually most of them return. If some of them have something in common, you wouldn't find it in our files."

Innocent as sugar, Ginny asked, "You don't keep any record of the runaways who end up dead?"

"Dead?" Stretto demanded. "Are these girls dead?"

Now she let him feel some of the bite in her tone. "In the past two years, seven junior-high girls in this school system have run away from home and died."

"But"—the chairman was groping—"what does that have to do with us?"

"Those seven girls are connected in some way. And they're connected to the girls we're looking for. We want to find them before the same thing happens to them. We can't afford to overlook anything—and one possibility is that there are facts buried away in your files that could help us."

"This is very upsetting." Stretto looked upset. "Of course we want to help in any way we can." Probably because he didn't have any better ideas, he latched onto what Kirke had said earlier. "If you'll get written consent from the parents, we'll show you everything we have."

"We don't have time to do that," Ginny snapped. "Those seven girls died as a direct result of whatever made them run away. The process has already started for two more." She was laying it on thick. "Every delay could be fatal." I wanted to applaud.

"I'm sorry, Ms. Fistoulari." If you could trust his face, Paul Stretto really was sorry. "There's nothing I can do." But if he wanted us to believe him, he blew it a second later by turning to Kirke and asking, "Is there, Julian?"

Kirke said, "No." He made the word sound like he'd chewed it out of pig iron.

Ginny considered for a moment. Then she said, "Give me the notes, Brew."

I dug them out and handed them over.

"Mr. Stretto," she said grimly, "we have reason to believe that these girls didn't just die. They may have been killed. Murdered." She stressed the word. "Each girl sent her parents a note. I have some of them here, and I'd like you to read them."

One by one, she put the Christie, Larsen, and Hannibal notes in front of him.

He was confused, but her tone didn't leave him any choice. He read them, then read them again.

"Now please read these two," she said as she showed him Alathea's note, and Mittie's. "They were written by the girls we're trying to find."

He read them too, but he seemed to have difficulty understanding what they said.

"They're all written on the same kind of paper," Ginny observed roughly. "The watermarks are identical."

A minute later I was surprised to see a change come over Mr. Paul M. Stretto, chairman of the board of education. All of a sudden, he didn't look like a man who just happened to have an electable face. He looked like he'd earned it. "Julian," he said in a completely different tone, "get Martha and Astin in here."

If all this made any impression on Kirke, he didn't show it. He just got up and left the room. When he came back, he had a man and a woman in tow. The man looked worn out, like a pencil that's been sharpened too often, but the woman bristled with energy.

Stretto introduced us. The man was Astin Greenling, curriculum vice-chairman for the board. The woman was Martha Scurvey, budget vice-chairman. Aside from Stretto and Kirke, they were the only full-time members of the board. The other elected members served part-time.

Stretto gave Greenling and Scurvey a quick summary covering most of the facts, then handed them the notes.

Neither of them seemed to grasp the significance of what they read. Greenling muttered, "You'd think we didn't teach penmanship at all." Scurvey gave a sigh that puffed out her cheeks. "If this kind of thing gets out, we're in trouble. We already have a hard enough time selling our budget to the legislature."

"I didn't call you in here for your opinions," Stretto rapped out. Under his hair paint, he must've been a secretly decisive man. Or else he was doing a damn good imitation. "I simply want witnesses so that there won't be any confusion. These notes have convinced me that Ms. Fistoulari is right. As of now, I'm instructing Julian to give her our complete cooperation. I don't know what's happening to these girls, but I want it to stop."

There was silence in the room. Then Scurvey said, "Wouldn't it be better to call the police?"

"Leave that to me, Martha," the chairman answered.

Finally I figured out what he was doing. He was putting on a show for two influential—i.e., voting—members of the board. A display of power to consolidate his position. When a diplomat does it, it's called statesmanship. But it was a gift horse, and I didn't look it in the mouth. All I cared about was getting to see those files.

Stretto dismissed us. I picked up the notes, and we followed Kirke back down the hall to his office. There I gave him our list of names. Mostly because I didn't like him, I watched him carefully for a reaction to any of the names, but I didn't spot one. For all he cared, apparently, I'd read them out of the phone book. He wrote them down, then left us in his office.

He came back with the files fast enough to prove that he knew his job. But he didn't leave us alone while we read them.

It took us half an hour to go through them all. I hated to admit it, even to myself, but as far as I could see Kirke was right. The files didn't do us any good. I took a few notes— the girls' schedules on the days they disappeared, the names of their teachers, things like that—but the information didn't help. If Ginny found anything interesting, she didn't say so.

But I didn't expect her to, not with Kirke hovering over us.

When we were finished, she thanked him—which I thought wasn't called for—and led the way out of his office. As I followed her through the door, he stopped me. He stood up close and whispered so that Ginny couldn't hear him, "Do you always tag along behind her like this?"

"Like what?"

He shook his head, dismissed the question. "You're wasting your time. By the time they reach junior high, most girls are nothing but little whores. There's nothing special about the ones that run away. Did you know that we're having a near-epidemic of VD among the junior-high boys?"

I wrapped my left hand around his upper arm and dug my fingers in until his face turned white. "Watch your mouth," I whispered back at him. "You're talking about my niece."

I gave his arm an extra squeeze to remember me by, then hurried after Ginny. I was grinning, but I wasn't amused.

Once we were outside the office and on our way back to the parking lot, Ginny asked me, "What was that all about?"

"Kirke didn't much like the way he got overruled."

She nodded sharply. "Sonofabitch."

I agreed with her. But the main thing bothering me was the feeling that it was all wasted. We weren't getting anywhere.

9

We didn't talk about it. Ginny had a pinched look between her eyes, the one that meant she was thinking hard. I had no idea what she was thinking about, but I learned long ago to leave her alone when she looks like that.

I didn't even ask her where we were going. She headed straight for her Olds, opened the door and got in. I wedged myself into my Torino and followed.

We ended up at Mountain Junior High, where we had another session with Vice-principal Rumsfeld. She wasn't exactly overjoyed to see us again, but this time Ginny had a much clearer idea of what she wanted to know, and the vice-principal wasn't the kind of woman who could turn us down if there was any chance at all of helping one of her students. She took us to meet Alathea's PE teacher, and the two of them showed us Alathea's shortcut between her fifth and sixth periods.

"We don't normally allow our students outside the school buildings unsupervised," Ms. Rumsfeld said sternly, "but I understand that this was something of a special case."

"Alathea had an awkward schedule," the PE teacher said. "She had a hard time getting from the gym to her next class before it started. She asked permission to take this shortcut. I didn't see any reason to turn her down. She was a very dependable girl."

Very dependable. Yes. That's what I had to keep in mind. I didn't know any of the seven dead girls. For all I knew, every one of them might've been a raving lunatic. But I knew Alathea. She wasn't crazy, or on drugs, or a whore.

With the vice-principal and the PE teacher guiding us, we needed about five seconds to see why Alathea had wanted to use the outside route. For someone in a hurry, it was much easier than going through the buildings. But it was also a perfect place to disappear from, if that's what you had in mind. The buildings stood close to the street, and on that side most of them—the gym, the auditorium, one end of the library—didn't have any windows. Alathea hadn't just been alone, she'd been out of sight.

Which fit with what Ginny'd learned about Rosalynn Swift and Esther Hannibal. But it didn't mean anything to me. If you wanted to run away from school, would you do it when you were surrounded by kids and teachers, or when you were alone?

But Ginny seemed satisfied with whatever it was we'd learned. She thanked Ms. Rumsfeld and the PE teacher, told them we wouldn't bother them again if we could help it. Then we left.

This time she led me all the way down Paseo Grande to the Murchison Building. Back to her office.

Ted was there waiting for us. He looked like he'd spent the day in a dryer at the laundromat—hot, thirsty, and about two sizes smaller. But his eyes weren't bulging the way they did last night. They were sunken and sizzling, as if they were being cooked from inside by whatever he was thinking.

He didn't say anything until we were settled in Fistoulari Investigations' back room. Then he confronted Ginny. Standing in front of her with his hands on his hips, he looked like the losing end of a cockfight, plucked half to death and still ready to peck anything in sight. "You're wasting my time," he said.

That surprised her. She looked at him hard. "I thought you wanted to help." Even sitting down, she was practically his size.

"I want to find Mittie. This way isn't getting me anywhere."

Well, off and on I'd been thinking the same thing myself, but for some reason it irritated me to hear him say it. Apparently I felt that nobody but me was allowed to disagree with Ginny—which makes even less sense when you think about it. But I didn't get a chance to argue with him. She

was working on what he said faster than I was. "Why not?
Didn't you get anything?" she asked.

"Oh, I got what you wanted, all right." He took two half
sheets of paper out of his pocket and tossed them on the
desk. "I know we're in a grubby business, but it isn't supposed to be this bad. Nailing people who screw around,
clearing people who don't—that's what we're supposed to
do. Not this. It was bad enough talking to those Consciewitz
people. They're lunatics—all that stuff about an 'uncle in
Detroit'—but they miss their daughter so much it's making
them sick. They were practically desperate to make me take
their note. They say it proves she didn't run away. I don't
know how, their explanations didn't make any sense. As far
as I can tell, believing she didn't run away is the only thing
that stops them from killing themselves.

"But May-Belle Podhorentz's parents—My God, Ginny!
I practically had to extort that note out of them. It's the only
piece of her they had left. After what happened to her, they
had to put up with some half-wit cop who gave them a
bunch of shit. They spent ten months being eaten alive by
fear and shame and God knows what else. Then I came
along. Next time, just ask me to rape the rest of their kids.
It'll be easier."

Ginny still hadn't even glanced at the notes on her desk.
But if Ted made her mad, she kept it to herself. She just
held her eyes on him and asked, "Did they say if they
thought May-Belle's note was written under duress?"

"They didn't say, and I didn't ask. I was too ashamed of
myself."

She considered for a moment, then said, "All right. I don't
really need that. What about the schools?"

"Nothing," Ted rasped. "May-Belle Podhorentz and Dottie Ann Consciewitz were just like Mittie: They disappeared
when nobody was watching them."

Ginny sat up straighter in her chair. "What do you mean?"

"What do you think I mean? None of them walked away
from their friends or disappeared in the middle of a class or
snuck out the back way during lunch. They all waited until
they were alone. May-Belle was a piano student. One of the

practice rooms was assigned to her during her third period. She didn't show up for her fourth-period class. Dottie Ann liked PE, and she had a job in the gym during fifth period. She sorted uniforms and equipment. Alone. She didn't make it to sixth period. And Mittie—"

He started to shout. "It was the same goddamn thing with Mittie!" He couldn't help himself. "What the hell do you care? What does all this prove? We're not getting anywhere, and you know it!"

Ginny never flinched. "I think that what we're doing is pretty obvious. What else would you suggest?"

That stopped him. But not because he didn't have ideas of his own. His expression reminded me of the way he'd left the diner the night before. He had something in mind, no question about it. Whatever it was, however, he stopped because he didn't want to say it out loud.

"Spill it, Ted," I said softly. "We're all in this together."

He didn't move a muscle.

I went on. "And you need us. You don't have a client. You can't hire yourself to look for your own daughter. You'll lose your license."

I knew a thing or two about losing a license.

Then he turned to face me. His cheeks were as pale as frostbite. "I don't give a shit about that," he said. "I don't want any of this to be true."

I held his eyes.

Thickly he asked, "What do you think about—about prostitution? Where does that fit in?"

"Isn't it obvious?" I was trying to guess what he really had in mind. "That's probably the only thing the coroner was right about. They have to get money somewhere. How else are girls that age going to do it?"

Something like a spasm of rage or disgust jumped across Ted's face. He turned on his heel and left the office.

Ginny stared after him for a long time, frowning grimly. Then she picked up the notes he'd left on her desk. She read them, studied them, checked the watermarks, then handed them to me.

They fit the pattern exactly—paper, watermark, torn edge,

handwriting, everything. When I compared them with the notes we already had, I saw that May-Belle Podhorentz' was word-for-word identical with Mittie's.

After all, sixteen months is a long time for whatever bastard dictated these notes to remember exactly what they said.

"I should have told him what we've got," Ginny said. Still thinking about Ted.

"He didn't want to hear it." That was my first reaction. Then I said, "Besides, we haven't got anything."

"That depends on what you're looking for," she replied in a musing tone. "Things are starting to fit together."

"Oh, good." Being sober doesn't do much for my temper. "Now if the fit just made sense, we'd be getting somewhere."

It was her turn to stay calm. "We *are* getting somewhere. If Marisa Lutt's parents have a note like these, we'll have a case that can stand up under any kind of pressure—even if that fucker Acton tries to get us out of the way."

"That isn't what I meant." Even I knew how important those notes were.

She looked at the ceiling for a moment, then said, "I take it you didn't notice anything interesting in what Ted told us? About how Mittie, May-Belle, and Dottie Ann disappeared?"

"It's the same story as Alathea," I said sourly. "I knew all that already. I read it in Kirke's files. So what?"

"I'm going to have to check it out with the other schools. This is too iffy to take chances with. But I think there's something important in those files. According to them, these girls didn't just run away from school—they ran away *during* school. Never after or before. During. And every one of them was alone on a regular basis at some point in the school day. Being alone didn't happen by accident on a particular day."

"Which proves what?" She was on the edge of something. I could feel it. But I didn't have the dimmest notion what it was. I was like Ted—I had ideas of my own, and they didn't seem to relate to what Ginny was thinking.

"I don't know yet. Files don't always give a very clear picture of what really happens."

That was true enough. But it still didn't mean anything to me. Even if the other files checked out with the schools themselves, that only showed that every one of the girls had a regular chance to run away. Opportunity, nothing more.

I used to know some cops, back in the days when I was still on speaking terms with some of them, who believed that opportunity creates crime. People do things for the simple reason that they get the chance. Wives shoot their husbands because there's a gun in the house. Kids become junkies because drugs exist. Responsible executives take money out of the till and blow it in Las Vegas because Las Vegas is there. Opportunity. Those cops used to talk about preventing crime by getting rid of opportunity.

I think that's a crock of manure. In my opinion, people commit gratuitous crimes, crimes they aren't forced into, the way a starving man sometimes feels forced to steal, or a woman whose husband is cheating on her sometimes feels forced to shoot him, for the sake of power. If they can get away with it, it puts them on top of the world.

But right then I wasn't so sure of anything. If Ginny wanted to blame it on opportunity, I wasn't going to argue with her. I didn't have anything better to offer. Instead I said, "There's plenty of daylight left. What do you want me to do while I've still got wheels?"

"Marisa Lutt," she said without hesitation. "Let's make sure we've got everything. I'm tempted to call Encino, ask him to go farther back than two years. But I'm half afraid to find out if there're any more of these cases. And I got the impression that he's going to work on it anyway. Maybe he didn't know about the notes before, but he does now. He'll probably call us himself if he finds anything we need to know."

I agreed with that. "You're going to do the rest of the schools?"

"Yes. Ensenada and North Valley. I think that covers it, doesn't it?"

I made a quick mental check. "That's it."

"OK." She got to her feet. "Call my answering service when you're finished. Then you might as well get rid of that clunker."

"Yeah." I heaved myself up out of the chair. Collected all the notes and stuffed them in my pocket. This time I went out first. I wasn't trying to prove anything, no matter what Kirke had said. It was her office, and she had to lock up after me.

Alone again, I dug the Torino out of the garage and headed in the direction of the Heights. The Lutts lived in one of those newish suburbs where all the houses look nice even though they're crammed together on lots you can hardly lie down crosswise on, and all the streets and even the developments have cute irrelevant names. The Lutts' development was called Sherwood Forest—in this part of the world, of all places—and they lived on Friar Tuck Road between Little John Street and Maid Marian Lane. As first impressions go, it didn't raise my expectations about Carson and Lillian Lutt, but I suppose with real estate prices being what they are you pretty much have to live wherever you find a house you can afford. If I wasn't mistaken, Sherwood Forest's big selling point was that the houses were less expensive than they looked. That, and a chance to send your junior-high kids to Ensenada Middle School.

I parked in the street, even though that left precious little room for the rest of the traffic, and went up the walk to the Lutts' front door. Paint and trim aside, their place was identical to every fourth house on the block. And they had one chest-high piñon growing out of their front lawn, just like every other property in sight.

Unfortunately you can't tell what's going on inside a house from the outside. When Carson Lutt opened the door, it took me just one second to be sure that he was drunk.

He looked me up and down blearily, as if I were some kind of obnoxious consequence of his drinking, then said, "What the hell do you want?" His voice was smeared around the edges in a way that showed he wasn't really very good at drinking. It takes practice to learn how to speak clearly when you're full of booze.

I groaned to myself. The smell of his breath made me as thirsty as a dog. And I was already in no mood to put up with a belligerent drunk. I had to make a special effort not to sound too hostile myself. "My name is Axbrewder. I'd like to talk to you about your daughter."

"That punk?" he snorted. "What's she done now?"

"Nothing as far as I know."

"Oh." That seemed to surprise him. For a minute he forgot to be angry at me. "Come on in." He waved me into the house and shut the door. "Have a drink."

"No, thanks." The living room looked better than I'd expected. Whoever decorated it had spent enough money to make the atmosphere soothing and the furniture comfortable, but stopped before the place looked like those implausible pictures in home decorating magazines. It was the kind of room where you'd expect a quietly successful businessman and his wife to give quiet parties for friends they actually enjoyed.

Well, Lillian Lutt was sitting there on the couch quietly enough—but if she'd looked any more miserable you could've stuck her head on a pole and used her to ward off evil spirits. She had a tall glass in her hands, the kind you use for heavy drinking. It took me a couple of seconds to pull myself together enough to add, "I'm on the wagon today."

Carson Lutt peered at me. "Did I hear you say no?"

"Offer him a drink, Carson," Lillian Lutt said from the couch. "I hate to drink alone."

"You're not drinking alone," he said. "I'm drinking with you."

"That's nice." She almost smiled.

"Have a drink," he said to me. "I'm serious."

I said, "So am I. I don't want a drink. I want to talk about your daughter."

"What's she done now?" Mrs. Lutt asked. The pain in her face was terrible to look at.

"Nothing," I snapped. The smell of all that alcohol made my nerves jumpy. My control wasn't as good as it should've been. "She's been dead a little too long for that."

That took a minute to sink in. Lillian gave me one straight look as if she were about to scream, then got up and walked out of the room.

"All right, you, whatever your name is." Suddenly Lutt's voice was clear and sharp and determined. "Get out of here."

"Tell me about Marisa first."

He didn't even blink. "You're a lot bigger than I am. I don't think I can throw you out. But I'm going to try. And I'm going to keep trying until you"—his voice jumped into a yell—"*get the hell out of here!*"

I didn't have anything to say to that. It was his house. And I understood what he was doing with his pain. So I just shrugged and let myself out the front door.

But I didn't leave. Instead I sat down on the front porch and tried to think of a way to handle the situation.

Part of me wanted to go back and accept his offer. I had a feeling that he'd tell me everything I wanted to know and more if I just had a few drinks with him. People who aren't used to being drunk are like that. But I wasn't ready to pay that much for the answers to a few questions. Once I got started, I wouldn't stop. On the other hand, I was seriously tempted to go back into the house and pound on him for a while.

I was still considering my nonexistent options when a kid came up the driveway toward the house. She looked to be about nine or ten—a cute kid with straight blonde hair, braces, and one of those loose-jointed tomboy bodies that promises a lot of future development. She stopped in front of me, studied me gravely for a long minute.

Not having any better ideas, I said, "Hi."

"Hi," she said. Then abruptly, "Are they drunk again?"

That sounded like a dangerous question, and I was leery of it. But the seriousness in her child-face demanded an honest answer. Finally I said, "I think so."

"Oh, damn." She made *damn* sound as innocent as sunlight. All at once, she dropped herself onto the porch beside me and put her chin on her knees. "They're going to blame it on me."

"Why would they do that?"

"I'm late. When I'm late, they always use it as an excuse. They say they're worried sick about me." Her sarcasm underlined the hurt in her voice.

I waited a moment. Then I said, "But you don't think that's the real reason."

"Of course not." This time I heard real bitterness. "I come home late because I know they're going on one of their binges. I stay away as late as I can."

I nodded. "It must be rough."

"Yeah." She stared in front of her as if her whole future were a desert. "They think I'm going to turn out like Marisa."

All of a sudden, the Lutts went *click* in my head and started to make sense. Now I knew what they were going through. I'd seen a lot of it in the last two days. Your thirteen-year-old daughter suddenly runs away for no reason in the world, and when she turns up dead months later you're told she's a junky whore. So who do you blame? It must be your fault, she's a little too young for you to pin it all on her, but to save your soul you can't think what you did wrong. Pretty soon you start to think that you did everything wrong. You can't trust yourself anymore—and that means you can't trust anybody. Not even your ten-year-old.

"That's why they drink," I said quietly. "Because of what happened to her."

"Yeah," she assented. "And then that pig came. The cop. At first I thought you were him. He was big, too. I didn't hear what he said, but when he was gone Mom was crying and couldn't stop, and Dad looked like he was going to be sick."

I was thinking fast now—and what I came up with disgusted me. I felt rotten just considering it. But I didn't see any other way. After a minute I said, "My name is Brew."

She looked over at me, made an effort to smile. "I'm Denise."

"Denise," I said carefully, "I'm a private investigator. I'm trying to find a girl who ran away from home. Just like Marisa. Right now, it looks like they're connected. The same thing is going to happen to this girl unless I can find her in time. But I'm not getting anywhere, and I need help. Your parents—well, they're too upset to understand why I need to talk to them."

She peered at me intensely. "You can ask me. I know all about it. They didn't want me to hear, but I listened at the door." She was eager to help. Probably her own self-respect wasn't exactly in great shape. She needed to do something, make a positive contribution in some way.

I gave her the best smile I could muster. "There's just one thing I really need. After she ran away, Marisa wrote your parents a note. That's where the connection is. In the note. I need it."

For a second while she looked at me, her eyes brightened. Then she jumped up. "I know where it is." Before I could regret what I'd gotten her into, she hurried into the house.

She wasn't gone long. I heard shouts as if her parents were yelling at her. Then she came back out and handed me a piece of paper.

A half sheet of good twenty-pound bond, neatly torn along one edge. What the messy handwriting had to say wasn't more than three words different than Alathea's note. By this time I could recognize the watermark at fifty paces.

I got to my feet. Talking fast so that I could finish before either of the Lutts came out after Denise, I said, "Now listen. When your parents are sober, I want you to tell them about me. Tell them Marisa didn't run away. She was kidnapped. I don't know how or why, but I'm going to find out. I'm going to nail whoever did it. Your parents don't have any reason to hate themselves. And they don't have any reason to be worried about you."

If Ginny had been there, she would've tried to stop me during that whole speech. I didn't have any business making promises like that, and I knew it. But I felt dirty about the way I'd used Denise, gotten her in trouble with her parents when she already had more than she could handle. I had to give her something in return.

If it turned out that I couldn't keep my promises, I could always go back to drinking. One shame more or less wouldn't make any difference. Alcohol doesn't care about details like that.

10

Rush hour traffic slowed me down, so by the time I'd returned the Torino and walked back down Cuevero to my apartment I needed supper. I didn't feel much like cooking for myself, but in my neighborhood there aren't any restaurants that don't have bars attached, so I didn't have much choice. I fixed whatever was left in the refrigerator and ate as much of it as I could stand. Then I called Ginny's service and left a message telling her everything I knew.

Afterward I spent about an hour cleaning my apartment, which is something I do whenever I'm feeling particularly grimy inside—and trying not to think about it. You'd be surprised how much cleaning you can do in a one-room efficiency apartment if you really put your mind to it.

By then it was dark outside. But not dark enough to suit me. Looking for chores to pass the time, I stripped the .45 and cleaned it. It didn't need much. In the past few years, I'd probably cleaned the damn thing three times for every shot I'd fired. But it's another job that can take a while if you go into it with the right attitude.

When I was done, I took a long shower.

The night still felt too early, but I couldn't stomach any more waiting. After my shower, I got dressed, loaded the .45 and stuffed it into my shoulder holster, and went out.

Looking for Manolo, the information dealer.

I'd spent the whole day doing what Ginny wanted me to do. Now I wanted to check out an idea of my own.

Manolo was the man who could help me.

Most of the traffic had died out on Eighth Street. I could smell the alleys as I walked past them, hear the jukeboxes in the bars. Women shouted at their children, husband, loan sharks. Young studs swaggered in the road, catcalling at every girl they saw. Grizzled patriarchal Indians, Chicanos, Mestizos tried their best to walk in straight lines. Couples stood and necked in doorways and around corners. I didn't pass five Anglos between Cuevero and the center of the old city, where Paseo Grande would've continued on if it hadn't turned into a pitiful narrow thoroughfare called Coal Street. For the first time today, I felt like I knew what I was doing. Things can happen at night.

Not that my search promised to be easy. Old Manolo was a man of regular habits—and he made it his regular habit to be wherever the listening was good. Which on any given night could be any one of twenty different places. Sometimes he seemed to be everywhere and nowhere, and you had to know the history and fate of every bottle of anisette in the city to find him. Not a very reassuring prospect, but I didn't see any way around it.

I was trying to decide where to start when I got lucky. A kid came running toward me down the sidewalk, and I recognized him before he got to me. His name was Pablo. I knew him because I'd met his family two years ago, when Ginny and I were working on a protection-racket case. He was in a hurry, and there was a strange bulge under his shirt. He had a packet of some kind tucked into the front of his pants.

Apparently he was running for a numbers racket.

I suppose you could say that's a relatively harmless way for a kid to hustle a few bucks. He was a messenger boy, nothing more. And anyway it was none of my business. But that didn't stop me. I caught his arm as he went past and swung him to a halt. "*Hola,* Pablo. There is no dignity in such haste," I said in Spanish.

"I must run, Señor." He didn't even look at me. He was trying to break my grip without making a production out of it. Probably afraid of attracting attention. "If I go and come swiftly, I will be given a dollar."

"A man does not run to do the bidding of those who are themselves not men enough to do their own running." Stern Uncle Axbrewder. If Ginny heard me, she would've had real trouble keeping a straight face.

Now he looked at me. "Ay, Señor Axbrewder?"

"It is I myself, Pablo."

Then he put on a whine. "Señor Axbrewder, my arm is being broken."

"An arm will mend, Pablo. When it is the self-esteem which breaks, mending is not done easily."

"Yes, Señor. For what have I been stopped?"

Well, I could see that I wasn't getting through to him. I got down off my high horse. "I wish to have speech with old Manolo, the drinker of anisette. Where is he to be found?"

"God knows, Señor."

"That is very true. But a cunning boy like Pablo has surely taken thought on the matter."

He twisted against me for another moment. Then he gave up. "It is possible that he takes his anisette in the place of Juan Cideño."

I said, "*Gracias,* Pablo," and let him go.

He stared at me for a moment as if I were as crazy as all Anglos. Then he turned and started running again.

Like I said—lucky. Juan Cideño's bar wasn't more than a block from where I stood.

On the inside, it resembled the Hegira. Its major distinction was a life-sized poster of Raul Ramírez on the wall opposite the bar. The poster wasn't old, but stale air and smoke had stained it until Ramírez seemed like a champion from another generation.

Old Manolo sat in a booth at the back.

His eyes were closed—he looked sound asleep. Even knowing him the way I did, I half expected him to topple slowly to the floor and start snoring. But there was a small glass of anisette on the table between his hands, and after a few seconds he picked it up delicately with his fingertips, tucked it under his gray walrus mustache, and took a sip. Then he set the glass down, swallowed, and went back to looking like he was asleep.

I glanced around the bar, just making sure there wasn't anyone nearby who might be offended if he happened to overhear me. None of el Señor's men, for example, would take kindly to the questions I wanted to ask. Then I went over to the barkeep. Old Manolo is like an oracle—there are ceremonies you have to perform if you want answers from him. I bought a bottle of anisette and took it over to his booth.

Hoping he wouldn't try to make me drink it with him. Wondering what I was going to say.

He spared me the effort of finding an opening line. When I arrived at his table, he said without opening his eyes, "*Hola*, Señor Axbrewder. Have you come to sit with an old man and tell him interesting tales? That would be very welcome."

His English was distinct. But I answered in Spanish. "*Hola*, Manuel Sevilla y Acclara de los Maestos." Speaking Spanish with him was part of the ritual, like knowing his proper name. "Alas, all my tales are poor things in comparison to your own legendary knowledge." I was trying to figure out how he'd known who I was without opening his eyes. "Yet I would sit with you, and share speech, if I am not an intrusion."

He nodded as if he knew exactly what I had in mind. "You bear with you a thing more precious than many tales. Please sit."

Huh? I said to myself. But then I figured it out. He was talking about the bottle. He must have heard me buy it, recognized my voice. I kept forgetting just how good he was at picking up on everything around him.

I said, "*Gracias,*" and slid into the booth. Then I unscrewed the top of the bottle and refilled his glass.

He nodded again, smiling faintly under his mustache. But a moment later his eyes opened, and he looked at me with an air of mild surprise. His eyeballs were a muddy color, as if they'd been stained by all the secrets he carried around in his head. "You do not accompany me, Señor?" he asked. When I didn't answer right away, he went on, "Perhaps tequila would be of more pleasure to you. Not all are equally enamored with anisette."

He was being perfectly magnanimous. But his graciousness cut both ways. He was offering me a chance to get out of being rude—and warning me that I'd better take him up on it.

"Unhappily, I must decline," I said carefully. "I am like other Anglos. Drink plays upon my wits discourteously." That was like admitting a failure of manhood, but I couldn't think of an alternative. "The matter before me is urgent. I must practice great sobriety if I am to speak clearly, and to hear what is said to me without confusion." I shrugged as eloquently as I could.

Old Manolo considered for some time. But he didn't close his eyes. Finally he made up his mind. "It is said of you, Señor Axbrewder, that you suffer an infirmity of the heart, arising from the greatly-to-be-regretted death of your brother. Such things must be understood and accepted." Solemnly he took a sip of his anisette.

Deep inside me, I gave a sigh of relief. He wasn't offended. The oracle was still open.

I didn't say anything. I knew better.

He didn't keep me waiting long. He scanned my face for a moment, then said, "You spoke of urgency. Is it permitted to inquire concerning this matter?"

"Señor Sevilla, the young daughter of my brother's widow has gone from her home."

"Ah," he said politely. "That is to be regretted. But many girls both young and old have gone from their homes, Señor. The world has become corrupt in every place. Girls no longer honor their homes, or the wishes of their parents. What can be done? The world pays no heed to the sorrow of parents."

"That is very true. But I have cause to think that the corruption does not lie in this widow's daughter. Hear what I have learned in seeking her." Speaking formally, precisely, I told him about the seven dead girls. I described the connection between them and Alathea. When I was finished, I said, "Such evil does not befall so many young girls by chance. It is deliberately done. My thought is that for each the corruption comes from one source, one supplier of drugs. I must find that man if I am to save my dead brother's child."

Old Manolo had closed his eyes while I was speaking. Now he was silent for a long time. I didn't rush him. Information dealing is a touchy profession. He was alive after all these years because he was cautious and selective. But by the time he decided to speak, my knuckles were white from clutching the edge of the table.

"Señor," he said softly, not opening his eyes, "I think perhaps you have made the acquaintance of my son's wife's father's sister's daughter. You were not properly introduced. So few things are now done properly in the world. But her name will be known to you. She is Teresa María Sanguillán y García."

He paused, and I said, "I have been given the honor of knowing her name."

"Then you will understand that I wish to assist."

"I believe it." His family was in my debt. That meant something to him.

"Unhappily, I can offer you nothing. Indeed, the fate of these young girls has been known to me. But the supplier, he who works this evil—That one is not known."

I was trembling. "Señor Sevilla, it is said that no grain or gram of heroin passes from hand to hand in Puerta del Sol without your knowledge. In the matter of drugs, all tales come to your ears."

"I hear much," old Manolo assented. "No man hears all."

"Can it be that el Señor has such evil dealings, and there is no talk of them? Or that men talk of the dealings of el Señor, and you do not hear?"

At that, he opened his eyes. I half expected him to be offended, but he wasn't. There was nothing in his gaze but sadness. "Señor Axbrewder, the knowledge you seek is dark and mysterious. I can shed no light upon it. But I ask you to believe that no hint of this knowledge has touched my ears. That in itself is knowledge for you, is it not?"

When I didn't answer, he went on, "I will speak further. There are many drugs, and much passing among hands. But in the matter of heroin, all passing begins in the hands of el Señor. That is his pride, and the source of his great wealth. I do not speak this to mislead you. El Señor is a man of honor, placing great value upon his family and his children, and the purity of his daughters. Such corrupting of young girls is a terrible evil, and he would in no way permit it."

"These girls are Anglo," I said. "Does el Señor's honor extend itself to Anglos?"

"In truth, it does. He has no love for Anglos. That cannot be denied. But I speak absolutely. This corrupting of young girls does not come through him."

Well, probably that wasn't the whole story. If the bastard I wanted was cutting into el Señor's profits, el Señor would've slapped him down long ago. So I could assume that those profits weren't in any danger. Which fit with what old Manolo was saying. Apparently Alathea's kidnapper made his own clientele out of people el Señor didn't want.

But that didn't help me any. I was still stuck. I couldn't keep the bitterness out of my voice as I said, "El Señor controls all heroin in Puerta del Sol—and yet he does not supply these girls. Still they die from heroin. What, then, can I do? My brother's widow's daughter will surely die also."

Manolo poured himself another drink, then recapped the bottle and stuck it in the pocket of his coat. He emptied his glass and got to his feet. My audience was over—he was going somewhere else. But before he left, he bent close to me and whispered so that no one in the bar could overhear him, "Possibly you must go to el Señor himself. If you wish to have speech with him, you must know his name. It is Héctor Jesús Fría de la Sancha."

A minute later he was gone.

I stayed where I was. Go to el Señor for help. Sure. That sounded like a polite way of telling me to go to hell. El Señor was what the newspapers probably would have called "the crime czar of Puerta del Sol," if they'd known of his existence. A man of honor. Oh, absolutely. He would chew me up into little pieces and spit me in the gutter. No thanks. I wasn't that desperate. Not yet.

So I didn't go looking for el Señor, even though I knew where to find him. I left the bar and started for home. Feel-

ing like shit. Because I'd failed Alathea. I'd played the only
hand I had, and lost. Now the only thing left was to be
Ginny's errand boy while she tried to crack this case her
own way.

My depression must've showed in the way I walked, because this time the *muchachos* felt free to notice me—which
they don't usually do, even when I'm drunk. Most of the
time I'm a little too big for them. But not tonight. They
weren't exactly aggressive about it, but they whistled from
across the street and muttered obscure Spanish insults at my
back as I went past. The whole community seemed to know
that I hadn't been able to get what I needed out of old
Manolo.

When you're in that kind of mood, it's hard to stay away
from the stuff. Alcohol is the only magic in the world. When
you're working, you're trying to change things around you
so that you fit into them better. But when you're drinking,
the fit comes from inside. And if it isn't real, at least it's
easier than straining to figure out puzzles when no one will
tell you the secret. On my way home I had a tough time
staying out of the bars.

But I did stay out of them—for Alathea. Because the one
thing alcohol would never do was help me find her. Until
she was found, being Ginny's errand boy was better than
nothing, and it was probably about all I was good for.

I ignored the bars. I ignored the *muchachos* and their
insults. I just lumbered my way up Eighth Street in the direction of home.

As I approached my apartment building, I noticed a long
black Buick parked at the corner of a side street. All the
lights were off, but the motor ran softly. Three men sat
inside.

Just when I got abreast of the car, its doors thunked open,
and the men got out. They wore neat businessmen's suits,
with crisp businessmen's ties and shiny businessmen's
shoes. At that time of night in that neighborhood, they might
as well have worn sandwich boards saying, "Plainclothes
Cops." They were all big, and the biggest one was a chunky
individual about my size and maybe thirty pounds heavier.

He said, "Axbrewder," in the kind of voice you'd expect if you taught a bulldozer to talk.

The muscle with him stayed back and didn't say anything—and the light was bad, so there was a chance I might not recognize them if I saw them again. But the goon with the diesel voice I got a good look at. He had a jaw hard and square enough to set rivets, a nose that could moonlight as a can opener, and a forehead that looked like it was made out of reinforced concrete. He flashed his badge at me and said, "Detective-Lieutenant Acton."

But he wasn't trying to introduce himself, or even prove he was a cop. He just wanted to get close to me. As he put the badge away, his other hand came up to my chest and shoved.

I wasn't braced for it, and it wasn't exactly a gesture of undying friendship. He got his weight into it. It sent me backward, smacked me hard against the wall of the building.

I was already rebounding at him when I saw that his backups had their guns out. Acton grinned like the blade of a plow, and suddenly I could picture him writing his report. "Shot while resisting arrest."

I stopped with a jerk.

"Acton," I said, trying not to show how much breath he'd knocked out of me. "What a pleasant surprise. I've been wanting to talk to you."

"Is that a fact?" His hand came up again, but this time he just poked me with one finger. He aimed to jab me in the solar plexus, which is a nice way to hurt someone when you don't want to leave any marks. He missed, but that didn't stop him. "Well, I want to talk to you, too"—he poked again—"Mick."

Mick. Instantly a wind began to blow inside my head, and my balance shifted. Nobody calls me Mick. Nobody. Not since my brother died. The night seemed to congeal at Acton's back, and I lost sight of the two cops with the guns. My chest was so full of rage and pressure that it felt like my ribs were going to crack.

"What's the matter, Mick?" Poke. "Don't you like being called 'Mick?' " Poke. Any second now, he was going to rupture my self-control, and then I'd have to take his face off with my bare hands.

But then his partners registered on me again. They had guns. If I touched Acton, they'd probably beat me half to death before they threw me in jail. Ordinarily I wouldn't have cared much about being locked up, but if it happened now I wouldn't be able to help find Alathea. Right this minute, she was somewhere in the city prostituting herself to get money for drugs. If we didn't find her, she was going to end up dead.

Just holding the knowledge in hurt so bad that I thought I was going to pass out. But I stood there. Let Acton do whatever he had in mind.

He must've seen me make the decision, because he eased off with his finger. "That's nice, Mick. That's a good boy. Swallow your pride. A drunk like you should be used to it by now."

I didn't say anything.

"Give me the notes, Mick."

The notes—That surprised me. Who the fuck told him about the notes? But I was already clenched, and I didn't show anything. Through my teeth, I said, "I don't have them." If I'd opened my jaws, I wouldn't have been able to hold in my rage.

"Where are they, Mick?"

"The safe. Fistoulari Investigations."

"Ah, that's too bad." He never stopped grinning. "That means I'll have to get a warrant. What a shame. It's a good thing you're a liar, Mick."

I couldn't do anything about it. I had to stand there while he searched me. When he found the notes, he glanced through them, counted them, then stuffed them into his coat pocket.

I stopped looking at him. Instead I stared into the darkness past his shoulder. That grin of his was going to give me nightmares.

"Now, Mick. I'm going to let you have a little friendly advice. Get off my case. Stay off it. I hate your guts, Mick,

and if you get in my way I'll slap you down so hard you'll
have to reach up to touch bottom."

Staring into the darkness was a good way to watch his
shoulder muscles. If he intended to hit me again, I wanted
to know about it. "Why?"

He laughed, but it wasn't because there was anything
funny. "Rick Axbrewder was a good cop. He was also a
friend of mine."

I shrugged. What else could I do? "How did you know
about the notes?"

He stepped closer, and I almost flinched. But he didn't
hit me. His tone was soft and bitter as he said, "That bastard
Stretto lit a fire under the commissioner. Now the commissioner wants my hide. I'm in trouble because I didn't make
the connection with those notes. So I'm warning you. This
is the last time a punk drunk like you is going to make me
look bad."

"I don't have to," I said. "You're already doing it to yourself. Why did you scare the Christies like that?"

That did it. His shoulder bunched, and he swung at me
hard, fingers stiff, gouging for my solar plexus. I blocked it
as best I could, but his fingers still dug deep into my gut.

I hunched over, staggered back to get out of the way of
another hit. However, he didn't swing again. He and his
goons got back into their car and drove off, roaring the
engine and squealing the tires to convince me that they
meant business.

For a couple of minutes, I stayed where I was, almost
retching. Then I went the rest of the way to Cuevero Road
and struggled up the stairs to my apartment.

Losing the notes made me a whole lot sicker than just
one jab in the stomach. But there was no way around it—I
had to face Ginny. While I was still mad enough to make
decisions, I yanked up the phone and called her service. As
it turned out, she was at home, and they patched me through.

"Brew. What's happening?"

Almost puking with self-disgust, I told her, "I just had a
run-in with Acton. He took the notes."

My fault entirely. A Mongoloid idiot could've warned me to take better care of the evidence.

She must've heard most of the story in my voice. She didn't ask me how it happened. Or how I could've been so stupid. She asked, "Are you all right?"

"I'm not in jail."

"Thank God for small blessings." Somehow she made her tone just right for my mood. "How did he even find out about them?"

"Stretto. It seems he went to the commissioner. Apparently he doesn't think the cops are doing their job. The commissioner took it out on Acton."

"Surprise, surprise," Ginny muttered. "I wasn't sure the illustrious Mr. Stretto had that much in him."

"Anyway"—I gritted my teeth and said it—"I've pretty well blown our case. Now we've got nothing."

"He's a cop," she snapped. "What could you do, eat the damn things?"

"I shouldn't have been carrying them around."

She dismissed that without hesitation. "Forget about it. They were safe enough. We just didn't know Acton was going to get desperate. Anyway," she went on before I could object, "we don't need them now."

I said, "Huh?" Always the brilliant conversationalist.

"Acton won't destroy them. Too many people know about them. And I've already got what I need out of them."

"Which is what?"

"Brew, I finished checking out the other schools." My head must've been clearing—I finally started to hear the vibration of excitement in her voice. "I'll spare you the details. The point is that everything fits. Every one of these girls disappeared from school at a time when she was scheduled to be alone."

"You already knew that. It's in the school board files."

"Exactly!"

"Exactly what? It still doesn't prove anything. Why call attention to yourself running away when you've got a perfect chance to sneak off every day of the week?"

"Well, that's true, of course," she admitted, "if you look

at it that way. Let me ask you a different question, Brew. Is there any proof in those notes? Proof the girls didn't write them, or wrote them under duress? I'm talking about hard evidence, the kind that stands up in court."

I thought about it for a long time. Then I said, "No."

"Damn right. As far as we know, they were all addressed correctly. But that's minor. The main thing is that all the notes were addressed to the right parents."

I said, "Huh?" again. It was getting to be a habit.

"Marisa Lutt wrote, 'Dear Mom and Dad.' So did Esther Hannibal. So did Ruth Ann Larsen, May-Belle Podhorentz, Dottie Ann Consciewitz, Carol Christie. We don't know about Rosalynn Swift. But Alathea wrote, 'Dear Mom.' Mittie wrote, 'Dear Dad.' "

It still didn't mean anything to me. "So what? Most kids know how many parents they have. If they've only got one, they can usually tell if it's male or female."

"Of course! That's the point!" She was hot on a trail I couldn't see. "Just look at it from the other side. We know those notes are wrong. We have good reason to believe they were all dictated by the same person. Well, nine girls who live in nine different neighborhoods and go to six different schools aren't going to end up having the same person dictate their notes by accident. So what does that tell you?"

"Kidnapping." I grated. I already knew that.

"Right! But if that's true, then the girls didn't run away at all. So it isn't a question of figuring out why the girls ran away while they were alone. The question is, how did the kidnapper know they were going to be alone? How did he know they were going to be somewhere that he could get at them without being seen? For that matter, how did he know he could get them to come with him? And how did he know their addresses? How did he know how many parents they had?"

I said, "Research?" Feeling like an idiot.

"Now you're getting it. Tell me, Brew. If you wanted to research nine different girls in six different schools, and find out the answers to all these questions, where would you go?"

That was it. Finally I understood. "The school board. The files." She was right, I could feel it. The bastard we were looking for got his information from those files. It was the only answer that made sense.

Maybe he was even on the board.

PART THREE

Thursday Night/Friday

11

Of course, it all rested on the assumption that the girls were being kidnapped. I had no problem with that. But it had one crucial flaw.

There didn't seem to be any payoff. No ransom demands. And in any case, half the families involved couldn't have scraped up a self-respecting ransom to save their souls.

Which brought me back to drugs. Some pusher in town was hot for new business. A very particular kind of new business.

Some pusher old Manolo had never heard of.

There must've been a hell of a lot of money in it to make it worth a possible kidnapping rap. Or a hell of a lot of hate. The kind of hate that makes serial killers.

I didn't say anything to Ginny about that. Instead I said, "That's going to be a big job. How many people are on the school board these days? Twenty?"

She said, "Fifteen."

"And then there are all those secretaries. And on top of that, some people from the individual schools may have access to the general files. You're talking about thirty suspects." Or more. "Where do we start?"

"By whittling down the list."

I said, "Oh." Heavy on the sarcasm. The sense that we were finally getting somewhere made me feel a little better about Alathea, but it didn't do much for my opinion of myself. "That shouldn't be too hard. We'll just call people up and ask them how they feel about stuffing dope down thirteen-year-old girls."

"So we'll have to work at it," she said evenly. "Where did you get the idea it was supposed to be easy?" When I didn't answer, she went on, "There's a lot we can do, but to save time we'll start with the obvious, the full-time people: Stretto, Scurvey, Greenling, and the secretaries."

I couldn't argue with her, so I asked, "What about Acton?"

"I'll check on him tonight. Find out if he was lying about the commissioner. If he was telling the truth, we'll have to assume he's in the clear—and Stretto, too, for that matter. Until we know more, anyway."

I couldn't argue with that either. If Stretto was involved, he wouldn't have called the commissioner. As for Acton—If he was dealing drugs, we'd put him in a real bind. As long as the commissioner knew about those notes, Acton couldn't risk destroying them. *If* the commissioner knew. After chewing it around for a minute, I asked, "What do you want me to do?"

"Get some sleep," she said promptly. "At this point, there's nothing more we *can* do until morning. Get a cab and come to the office tomorrow early. By then I'll have something set up."

After that, it was too late to argue. I didn't have anything else to offer. It was her case now. When she hung up, I went to bed.

And I went right to sleep. Being sober makes you more tired than you'd expect. But I spent the whole night dreaming about amber, and the next morning I was up with the birds. My face ached as if I'd been grinding my teeth for hours. Nevertheless I ignored it, ignored the feeling of stupidity that filled my chest, ignored the dry wish for alcohol in my mouth. Someday I'd have to find a way to feel proud of being sober, but right then I wasn't up to it. By eight A.M. I was out on Cuevero Road looking for a cab.

Which was not a good time of day for cabs, but I finally found one. Then it wasn't long until I was riding up the elevator of the Murchison Building to Ginny's office.

She was there already. When I went into her back room, I found her on the phone. I dropped into a chair. Whoever she was talking to, it didn't take her long. A couple of minutes later, we had an appointment with somebody or other for nine thirty.

"That was Dr. Sandoval," she said. "Camilla Sandoval, pediatrician. How long has it been since you voted?"

I shrugged. How can you answer a question like that?

"Well, you probably don't know she represents your district on the board of education. This is her fifth term—she's very popular. One of the part-time members." She looked at me sharply, as if she expected me to be surprised. "Your friend Encino speaks highly of her."

If she wanted a reaction out of me, she was going to be disappointed. We errand boys try to keep our opinions to ourselves. Especially when we're ashamed of our own bitterness. I got out my pocketknife and pretended to clean my fingernails, letting her hang for a moment before I asked, "What else did he have to say?"

She frowned, but she didn't look serious about it. I wasn't fooling her any. "Not much about Dr. Sandoval. But he told me a little something about Acton and the commissioner. Apparently Acton was giving it to you straight. Encino wasn't there, but when the commissioner personally goes to see a lieutenant instead of sending for him, and chews him out in front of half the duty room, word gets around pretty fast. Stretto called the commissioner, all right. We can count on it."

"Politicians," I muttered, mostly to myself. They know how to talk to each other. If I'd gone to the commissioner with those notes myself, I would've gotten in trouble for "obstructing an official investigation." Paul M. Stretto makes one phone call, and all of a sudden the air's full of shit. "So scratch the chairman of the board. Put Acton on the back burner. What's next?"

Ginny frowned again. This time she meant it. "We've got a lot of ground to cover, and everything we do takes time. I can't find Ted, so I bit the bullet and hired some help. I called fat-ass Smithsonian."

All things considered, that probably shouldn't have surprised me. We had between ten and thirty suspects lined up, and every passing day put Alathea in that much more trouble. But Ginny is an independent cuss, and she doesn't like farming out work to other agencies. And of all the private investigators I know, Lawrence Smithsonian is the one she actively hates. He isn't all that fat, but he as sure as hell *looks* fat, probably because his fees are overweight. And on top of that, his way of condescending to Ginny sends her blood pressure through the roof. Hiring his help probably cost her a pound of flesh. I had to stare at her for a while before I recovered enough to ask, "Why him?"

"Because he knows money." She was practically spitting. "He can learn more about the personal finances of our suspects in one morning than we could in a week. He'll start with the full-time board members and the secretaries, try to find out if any of them are getting rich in private, or living over their heads, or gambling with money they haven't earned, or rolling too high on the stock market. Anything. He has half the bank presidents in this town in his back pocket. I think he blackmails them."

After a minute I said, "Lona can't pay you."

"I know that." She wasn't thinking about money. She was still steaming about Smithsonian.

"I can't either."

That made her look at me. "Who asked you?"

I got up, went over to her. Cupped her head with both my hands and kissed her on the mouth.

She didn't kiss me back. She just sat there and took it. When I stopped, she looked at me like the barrel of a gun and said, "The next time you do that, you better mean it."

Well, I meant it all right. My shoulders were trembling, and my pulse beat in my head so loud that I could hardly hear her. But that wasn't what she was getting at. What she had in mind was something even more serious than the way I felt about her. We'd been through it before. She wanted me to quit drinking. Completely. Forever.

That was something I couldn't do. I wasn't worth it.

I went back to my chair and sat down, trying to hold myself so that she couldn't see me shake. When I thought I could control my voice, I asked, "When is he going to call back?"

"When he finds something. Or this afternoon. Whichever comes first."

"And in the meantime?"

"We'll go talk to Dr. Sandoval. Then we'll go back to the school board and see what we can run down this time." Her composure was too perfect. I'd confused her and probably hurt her—which was something I had definitely not meant to do. While she got herself ready to leave, I spent a few minutes trying to think of a new way to curse myself.

She was still holding up her wall of businesslike professionalism as we rode the elevator down to the garage and took the Olds out into the morning glare. But after that she unbent enough to tell me what her plans were. They sounded reasonable, and if they worked, we could probably cross half the people off our list today. I let it go at that. I'd already pushed my luck too far with her.

The office of Dr. Camilla Sandoval was on the opposite side of the old part of town from where I lived. It was in a squat dull-red adobe structure that looked like it moonlighted as a bordello. Already the waiting room was full of mothers with babies in various stages of stupor or hysteria. Most of them were either Chicano or Indian, and all together they gave a pretty good capsule summary of what life was like in the old part of Puerta del Sol. After half an hour in that room, Ginny and I'd seen every degree of squalor, sickness, flamboyance, passivity, color, resentment, joy, hunger, love, and rage. A real education, if you can stand to hear babies squall. And see mothers hit them.

When Ginny told the nurse we had an appointment for 9:30, she just shrugged and gestured at all the people ahead of us. It looked like it was going to be a long wait, and I didn't see any way around it. In this part of the world, the Anglos have spent the past hundred fifty years or so barging in line ahead of Chicanos and Indians, and I didn't want to add to the resentment in those faces. But in situations like this Ginny has a thicker skin than I do. She stood it for that first half hour. Then she dug some paper and a pen out of her purse, wrote a long note, and gave it to the nurse. Her way of presenting it didn't leave the nurse much choice. Three minutes later, Dr. Sandoval called us in to see her.

She was a chunky little woman, too small to be a football

player and too big to be a fireplug. If she was married, she didn't advertise it by wearing a ring. In fact, she didn't wear any jewelry at all. Her manner was tough, but it was a particular kind of tough, the kind that can look pain straight in the face and make it hurt less without being hurt herself. Or without showing it, anyway. By the time she asked Ginny and me to have a seat in the square cubicle she used for an office, I liked her.

She sat down behind her desk and studied us for a second. Then she picked up Ginny's note and slapped it with the back of her hand. "Nine junky whores," she said, "thirteen or younger. Seven of them dead. What do you want from me? Do you think they were my patients?"

"Dr. Sandoval"—Ginny matched her tone evenly— "we're private investigators." She flipped the photocopy of her license onto the desk. "We've been hired to find the two girls who are still alive. I don't think you know anything about them. That's why we want to talk to you. We want to ask you some questions about the people you work with on the board of education."

That was confusing enough to short-circuit some of Dr. Sandoval's hostility. She didn't exactly retreat, but she eased back a bit. "I don't understand."

"I know it's complicated," Ginny said, "and I can't tell you much without violating the confidence of my clients. But I can tell you this: We have reason to believe these girls were kidnapped. And we suspect the kidnapper has some sort of connection with the school board. We'd like you to give us background information about a few of the people who work there."

Now that the first surprise was over, Dr. Sandoval had started to fume. "This is insane. Do you understand what you're saying? Perhaps you don't know what the school board does. It exists to help children, to provide them with an education. Not all the members are idealists, of course, but they believe in education. We all believe in children. What you suggest is inconceivable."

Ginny didn't falter. "Criminals come in all disguises, Dr. Sandoval."

"I repeat. It is inconceivable."

"Then you believe Paul Stretto is pure as the driven snow?"

The doctor hesitated. Not a long hesitation, but a hesitation nonetheless. When it was over, she answered the question with a question. "If you're right," she asked, "why aren't the police involved in this?"

"They are," Ginny drawled. "It wouldn't surprise me a bit if you have cops on your doorstep before the day's over. The only difference is, they're trying to catch a pusher. We're trying to find two little girls."

"I see." She scanned both of us, and after a minute she looked like she really did see. "I have patients waiting. Please be as quick as you can."

Ginny's gaze didn't shift an inch. "Paul Stretto?"

"Mr. Stretto is a politician. I doubt that he has so much as glanced at a textbook since fifth grade. He is on his way to an exalted career as a public servant." Her mouth twisted sourly around the words. "I can't believe that he would risk his future by involving himself in kidnapping."

"Maybe he has friends who just ask him for information."

"How would I know that?"

"Have you heard any rumors?"

"The rumor," Dr. Sandoval said, "is that Paul Stretto wants to be president. Of the United States."

"All right," Ginny said, "How about Astin Greenling?"

"That man is the salt of the earth." No hesitation at all. "His life has been very unhappy, but he burns himself out every day struggling to provide the children of this city with a decent education. Every year when the levies are voted down, the budget cuts always come out of curriculum. He'll have heart failure some day if he doesn't stop trying to raise the quality of education with less money every year."

"You say unhappy? In what way?"

"His wife has leukemia." Dr. Sandoval's tone made it clear that she didn't intend to say anything more about Astin Greenling's unhappy life.

Ginny nodded. She was thinking the same thing I was. Treating leukemia costs money. Reams of money. But she didn't make any comment. Money was Smithsonian's job. Instead she went on down the list. "What can you tell us about Martha Scurvey?"

The doctor frowned, took a moment to decide on an answer. Then she said, "I don't like her personally. But since she was elected budget vice-chairman last year, our accounting procedures have started to climb out of the Dark Ages. And she seems to have a talent for procurement: She gets lower prices for our supplies. I have to respect that. It takes a little pressure off Astin."

"How long has she served on the board?"

"Just a year." Dr. Sandoval was sardonic. "For some reason, most people don't seem to know that the full-time members of the board of education are elected by the city at large. As far as I know, she's never been elected for anything before."

I sighed to myself and mentally crossed Martha Scurvey off the list. She hadn't been on the board when the first four girls disappeared. But Ginny went right on, not wasting the doctor's time. "And Julian Kirke?"

"He isn't an elected officer. We hired him. The board decided to get into this business of computerizing the files—which, incidentally, I've resisted every step of the way. It's expensive, and I think the money should be spent on the children. But quality education doesn't have as much prestige as computers. Machines have more dignity than human beings."

I liked her more and more all the time.

"But that's beside the point," she went on. "When I was outvoted, the board looked for someone who could handle the nuts and bolts of this grand system. They found Julian. He's a data-management expert, and had a good job with NCR, but they didn't promote him fast enough to keep him. I think he is a petty tyrant, but that doesn't prevent him from doing a good job. The fact is, in his hands the whole project has been less expensive than I thought it would be."

"How long ago did you hire him?"

"Two and a half, maybe three years."

"All right, Doctor," Ginny said briskly. "Just a couple

more questions. How much do you know about the secretaries who work under Mr. Kirke?"

"Very little. That's his department. I'm not involved with it. It's my impression that he's pretty hard on them. For that matter, he's barely civil to me. But they do good work." She sighed. "Our correspondence looks professional now. Finally."

I wanted to think about that for a while. I didn't know whether Kirke was a perfectionist or just a cantankerous sonofabitch. But it was going to have to wait. Ginny was asking, "How many people have access to those files?"

"In theory, everybody in the school system. They aren't intended to be secret. They're supposed to help the schools run better. But the process hasn't reached that point yet. In practice, the files are primarily accessible to the full-time people. When the rest of us want information, we ask Julian or one of the secretaries."

Ginny glanced at me, looking for more questions. But I didn't have any. This was her type of investigation, not mine. If it'd been up to me, I would've told the doctor exactly what we were looking for and asked her for some kind of intuitive answer. Her intuitions I would've trusted. So I shook my head, and Ginny got to her feet.

Without seeming rude about it, Dr. Sandoval ushered us out quickly. About a minute after we stood up, we were past the resentment of all those mothers and in the Olds. By then the doctor was probably examining her next patient.

I pushed my sunglasses onto my face, but they didn't help much. While Ginny started up the Olds, I muttered at her, "That was fun. What did we get out of it?"

She jerked around to me. "That's a cheap shot."

I looked away. I couldn't face her.

"I know. I just said it because I feel useless. It's my niece we're trying to find, and you're spending money like it was water, not to mention working your tail off, and my contribution is nil."

"Stop that," she snapped. "You know what we got out of it. Now when we go to talk to these people, we'll have a handle on who we're talking to."

"How will that help?" Trying to sound neutral.

With grim patience, she said, "We'll finally be able to put on some pressure. Maybe we can get our kidnapper to make a mistake."

I couldn't argue with that. It was something to do. It might even work. So I just sat there while Ginny stamped down on the accelerator and took the Olds squealing out of Dr. Sandoval's parking lot onto the highway.

12

I knew that Ginny and I were headed for a showdown.

I wasn't looking forward to it. It was a guaranteed no-win situation for me. In this day and age, there's no way to talk about shame and guilt without making it sound like self-pity. That's why people with any integrity keep their goddamn mouths shut. A nice trick, if you can do it.

But the fireworks weren't going to start yet. We didn't have time for them. We were on our way back to big Central High and the school board to take a crack at one of Ginny's plans.

When we got close to the school, we started hunting for a phone booth. Ginny's idea was to begin with Kirke. She didn't have anything particular against him—she just wanted to take advantage of the way he treated his secretaries. I had to admit it was a good idea. If he felt the pressure, it might shake him up a bit. And if he didn't, he might pass the joy on to someone who did.

When we found a phone, Ginny said, "I'll give you ten minutes."

"Should be enough. How long can you keep him?"

She got out of the Olds, and I slid over into the driver's seat. "I'll try for half an hour," she said, "but I can't guarantee it."

I put the car in gear. "That's OK. If he catches me, it'll just make someone more nervous."

She said, "Right," and I drove off.

I parked in the Central High lot and went into the building. Ten minutes didn't turn out to be too much time. It was between class breaks, and the halls were full of kids, half of them apparently trying to run into me. On top of that, with all the kids coming and going every which way, I missed a turn and had to ask directions. And the whole time I had to fight this crazy impulse to stop what I was doing and just go hunting for Alathea. Seeing so many young girls made me feel more desperate than ever. What with one thing and another, it took me more than eight minutes to reach the board of education door.

From there I went back down the hall and tucked myself around a corner where I could watch the door without much chance of being seen. Then I waited.

Exactly three minutes later, Kirke left the office. He looked a little more awake than he had the day before, and he was moving fast. Not hurrying, really. Just going like a man who couldn't afford to waste any time. Ginny knew how to get results over the phone.

When he disappeared around a corner, I gave him a minute for second thoughts, then went to the door and let myself in.

The front room hadn't changed. It still reminded me of the police duty room in the Municipal Building. But it was busier. Several kids at the counter occupied the attention of five secretaries. Fortunately the one I wanted wasn't one of them. I was looking for the secretary that Kirke had chewed out in front of Ginny and me the day before.

She sat at her desk with a harried look on her face.

I caught her eye, and she came over to the counter. I said, "Sondra?" She nodded. My face didn't register with her, so I said, "My name's Axbrewder. I was here yesterday."

"Oh yes, I remember." For a moment her expression relaxed, and she turned pretty, the way she was born to look. She leaned toward me and said softly so that the kids couldn't hear, "You're the private detective." Word gets around.

"That's right." I took a stab at trying to look charming, but for some reason my smile didn't feel right, so I dropped it. "I'd like to talk to you."

The way she turned her eyes up at me conveyed the impression that she gave my smile credit for good intentions. "What about?"

"I can't tell you here. Can you take a break or something? I'll buy you a cup of coffee."

At that her face closed like a shutter. "I can't."

"Oh, come on." Axbrewder at his most persuasive. "Kirke won't catch you. My partner has him, and she won't let him go for at least half an hour. And if he comes back sooner, I can cover you." I was prepared to try almost anything. "He'd look better with his nose sticking out his ear, don't you think?"

Well, I was right about one thing, anyway. Kirke had been leaning on her hard. Too hard. Even timid people have limits, and Sondra had just reached hers. Her smile looked brittle and vaguely feverish, but it was a smile. "Where shall we go?"

This time my own smile was a lot more genuine. "How about the cafeteria?"

"OK." She went to her desk and got her purse, then said to one of the other secretaries in a determined little voice, "I'm going to take my break now." A minute later she was guiding me down the hall in the direction of the cafeteria.

I kept my mouth shut for a while, giving her a chance to feel as indignant and defiant and maybe scared as she wanted. But when we'd poured ourselves some coffee and found a table in the oversized mausoleum they called the cafeteria, I got started.

"How long have you worked here, Sondra?"

"About a year." She was so preoccupied with the risk she took that she seemed to have forgotten I had a particular reason for wanting to talk to her.

"A year," I repeated, crossing her off my list. "How do you like it?"

She grimaced. "It's a job. I don't have much choice. I've got to work somewhere."

"But you don't get along with Kirke."

"Who does?" Defiance had the upper hand at the moment. "What's his problem?"

Bitterly she said, "He thinks secretaries shouldn't make mistakes. He thinks secretaries shouldn't be human. And," she added after a moment, "he doesn't like women."

I scanned her with what I hoped was an appreciative gleam in my eyes. "He's a little confused."

She rewarded me with another smile. If her color hadn't been so high already, she might've blushed.

I took a slug of my coffee, then fought down an almost overwhelming desire to throw up. What could they have made the stuff out of, Clorox? When the impulse to puke passed, I asked carefully, "Sondra, how much do you know about this new filing system Kirke is working on?"

"Not much." The coffee didn't seem to faze her. She must've been used to it. "He only lets three of us touch it, and I'm not one of them. Just Mabel, Joan, and Connie. The rest of us do ordinary office work. Letters, transcripts, reports, newsletters, stuff like that."

"What do you do if you need something in those files? Say you need to look up the records for a kid who goes to Ensenada Middle School."

"Usually I ask Mabel. Or Connie or Joan, if Mabel isn't around."

"I see." I pushed my coffee away. Just looking at it made my stomach queasy. "Besides them and Kirke, who knows how to use the files?"

"Well," she considered, "there's Mr. Greenling—he's nice—and Mrs. Scurvey. Mr. Stretto never touches anything. If he wants something, he asks Mr. Kirke for it. I think that's all."

"None of the other people on the board?"

"No." She was sure.

"What about people from other schools? What if the vice-principal of Mountain Junior High, for instance, wants to know something?"

"They ask for it, and Mabel or Connie or Joan gets it for them. Or maybe Mr. Kirke. Those files aren't easy to use. They're sort of in-between, you know? You don't just look in a filing cabinet alphabetically and pull out what you want. They're getting ready to be put in a computer, so they aren't handy. Mabel says they're all in pieces, cross-indexed every which way. Besides"—her tone went sour again—"Mr. Kirke doesn't like other people to touch them."

"That figures." I paused for a moment, trying to guess how far I could go with her without losing her spontaneity. Then I said, "Would you mind telling me a little more about Mabel and Connie and Joan?"

"Like what?" She must've felt giddy with courage. She sure as hell wasn't feeling suspicious.

"Well, take Mabel. What's her last name?"

"Allson. Mabel Allson."

"What's she like? Is she married?"

"I like her. She's the only one who ever stands up to Mr. Kirke. I think it's because she doesn't need the job. Her husband is a bank president. Flat Valley Savings and Loan, I think. She works because she likes it."

"How about Connie?"

"Connie Mousse." Sondra giggled. "We call her the Moose. She's a frustrated old maid. She hates everything. She works here because she likes hating it. If she had a husband, she wouldn't need the job, she could hate him instead."

"And Joan?"

"She's Joan Phillips. We get along OK, I guess, but I don't feel close to her. All she ever talks about is her fiancé, Jon, what's his name? Jon Gren, that's it. I ought to know all about him by now. He's a second-year intern at University Hospital. They're going to get married when he graduates."

She said some more, but all of a sudden I wasn't listening. I was thinking, *intern*. Who else besides pushers know where to get drugs? Doctors, that's who. Not Camilla Sandoval. It would be too risky for her. There was a hell of a lot of junk involved, and all the records would be in her name. But how about a second-year intern in a major hospital? If he knew what he was doing, he could rip off any drug he wanted by the pound.

"Sondra," I said, "you're a delight. I haven't been delighted in a long time, and I need it. But we're just about out of time." I fished out one of Ginny's cards and handed it to her. "You can get me with that number. If there's ever anything I can do for you, call. Day or night, it doesn't matter. Especially give me a call if Kirke hassles you about talking to me. I'll make a pretzel out of him."

She smiled bravely. But the mention of Kirke brought back her fear, her smile betrayed a hint of the old despair.

"I mean it," I said. "Nobody pushes my friends around."

"All right, Mr. Axbrewder," she said brightly. She was determined to carry it off. "I'll keep that in mind."

It wasn't until we were on our way back to her office that I remembered there was something else I had to ask her. "Just one more thing, Sondra. People like Mabel, Joan, Connie—how long have they worked here?"

"I'm not sure. Longer than I have. I know it's been a long time for Mabel. The Moose has been here forever. And Joan—I don't know, maybe a couple of years."

I thanked her again and we went back through the school board door. The whole time I'd been with her, she hadn't once asked what all these questions were about. When she sat down at her desk, her face was white and her hands shook.

Apparently I'd underestimated just how scared she was of Kirke.

I found it a little hard to understand. He wasn't back yet, and unless someone ratted on her, he wouldn't know that she'd been talking with me. But she seemed to think he'd know. Just know.

Then he came back. Stalked into the office so quickly that he almost hit me with the door. We glared at each other for a second. A hot red spot marked each of his pale cheeks, and his chain-saw mouth was gripped tight. Ginny had put pressure on him, all right.

"I just finished telling your partner where to stick it," he rasped. "What the hell do you want?"

I grinned unkindly. "I'm waiting for her. When she gets here, we want to talk to Mr. Greenling."

Kirke turned on his heel. The kids were gone now. He had a room full of women at desks to consider. But he homed in on Sondra as if she'd sent up a flare. He had a good eye. There was something scared in the way she hunched over her work, not looking at anything except the paper in her typewriter, and he spotted it. At once he went over to her, stood beside her. He didn't say anything. All he did was drum lightly on the desktop with his fingers. And watch her fall apart. The shaking of her hands got worse. Her fingers tangled, and in a minute she'd made a hopeless snarl out of what she was typing.

"When Miss Fistoulari gets here," he said, "take her and Mr. Axbrewder to see Mr. Greenling." He made it sound like a form of torture. Then he went into his private office and closed the door.

"Nice guy," I said to the room.

It might as well have been empty. Nobody even glanced at me.

"Thanks," I said. "I think I'll wait outside."

Stepping into the hall, I closed the door behind me. Mostly for my own protection. I couldn't stand the reproach of Sondra's hunched shoulders.

Before long Ginny came down the hall. There was a fighting flare to her nostrils, but mostly she was just alert and ready, like she'd gone the distance with him, and he hadn't laid a glove on her.

"This better be worth it," I growled. "That man is a solid-gold bastard."

She considered for a moment, then shrugged. "We'll find out."

"What did you get out of him?" I asked.

"Not much. I don't know whether he's tough or not, but he's hostile as all hell. At first I couldn't figure it out. I wasn't hassling him in the beginning. But then it hit me: He hates women. According to him, he left his job at NCR because his boss was a woman. 'All women are bitches'— that's a direct quote." A fighting light shone in her eyes. "That's when I cut into him."

"I guess you did." Sondra had just said the same thing. "He's taking it out on his secretaries."

"That's their problem." She was in no mood to sympathize. "If they don't like it, let them stand up for themselves."

For a minute we stood there scowling at each other—or

rather scowling past each other. Then she asked, "How about you?"

I shook myself, made an effort to haul my insides into some semblance of order. Then I told her about Mabel, Connie, and Joan—and Jon Gren.

She wasn't as impressed as I'd expected by the news about Joan Phillips' intern boyfriend. "You're assuming that if somebody is leaking those files, they're leaking to somebody they know personally. That doesn't have to be true. It could be pure business. They're just doing it for money."

"At the moment, that doesn't matter," I countered. "The point is, it gives us a place to work." She nodded, and I went on. "Anyway, our list is down to five; three secretaries, Kirke, and Greenling. And it isn't even lunchtime yet."

She looked at me sharply. "You're feeling better."

"I'm making a contribution."

"Glad to hear it."

Her tone was sardonic, but I knew that it wasn't aimed at me. Sardonic was just her way of keeping herself distant, objective. She was working. She didn't have time to worry about my poor dismal ego. I wanted to kiss her again, but I knew better.

"Who do you want to tackle next?" she asked.

"We have an appointment with Mr. Greenling." Axbrewder playing at formality.

"Let's go."

I opened the door for her, mainly to remind her I wasn't Julian Kirke, and followed her back into the office.

Sondra's face had that swollen almost-crying look, and she wasn't willing to meet my eyes. But she came over to us right away and guided us down the back hall to Astin Greenling's office. In a minute we were standing in a room that would've made a perfectly comfortable broom closet if it hadn't been crammed to the ceiling with files and textbooks. In a tired voice, the curriculum vice-chairman offered us seats. When I sat down, my back was jammed against a bookcase and my knees were pushing the edge of his desk.

He looked vaguely more rumpled than he had the day before, but other than that he seemed pretty much the same.

He gave the impression that he was too obsessed with and exhausted by his work to get dressed in the morning without help. No matter what Dr. Sandoval said about him, he belonged on the list. He looked like a moral wreck. There aren't very many people in the world so good that they wouldn't sell their own mothers into slavery—if you got them tired enough and desperate enough. Especially if they needed the money for some "good" reason.

But he didn't make any effort to put us off, didn't tell us how busy he was. He didn't say anything at all. He just sat behind his desk and looked at us with those exhausted eyes, waiting for us to let him know why we were there.

Ginny took a few moments deciding what approach to use. Then she said, "When Mr. Stretto showed you those notes yesterday, the only thing you had to contribute was an inane comment about 'penmanship.' Didn't you understand what you were reading?"

Apparently she'd decided on the hard-headed approach.

Greenling made an aimless gesture with his hands. "It doesn't have anything to do with me." He didn't sound hopeless. For him hopeless was so long ago that he didn't remember what it felt like anymore.

"I disagree." To hear her, you would've thought she'd already made up her mind about this case. "There are only five people in this entire school system who could've kidnapped those girls. You're one of them."

"Kid—?" If she'd suddenly ripped off her clothes and jumped him right then and there, he couldn't have been more surprised. "Kid—?" He couldn't even get the word out. Probably his reaction would've been the same if he were innocent or guilty. It's amazing how hard it can be to tell the difference in this lousy world of ours.

"That's not all," she went on. "Of those five people, you're the only one who has a motive."

"Motive?" He was gaping like a fish. "I—? Motive?"

"You need the money. For your wife."

Wife was the magic word. It transformed him. Not all at once. He had to struggle with it for a minute. I watched with a kind of nauseated fascination while terrible things went on inside him. He looked like an alcoholic going through withdrawal. Then it was over. His eyes burned, and all the lines of his face were sharper. In a tight voice, he said, "Get out. My wife is dying. Get out of here."

Ginny didn't flinch. "How are you paying for it, Mr. Greenling?"

But he didn't flinch either. "We have security guards. I didn't want them. The money for these things always seems to come out of curriculum. But now I'm glad we have them. Get out!"

Ginny studied him for a moment. Then she got to her feet. She'd done what we came for—she'd turned up the heat. There wasn't any point in trying to call Greenling's bluff. And right then he didn't look like a bluffer.

"We're going to find those girls, Mr. Greenling," she said evenly. "Whoever kidnapped them we're going to nail to the wall."

Then she left the room.

I stayed where I was. Sometimes that works. Sometimes when people get mad at her they're willing to talk to me. Innocent people, usually. When she was gone, I said, "Come on, Greenling. Save yourself some grief. Tell me how you pay for it."

He picked up his phone, pushed a button. When a voice answered, he said, "Connie, get Security. Now."

I didn't argue with him. It was his play. He could call it any way he wanted. I wedged my way out of his closet and closed the door behind me.

Ginny was waiting for me in the hall. I said, "Nothing," and she nodded. But she wasn't really paying attention. She was on some other trail. She had a hunting look in her face.

After a moment she said, "Did you see it?"

"See what?"

"Over on the right side of his desk. A stack of paper. Probably for notes. White stuff. Half sheets.

"They looked like they'd been torn along one edge."

13

I said, "I don't believe it. That man is as innocent as the day he was born. Even if he has something to be guilty about, he's still innocent."

She looked at me—not challenging, just questioning. "What makes you say that?"

I was about to answer, *Because I've been there and I ought to know.* But I couldn't say that to her, not the way things were going today. So instead I said, "He's got too much dignity." It was lame, but I didn't have anything better to offer at the moment.

Ginny said, "Dignity covers a multitude of sins. I'd rather have proof."

"Yeah? I thought you were the one who said we didn't need proof."

She grinned quickly. "That's true. But I wouldn't turn it down if you offered it to me."

I loved that grin. "What're we waiting for? Let's go find some."

"Right." She went about three steps down the hall, then knocked at a door with a sign on it saying:

MRS. MARTHA SCURVEY
BUDGET VICE-CHAIRMAN

From inside, a woman's voice snapped. "Go away. I'm busy."

Ginny opened the door, stuck her head in, then looked back at me with a sudden ferocity in her grin. She gestured for me to follow her.

"I told you to go away!" the woman said angrily.

When I got into the office—which was about the same

size as Greenling's, but a hell of a lot neater—I found out why. The air was thick with sweet gray smoke. Martha Scurvey sat stiffly behind her desk with a hash pipe in her hands. Probably she didn't want anyone to come in until the air-conditioning cleared the air. Or maybe until she smoked a cigar to cover the odor.

"I'll tell you what, Ms. Scurvey," Ginny offered. "You give us a little of your time, and we'll forget what that stuff smells like." I could hear the grin in her voice.

"That's blackmail." Martha Scurvey was angry enough to pluck chickens, but she was also under complete control. A dangerous combination. She must've had a lot of charm on tap, or she wouldn't be sitting where she was. At the moment, however, it didn't show. The only thing she showed was stainless steel. I wondered where she picked up the hash habit. Offhand, she didn't look like the kind of woman who needed it.

"Not at all," Ginny said smoothly. "Just persuasion. The only thing we're interested in is a little talk."

Ms. Scurvey didn't want to talk. She wanted us to get the hell out of her life. But she knew how to concede without losing face. With a gesture that might've looked gracious if her eyes had backed it up, she offered us chairs. While we seated ourselves, she stashed her pipe, pouch, and matches in a briefcase, which she locked. Then she leaned her elbows on the desk and said, "I prefer Mrs., not Ms. I'm a married woman and proud of it."

That sounded as phony as her graciousness. How she felt about her marriage was irrelevant. She was just trying to get on top of the situation.

Ginny let her try. "Certainly, Mrs. Scurvey. We're not here to give you any trouble. As far as we know, you're in the clear."

I had to admire her. Ginny plays control games as well as anyone. Mrs. Scurvey had already been outmaneuvered, and she didn't even know it. "In the clear?" she asked. "I don't understand."

After that I stopped listening for a minute. I was distracted.

In a neat stack off to one side of her desk, Mrs. Scurvey had a pile of white writing paper. A handy size for notes—full sheets torn neatly in half. From where I sat, the paper looked like good twenty-pound bond.

I felt a childish urge to nudge Ginny and point, but I resisted it. Instead I shifted my weight, sneaked a couple of deep breaths, and went back to paying attention.

Ginny was saying, "—your opinion of Mr. Greenling?"

Mrs. Scurvey looked at her hands, checked her fingernails. "He's conscientious—very conscientious—but hopelessly out of date. His ideas of education have yet to reach the twentieth century. I'd love to do a strict cost analysis of his department, but he won't let me touch it. I'm expected to take his word for everything. At present." She made it clear that Astin Greenling wouldn't have the power to turn her down much longer.

"Do you know about his wife?"

"He doesn't talk about her, and I don't ask. I've heard she's ill. That's more than I want to know."

"What about Paul Stretto?"

"Paul is a forward-thinking educator with a keen appreciation for economic reality. He's brought this school system a long way toward facing the facts of life and doing the job it's supposed to do."

I was glad Ginny didn't ask what kind of job that was. The smugness in Mrs. Scurvey's tone made my scalp itch. I didn't like what it implied about her relationship with Stretto. Fortunately Ginny wasn't interested in theories of education. Instead of pursuing Stretto, she asked, "How do you feel about Julian Kirke?"

"Personally, I think he's odious. Professionally, he does great work. His new filing system will save us thousands of dollars a year—once he gets it into the computer."

"Do you see him socially, know anything about him?"

Mrs. Scurvey gave Ginny a withering stare and said, "No." Kirke was probably too low for her. He wasn't chairman of anything.

"Who works on the files with him?"

"Three of his girls," she said stiffly. "Mabel, Joan, and—and Connie? I think that's her name."

"What do you know about them?"

"What should I know about them? They're his girls. Ask him."

"Do they ever do any work for you?"

"Just routine typing."

"They don't help you with the files?"

"When I want something out of the files, I get it myself." Mrs. Scurvey was running out of endurance. Her tone would've curdled milk. All of a sudden, I guessed that she didn't smoke hash because she liked it. She smoked it because she needed it. She was brittle inside and didn't want anybody to know.

Before I could think about it, I asked her, "How long has your husband been dead, Mrs. Scurvey?"

Milk, hell. She practically curdled me. "That's none of your business."

Which told me what I wanted to know. Now she made sense to me. Her high-pressure approach to her job, her relationship with Stretto, the hash—she was running away from grief. I half wanted to ask Ginny to leave her alone. A married woman, and proud of it. It's a hard life when you lose everything that used to tell you who you are.

But Ginny was almost through anyway. "Just one practical question, Mrs. Scurvey. What's the phone setup around here?"

"The phone—? I don't understand."

"If I wanted to call you, could I reach you directly, or would I have to go through one of the secretaries?"

"Through the secretaries."

"And when you want to make a call?"

Mrs. Scurvey sighed. "Through the secretaries."

"So they can make calls that you don't know about, but you can't make or receive any calls that they don't know about. Right?"

Mrs. Scurvey was hugging herself with her arms. "Are you finished?"

"Yes, I'm finished," Ginny said. "Just let me make a note

of that." Before Mrs. Scurvey could stop her—if Mrs. Scurvey wanted to stop her—she reached over and took a sheet off the stack of white paper. She got a pen out of her purse, scribbled something on one end of the sheet, then put it and the pen back in her purse.

"Thanks for your time. We're sorry we troubled you.

"Come on, Brew." Thirty seconds later, we were out of the school board offices and walking down the halls of Central High.

I wanted to see that sheet of paper. But Ginny didn't seem to be in any hurry to look at it, so I asked her, "What was all that about the phones?"

"Just fishing," she said. "Whoever we're looking for doesn't work alone. One way or another, I think there have to be at least two of them. It's hard for me to picture somebody who works here moonlighting as a pusher successfully. Too many things could go wrong. I figure we're looking for somebody who gets the information, then passes it to somebody else. Somebody else who handles the girls."

I stopped her. "They wouldn't be stupid enough to call each other at work."

"That depends." She pushed open a door, and we went out into the glare of the parking lot. The asphalt swam with heat. "Greenling or Scurvey wouldn't because their calls go through the secretaries. But that doesn't apply to the secretaries."

When we reached the Olds, she put her purse on the hood and took out the sheet of paper.

Sure enough, it was twenty-pound bond. Neatly torn along one edge. The watermark matched all the other notes.

"Damn it," Ginny muttered under her breath.

"For sure." I couldn't figure out what Martha Scurvey was doing with paper like this. She wasn't supposed to be one of our suspects. She'd only been on the board a year.

But Ginny was cursing something else. "I should've grabbed a sheet from Greenling, too. I wasn't thinking." She stuffed the note angrily back into her purse. "I swear to God, Brew," she rasped, not looking at me, "some days I don't know what I use for brains."

The frustration in her voice surprised me. I tend to get so involved in my own inadequacies that I sometimes forget she's human, too. Judging from the sound of things, finding this paper in Martha Scurvey's office must've broken one of Ginny's intricate logical chains. Ruined a theory or two and left her feeling stupid. "Don't complain to me," I said quietly. "I'm the guy who lost the notes, remember? I didn't even see that paper on Greenling's desk."

"Yes, well," she said, jerking open the door of the Olds, "that's a big consolation."

That crack irked me. But I didn't snap back. Reciprocity—it was my turn to stay cool. I got into the passenger seat, watched her while she took us out of the parking lot in the direction of her office. When I got tired of looking at her scowl, I said, "So who cares about your brains? It's your body I'm interested in."

For a second there I thought she was going to let go of the wheel and clobber me. But then suddenly the scowl broke. She threw back her head and laughed.

"Ah, Brew," she sighed after a minute, "if I ever figure out what to do with you, you're going to be in big trouble."

"Take your time," I said. "I can wait."

We chuckled together, and while it lasted I felt better.

About a mile from the Murchison Building we stopped for a quick lunch. As we ate, Ginny looked at me abruptly and asked, "How did you know Mrs. Scurvey's husband was dead?"

"Intuition," I said. "She doesn't have any kids. She's having an affair with Mr. Paul M. Stretto. I don't know how I knew. It just came to me."

"Are you sure you didn't figure it out from the name on her door? It didn't say, 'Mrs. George-or-whatever Scurvey.' It said, 'Mrs. Martha.' "

"That," I said flatly, "never occurred to me."

She shook her head. "You're not a well man. You ought to see a doctor. Maybe there's a treatment for it."

I didn't try for a comeback. Her eyes were focused somewhere else, and her voice had an abstract sound. She wasn't even listening to herself. Instead she was groping for some-

thing, some kind of link that would tie this case together. I
knew better than to distract her.

When we were finished eating, we went on to her office.

While she called her answering service, I started a pot of
coffee. But after that I didn't have anything to do except sit
and watch her think some more. I didn't mind at first. Ginny
thinking is Ginny making progress. But after half an hour
or so I started to get restless. I was just about to interrupt
her when she reached a decision. Without warning, she came
back from wherever it was she'd been and pulled the phone
toward her. "The hell with him," she muttered. "I can't wait
any longer."

There was a kind of suppressed violence in the way she
dialed, and when she started talking her face was knotted in
a grimace, but she managed to keep her voice tolerably
smooth. Once she got past the people who fronted for him
to Smithsonian himself, she put the call on the speaker so
that I could hear him too.

Even over that tinny amplifier he had the kind of voice
that makes you want to wash your hands. Oily and sticky.
You'd have to be a bank president to like it. "What's the
matter, Fistoulari?" he asked. "No patience? I told you I'd
call at three. You can't crack this case without me?"

Ginny picked up a metal letter opener, set the point in the
blotter on her desk, and slowly twirled it with her fingers.
"Of course not, Lawrence." Somehow she kept the acid out
of her tone. "You know I'm helpless without you."

"That's probably true." He couldn't have sounded more
self-satisfied if he'd just been propositioned by Miss America. Ginny stopped twirling the letter opener and began
slowly pushing it into the blotter. The expression on her face
said, *Why am I talking to this asshole?* "Under the circumstances," he went on, "I won't keep you hanging. I have
most of the information anyway. The only one I'm not satisfied about is this Stretto character."

"What have you got on him?"

"Nothing you want. For a politician, he looks pretty clean.
But I always double-check politicians. He keeps a higher
profile than he can afford on board of education money, but

right now it looks like it comes out of his campaign organization. Rumor is that it's clean money. Maybe it was born clean, and maybe somebody washed it. I'll know later on, probably by tomorrow."

Well, it was still possible that Stretto supplied files to someone who supplied him with money. But I didn't believe it. He'd been too quick to call the commissioner.

"How about the others?" Ginny asked.

"Scurvey and Kirke are clean. Martha Scurvey is a society broad"—the letter opener was starting to bend—"and she probably has more cash in her purse than she gets paid in a year. Her husband was Matthew Scurvey, the computer biggie. He left her enough to buy her own public school, if she wants it." He paused, then said, "It's possible she's one of Stretto's private contributors."

"I already know that," Ginny said. With malice aforethought. But she kept her voice bland.

"Yeah?" Smithsonian growled. He didn't like it when people already knew what he was telling them. "Then maybe you already know about Kirke, too."

"Not a thing. I can't get close to him."

"Well, then." Smithsonian mollified. "He's clean. He lives within his means—which aren't that much, let me tell you. His apartment has a certain amount of class, and he drives a car with a hefty price tag. A Citröen-Maseratti. But his bank financed the car. Take the payments on that, plus rent and taxes, out of his salary, and you still have enough for food, with something left over for a trip to Mexico every once in a while. Unless you're trying to support a little action on the side. He isn't. Absolutely no money he can't account for."

Ginny absorbed that for a minute. So did I. I hated to cross Kirke off the list, but at the moment I didn't see any way around it. About the only thing I was sure of in this mess was that whoever was kidnapping these girls and pumping them full of junk was making money out of it. Considering what can happen to you if you're convicted for kidnapping, it had to be a *lot* of money.

Then Ginny asked, "What about Astin Greenling?"

"Ah, Mr. Greenling," Smithsonian said, "the man with the sick wife. I took a good look at him. Medical expenses cause more crime in this country than anybody knows about. You can bet he doesn't pay his bills with his salary. And the kind of hospitalization the board carries is nothing special. I was a little surprised to learn that in fact Mr. Greenling does pay his bills.

"How? you ask. I'll tell you how." Smithsonian was enjoying himself. "That sucker is up to his ass in loan sharks."

"Loan sharks." Ginny sat up straight, tossed the letter opener aside. I could almost see her thinking, *How does he pay them back? Maybe he pays them with something besides money. Maybe he pays them with information.* "How long has that been going on?"

"About two years." Smithsonian chuckled. "I don't know why they haven't broken his arms yet."

"After two years? How do you think he's handling it?"

"Hard to tell without actually talking to him. No doubt every time one of them gets nasty he goes to another and borrows enough to save his skin for a while. If that's what he's doing, he's digging himself a hole they'll bury him in."

"All right, Lawrence," Ginny said. "You're giving me exactly what I want. Now I have some more names for you."

"More?" he barked. "You think you're my only client? I don't have better things to do than this—?"

Ginny cut him off. "I'll pay. Whatever it is. Just send me a bill."

"Believe it, Fistoulari. I'll send you a bill." He paused to give us a chance to feel like we were being threatened, then said, "So tell me the names."

"Mabel Allson," Ginny said promptly. "Connie Mousse. Joan Phillips. They're all secretaries for the board. And Jon Gren." She spelled out the names for him. "Gren is Joan Phillips' fiancé. An intern at University Hospital."

"Do not call me," he said heavily. "I'll call you. Tomorrow. Around noon." He paused again, probably waiting for Ginny to tell him how wonderful he was. When she didn't say anything, he hung up with a bang.

She switched off the speaker, and we stared at each other

for a minute. Or rather I stared at her, and she looked through me into empty space. I stood it as long as I could. Then I got up. "Let's go."

Her gaze didn't shift an inch. "Where?"

"Back to the school board. Or over to Greenling's house, talk to his wife. Somewhere. We can't just sit here."

She wasn't listening. "I've missed something. There's something here. Something that gives it all away. But I can't pick it up. Damn and blast! What's the matter with me?"

I said, "You're trying too hard."

I don't know why I bothered. It didn't register with her at all. "I'm going blind," she insisted. "It's right here in front of me, but I can't see it."

I didn't see it either, so I took a deep breath and said, "Acton."

That reached her. She looked up, and her eyes came into focus on my face. "What did you say?"

"Acton."

"What is that? More intuition?"

"No. I'm just trying to shake you up a little. You're in a rut. You've got Greenling on the brain."

She leaned back in her chair, put her hands behind her head. "You still don't believe he's the one?"

"Who, me? Do you think I'm crazy? Of course he's the one. Who else could it be?"

Her eyes narrowed, until I almost couldn't see the fighting gleam in them. "All right, ace. Maybe I'm in a rut. She's your niece. What do you think we should be doing?"

"I think we should go shake down Jon Gren."

"Wonderful. Try it with my blessing. Only there's one thing you ought to keep in mind. Hospitals don't keep heroin around. Morphine, yes. Heroin, no. He's just Joan Phillips' fiancé—that's all you've got on him."

What could I say to that? "Well then, let's talk to Mrs. Greenling." Trying not to sound defensive. No point in telling her that she'd just shot down the only theory I had.

She sighed. "That may be a good idea." Reluctantly she got to her feet. "So why do I feel like you're asking me to go hurt a sick woman?"

Under other circumstances, that would've made me mad. After all the things I'd done in the past three days without helping Alathea even a little bit, I was in no mood for her to turn finicky. But I was saved by the phone.

She snatched it up. "Fistoulari Investigations."

While she listened, all the blood drained out of her face and something else took its place—something that looked like murder. Then she said, "Hang on. We'll be right there."

She put the receiver down.

If I hadn't known better, I might've thought that it was me she wanted to kill.

In a tight voice, she said, "That was Lona. She's over at University Hospital. The cops just brought in Alathea. She's still alive, but she's in a coma. OD."

Maybe she wanted some kind of reaction from me. Maybe there was something she wanted me to say. I didn't know, and I didn't care. I was already on my way out to the elevator.

14

I hit the call button for the elevator, hit it again, pounded the damn thing. Finally the lights of the floor indicator started to move. They were slow, slow. By the time the doors opened, Ginny ran down the hall to catch up with me.

"Sorry," she muttered under her breath as she hurried into the elevator. She must've thought I was holding it for her. "Had too call my answering service."

I ignored her. I was thinking, *Coma. Alathea. In a coma. Bastards bastards bastards.*

"They'll get her out of it," Ginny said. "Doctors know more about these things than they used to. She'll be able to tell us everything we want."

"Leave me alone." I looked at her, let her see I meant it. "That isn't what I need."

For a second I feared that she would ask me just what it was I did need. But then the elevator opened into the basement, and we both hustled toward the Olds.

I wasn't driving, I didn't have anything to do, I was helpless. The sun shone cheerfully, the traffic took its own sweet time, and the man who designed the sequencing of the stoplights was a maniac—and there was nothing anyone could do about any of it. I just sat staring through the windshield with my hands clenched on my knees, trying to hold myself together while Ginny wrestled with things she couldn't change. I'd forgotten my sunglasses.

She made good time. She must've because I was still in one piece when she slammed the Olds into a parking space in the University Hospital lot. We hit the asphalt together. But when I started to run, she caught my arm, held me back so that we walked toward the entrance together.

I let her do it. When Ginny gives orders, I obey.

University Hospital is a tall structure built in two square sections. For five stories the sections have a common wall, then the east wing goes on up for another five stories. They built the place out of red brick, and when the sun catches it at the right time of day, it looks like blood. The emergency entrance is on the ground floor of the west wing, and with all the security guards they have around, it looks more like a top-secret military installation than a place where urgent hurts are treated. At least during the day. At night, with lights in all those windows, it looks a bit more comforting.

We went in, asked a guard for directions, and got ourselves pointed toward the waiting room. That was where we found Lona.

She stood at a window looking out into the parking lot. Sunlight glared into her eyes from the chrome and glass, but it didn't seem to bother her. When Ginny said, "Mrs. Axbrewder," she turned to face us.

I wanted her to take a step toward us, hold out her hands, do something that would give me permission to put my arms around her. But she was too much alone for that. Her pain cut her off from everything. She stood there small and brittle, with her mouth clamped shut because there was nothing she could say or even cry out that would relieve the pressure inside her. It was as clear as daylight that we'd failed her, failed Alathea. When from somewhere she found the strength or maybe the generosity to say, "Thank you for coming," I almost groaned out loud.

"How is she?" Ginny asked softly. She felt as much a failure as I did. I knew that. The difference was that she could keep it from interfering with more important things.

"I don't know," Lona said. Her voice quavered, on the edge of control. "I haven't seen the doctor since he came out to talk to me. Before I called you. He told me what he was going to do. I had to give my permission because she's underage. But I didn't understand it. He wouldn't let me see her.

"He said"—she didn't look at us, never lifted her eyes above my chest—"he said she's an addict. There are needle marks all over her arms."

"It's not her fault, Lona." What else could I say? "Someone did it to her. She was forced into it."

Very carefully, she said, "I know that."

Lona!

"How did they find her?" Ginny asked. "What happened?" She wanted to know if the cops had caught Thea's kidnapper. Hell, I wanted to know. But she was moving slowly, gently.

"I'm not sure. I don't understand it. I got a call. From Lieutenant Acton. He was one of Richard's friends. He said that she'd been found. He said she was wandering around somewhere. Out on Canyon Road, I think. Trying to get a ride back into town. Somebody saw that she looked sick and called the police. I don't know who it was. When they found her, she was already unconscious. In the dirt at the side of the road."

I wanted to throw up. She was only thirteen. Things like that shouldn't happen to children.

"Did he say anything else?"

"He told me she was here. He said I should come down here right away because the doctors needed my permission to treat her."

For a minute, I had an impulse to grab the Olds and head for Canyon Road, out toward the mountains east of the city, where only the richest of the rich people live. I wanted to bang on doors until I found wherever Alathea had come from. It was a crazy idea, of course. Maybe she hadn't been kept in that area at all. Maybe she'd just been dropped off there so that she would get killed by the traffic. But that didn't make sense. There isn't much traffic on Canyon Road. And anyway that part of town held at least a hundred houses.

Somehow I fought the impulse down.

"Is there anything we can do?" Ginny asked.

"No, thank you." Lona's eyes didn't leave the buttons of my shirt. "I'm all right." If she'd been any more all right, she would've been hysterical. "You don't have to stay if you don't want to."

Ginny's eyes were full of tears, but she didn't let them fall. "That's OK. We'll stick around."

If that meant anything to Lona, she didn't show it. She turned away from us, went back to staring out the window.

Then we waited. Just waited. Which is what makes the famous Chinese water torture so unbearable. It isn't the dripping of the water—after a while, your forehead just gets numb. No, it's the waiting between drops that does it. Drives you completely bananas. Other people came into the waiting room, left again. Two angry and anxious mothers told each other what their kids had done this time. A man fumigated the room with a cigar the size of a Glock while his aged father had an ankle X-rayed. A guy and girl who'd been in a minor car wreck came in and took turns sitting around while they were checked out for whiplash. Compared to waiting, sobriety is easy.

It was almost four o'clock when a doctor finally showed up, asking for Mrs. Axbrewder.

Lona whirled as if she'd been stung. Her face was so full of questions that she couldn't get them out. She just stared at the doctor and ached, dumbly begging him to take pity on her.

"She's stable physically," he said. "She needs care, but she should be all right. I'm having her taken up to a room. You can visit her there in a few minutes."

Relief blurred Lona's face. She looked like she was about to give way when the doctor's tone sharpened. "But I have to tell you, Mrs. Axbrewder. We haven't been able to rouse her. She's still in a coma, and we can't reach her."

Ginny was standing beside Lona, had an arm around her shoulders. "How do you treat that?"

"We take care of her body and wait. Maybe she'll pull out of it tonight. Maybe tomorrow, maybe next week. Maybe—I have to say this, Mrs. Axbrewder. Maybe she'll never pull out. It depends on what kind of damage has been done to her brain.

"Permanent coma is rare, but it does happen. Every body is different. An overdose can be like an eraser on a blackboard. It can wipe out the conscious mind. But more often only a small part of the brain is damaged, and after a while the person recovers.

"Of course, her situation is complicated by the fact that she'll be going through withdrawal. All we can do at this point is keep her body nourished and pray."

Lona had her hands in her hair, pulling it away from her face. A woman in danger of going over the edge. Ginny gripped her hard.

"Have you ever had a case like this before, Doctor?" Ginny asked.

"Personally, no. But I've read about them. Studies say that these conditions are more likely to develop when the addict resists the drug for some reason. The mind fights the body as hard as it can for as long as it can, and then there's a backlash."

That meant something. It was trying to tell me something. But I couldn't hear it. Pressure filled my ears. My heart. The doctor told us what room Alathea would be in. When Ginny and Lona left the waiting room, I followed them toward the elevator.

Then another question occurred to me. I turned, ran after the doctor, caught up with him at the nurses' station. "Did you do a complete physical on her?"

He looked at me sourly. "I don't know who you are. What's your interest?"

"My name is Axbrewder. Alathea is my niece."

He considered for a moment, then nodded. "I examined her. What do you want to know?"

It stuck in my throat for a second. Then I got it out. "Is she a virgin?"

He grimaced. Disgusted at me. Or at the question. Or at the answer. "Not by a long shot."

I tried to swallow the acid in my mouth, but it wouldn't go down. Clenching my fists, I went to catch up with Ginny and Lona.

Ginny was holding the elevator for me. She had the same question in her eyes. I said, "Goddamn it to hell. Yes." When she let the door close and punched the floor button, she looked mad enough to chew steel.

Alathea's room was on the eighth floor of the east wing. We found it without any trouble. The halls are laid out square and the doors all have nice big numbers on them. But when we got to her room, another doctor stopped us from going in.

He was about as tall as Ginny, with longish red hair curling around his ears, more paunch than he needed, and bloodshot little eyes. He had freckles so bad that they looked like smallpox. His white coat was buttoned up to his neck. There was a stethoscope in one of his pockets, and his right hand gripped the handle of a black medical bag.

He smiled blandly at us. "I'm Dr. Stevens. Now that she's out of Emergency, I'm responsible for her. You can see her as soon as I'm finished. It'll just take a minute."

Ginny nodded for Lona. We stood around in the hall while Stevens went into Alathea's room and closed the door.

He didn't take a minute, he took three. It felt like thirty, but we were in no position to complain. When he came out, he gave us his smile again. "Don't worry," he said. "She'll be fine."

With his hands in his pockets, he went down the hall away from the nurses' station.

There was something about him I didn't like. He had the look of a man who'd just told a dirty joke. But my opinion of him didn't matter. As long as he helped Thea.

We went into Alathea's room.

It was a semiprivate room. Alathea lay in the bed near the door. A curtain drawn halfway across the room between the beds kept us from seeing who else was there. Past the second bed was the window. The afternoon sun slanted in through it across a long section of the floor.

Alathea looked like death. A sickly paraffin color filled her face, and the scrubbed white of the hospital gown only made it worse. The sheets were tucked up to her armpits. From her bare arms, IV tubes ran up to bottles hanging from poles at the head of the bed. Around the slashes of adhesive tape that held the IV needles in place clustered other red marks like insect stings—tracks of them mapping the veins inside her elbows. Violation as bad as any rape.

Lona went close to her, gripped her hand, and started to cry. After that I couldn't see anymore. I was blind with fury and loss.

Trying to control myself, I shambled over to the window. For a bad minute or two, I couldn't do it. But slowly my eyes started to clear. I hit my knuckles on the windowsill until I could see straight again. Then I looked around.

The room was on the west side of the building. The window hung right over the roof of the west wing, three stories below me. That roof had been fixed up as a recreation area, with stubby trees growing out of little plots of earth, big umbrellas for shade, and plenty of wrought-iron tables and chairs. The place was full of people—nurses, patients, children, visitors. Men and women in hospital gowns walked jerkily around or sat in wheelchairs. They looked like they belonged there, catching a little sun to warm their bones.

Only Alathea didn't belong. And me. She didn't deserve it, and I hadn't earned it.

A faint breeze came in through the window. The window was double glass, insulated for the sake of the AC. But today the hospital was saving money. The air-conditioning wasn't on. Instead the window had been cranked open a crack at the top.

I turned my back on it, glanced at Alathea's neighbor. An old woman, as shriveled as a mummy, asleep and snoring. It surprised me to find that I had pity left to spare for her. She looked like she'd outlived herself long ago.

I wiped my face with my hands and went back to Alathea's half of the room.

Lona wasn't crying anymore. She sat in a chair beside the bed and held Alathea's hand as if both their lives depended on it. Ginny remained with her, standing behind her and gripping her shoulders with both hands—trying to squeeze some kind of strength into her exhausted body. I watched them for a minute or two, hunting for a way to tell them I was leaving.

I didn't get a chance. The door swung open.

Looking like a campaign poster, Stretto strode into the room.

"I came as soon as I heard." Maybe my ears were tricking me. I could've sworn his voice echoed in the room. Somehow he got past Ginny without actually pushing her aside. "Mrs. Axbrewder, I'm terribly sorry. All of us at the board are just heartsick."

He took her hands away from Alathea, held both of them himself. From where I stood, he looked like he was asking her to vote for him.

"In a way, I feel responsible. If Ms. Fistoulari hadn't alerted us, we would never have known this could happen. We should have realized it ourselves months ago and taken steps to prevent it. I promise you, Mrs. Axbrewder, I will use every resource at my command as chairman to make sure this kind of thing stops."

God save me from politicians. I wanted to slug him. But Ginny was in better control of the situation. "I'm glad to hear it, Mr. Stretto." The lash of her voice cut all his blather to pieces. "Now I'd like to hear how you knew she was here."

Which was a very good question.

But he was innocent the way only a politician can be. "The police called me. Since you and I spoke yesterday, I've been doing my best to prod them into action. I even spoke to the commissioner." He was still campaigning. "In no uncertain terms, I told him my opinion of the way this case has been handled. Now it appears that he made my feelings clear to the officer in charge, a Detective Acton. This Acton called me earlier, no doubt trying to compensate for his former inadequacy by keeping me informed."

Acton, huh? That name cropped up too often. I wondered just how many people he'd told about Alathea.

First things first. "Mr. Stretto," I said, "how many people did you tell that Alathea is here?"

He started to answer, but a knock at the door interrupted him.

I went over to it, yanked it open.

Ted Hangst stood outside.

I started to say, What the hell is this? Open house? But he caught my arm, jerked me out of the room. Or tried to anyway. People as short as he is can't actually move me around by brute force. I let him get me into the hall. After I'd closed the door behind me, I took a good look at him.

If he'd had any sleep—not to mention food—since I last saw him, it didn't show. There was fever in his eyes, and his hand on my arm trembled no matter how hard he held on to me.

"Ted," I asked, "what the hell's wrong?"

"Her answering service told me where you were. I've been looking for you all afternoon."

"Looking for us? Why?"

"Why the fuck do you think?" He was more than just feverish. He was hostile and excited. "Because you hotshots have been wrong about this thing from the beginning. That's why I gave up on you. Instead I've been talking to people."

"So have I. I didn't get anywhere."

"Hotshot!" he spat. He was also desperate. "You were talking to the wrong people. You and Fistoulari never figured out why Mittie was kidnapped."

I was in no mood to play games with him, but I didn't let it show. He was stretched to the breaking point, and I didn't want to tighten him any more. He had something to tell me, something he was going to say as soon as he found a way. I gritted my teeth and didn't touch him. "That's true."

"You've got drugs on the brain. You're so hung up on heroin you can't see what's going on."

"Tell me, Ted." Softly, softly. "What's going on?"

"Prostitution!" The word made him so mad that he turned purple. "She wasn't kidnapped by a pusher. She was kidnapped by a pimp! He just uses drugs to control girls, make them do what he wants. What his customers want. They're all sick!"

He fell into a fit of coughing—or maybe it was sobbing—and for a long minute he couldn't go on. It wracked him pretty hard. When he got his breath back, a lot of the hostility was gone.

"It's killing me, Brew." He sounded faint. "There are actually men in this city who want to screw thirteen-year-old girls. They want to screw my daughter. Or worse."

I couldn't stand it any longer. I caught hold of the front of his coat, yanked him off the ground until his face was level with mine. Through my teeth, I hissed, "What did you find out?"

I didn't scare him. He was past being scared. And he didn't get mad, either. He was too tired. "I'm sorry, Brew. I keep forgetting about your niece. I didn't get much. Just a description of the pimp. Or his front man. The guy who lines up the customers. He's the one you talk to if you want—want to—"

I put him down, straightened his coat. "Tell me what he looks like, Ted."

Dully he said, "Tall guy. Red hair, curly. Freckles. His name's supposed to be Sven Last."

I didn't listen to the name. Instead I concentrated on the description.

For a second it paralyzed me. I stood frozen while images of a man with red hair and freckles played inside my head.

He went into Alathea's room. Dr. Stevens—

Then I saw him come out of the room, walk away down the hall. There was something wrong with that picture, something I should've noticed before.

His hands—

They were in his pockets. Both of them.

Then I moved. Snatched open the door, charged into Alathea's room.

"Ginny!" I barked, "he left his bag!"

Lona and Stretto stared at me as if I were a lunatic. I ignored them, focused on Ginny. "That doctor was a fake. Stevens. He left his bag in here."

It took one more second to reach her. Then she whirled, started hunting.

In an instant, she dived under Alathea's bed and came up with a black medical bag in both hands. Carefully she put it on the edge of the bed, snapped it open.

We all watched her—me, Ted, Stretto, Lona. We all saw what was in the bag.

Three sticks of dynamite and some kind of detonating mechanism. The mechanism was ticking.

Lona fainted. Stretto caught hold of the bars at the end of the bed as if he were about to join her. I ignored them both, concentrated on Ginny. The detonator didn't look familiar. In any case, I didn't know much about detonators. Neither did she.

The one thing I *did* know is that you don't try to disarm a bomb if you have no idea what you're doing.

The whole scene didn't seem real to me. I couldn't believe it. Things like this don't happen right in the middle of the afternoon.

"Ginny," I said. Even to myself, I sounded like I was strangling. "Tell me what to do."

She stood up straight, closed the bag, snapped it shut. Carrying it by the handle, she walked out into the middle of the room.

"Ted," she ordered evenly, "go to the nurses' station. Tell them we've got a bomb in here. They have to call the cops. I'll keep in this room. Tell them to get everybody out. Start next door on either side and work away from here. I don't know how much damage this thing can do.

"Go!"

He went.

"Stretto!" She had his number now. Her voice cut into him and brought out the decisive man who'd let us see the files. "Take Lona. As far away as you can, the opposite side of the building."

He didn't hesitate. He scooped Lona up in his arms, started for the door. By the time he reached the hall, he was running.

"Brew, get the window open."

The window. Great idea. Toss the bomb outside where it couldn't get Alathea. I practically threw myself at the glass.

It was built into a heavy frame, opened and closed with a crank. But the crank wasn't there.

The window was open a crack at the top. I reached up and hooked my fingers over the edge of the frame. Next I braced my feet against the sill.

Then I ripped the damn thing out of the wall.

After that I remembered the sun roof.

I turned to Ginny, panted, "You can't. There are people down there."

She didn't flinch. "I don't know when this thing is going off."

I whirled back to the opening, leaned out, and yelled loud enough to tear my lungs, "Get away! Go inside! Get off the roof!"

A couple of people looked up at me. The rest didn't seem to hear a thing.

"Brew!" Ginny snapped. "Get Alathea out of here. Then this woman. Tell the nurses to clear out those people."

I jumped at Alathea's bed, tried to move it. It had wheels, but they were locked. I spent precious seconds kicking off the latches. Then the bed rolled. The IV stands were built into the frame, and the bottles clinked against the poles, but the needles in her arms were safe. Heaving my weight against the bed, I guided it through the doorway and out into the hall.

A moment later Ted and Stretto came toward me. "Take her!" I shouted at them. "Tell the nurses to clear that god-damned sun roof!"

They caught the bed by its corners, and I turned and rushed back into the room.

Ginny knelt at the window, bent over below the level of the sill. Her right arm was hooked over the sill. Using the wall to protect herself, she held the bag out the window.

"You'll kill yourself!" I shouted.

"What do you want me to do?" Her voice was flat and fatal. "Drop it? I'll kill everybody down there."

I didn't argue. I went to the old woman's bed, snapped off the latches.

By the time I got her out the door, a nurse appeared beside me. She was pale with fear, but she didn't let that stop her. "I'll take her," she said, voice shaking. "She's an old woman. If she wakes up with all this going on and doesn't see a familiar face, she'll be terrified."

I gave the bed a shove for momentum and let the nurse have it. Scrambling on all fours to keep my head below the sill, I went back to Ginny.

When I reached her, I said, "Let me do it. You're too important to waste."

She fixed her eyes straight at me. "Get the hell out of here. I don't want to lose you like this."

For a moment I didn't obey. I couldn't—couldn't leave her like that. But I didn't have any choice. If we both got killed, who would nail the bastard who caused all this?

"For God's sake, Ginny," I said. "Use your other hand."

I watched while she carefully shifted positions, moved the bag into her left hand. Then I started to crawl away.

I was halfway across the room when the dynamite went off.

The concussion knocked me flat. I thought my eardrums had ruptured—I couldn't hear a thing. All of a sudden the air was full of dust and sunshine and silence. Hunks of plaster dropped from the ceiling. Cracks marked the wall above and below the window. More cracks ran along the ceiling. Nevertheless everything held. I couldn't tell whether any brick had been blasted off the wall outside onto the sun roof, but I didn't hear any screaming.

Ginny lay beside me. White plaster dust covered her like a shroud. At first her eyes were open. Her lips said, "Brew," without making any sound. Then her head rolled to the side.

Her left hand was gone. Nothing remained of her forearm except mangled meat. But her heart went on beating. Blood pumped out of her stump onto the floor. It looked like all the blood in the world.

I couldn't think of anything else to do, so I clamped my hand around her arm just below the elbow and squeezed with all my strength until the bleeding stopped.

I Hung onto her like that until help arrived.

PART FOUR

Friday Night/Saturday Morning

15

While the doctors took Ginny to surgery, I stayed where I was, sitting on the floor in the gutted room with my back against one wall, staring through the dusty air at nothing. The doctors had wanted to take me down to Emergency, examine me for possible concussion, shock, hearing loss, whatever. I'd refused. I was in some kind of shock, no question about it. But they couldn't do anything to help me. I didn't even want them to touch me. I sat with my back against the wall, staring at nothing. Like a drunk.

Before long the door opened and Ted came into the room. He stood close to me, but I didn't have the strength to raise my head, so all I saw of him was his old jacket and his stale shirt and his ratty tie. For a couple of minutes he just stood there. His awkward hands twitched once or twice, but he didn't say anything. Then he managed to force out a few words.

"Stretto left."

I didn't answer. If there were an answer anywhere in the room, I didn't have it.

"Before he left"—Ted sounded like someone had gone over his vocal cords with a rasp—"he gave me a message for you. He said he wants you and Ginny to vote for him. The next time he runs for something."

Vote for him. Dear God in Heaven.

"Brew." Ted was pleading with me, but I had no response to give him. "Brew, get up. We've got to find Mittie." He didn't seem real enough to move me. The only thing I could see in the dust and the late afternoon sunlight was the blood pumping out of Ginny's forearm.

But then I saw something else too. Thin silver streaks that fell and splashed on the floor. They made me look up.

Tears oozed from Ted's face like booze-sweat.

He had the power to move me after all.

They all had power—Stretto, Acton, Ginny, even Ted. They could all make other people feel fear or grief or respect. The bastard who did this to Alathea sure as hell had power. I was the only exception. I didn't have any of my own, so I lived off other people's. And when I couldn't get that, I accepted the most convenient substitute. Convenient and forgiving. Alcohol. Being drunk.

I didn't seem to have any choice about it. I was on my feet.

"Brew," Ted said, "you look terrible." He tried to smile.

That finished the job. Despite myself, I started to function again. "*I* look terrible? How long has it been since you had anything to eat?"

He shrugged. Food was irrelevant. "We've got to find Mittie."

"We're going to. As soon as I know Ginny's all right. But while I'm waiting I'm going to take you down to the cafeteria and put food in you if I have to shove it down your throat."

He attempted another smile. "Sure, hotshot. But before you do anything you might regret, you ought to take a look at yourself."

The mirror in the bathroom had survived the blast. When I looked in it, I saw what Ted was getting at. Plaster powder caked me so thickly that I looked like a spook. White dust made the rims of my eyes and my gums look red as fever.

I slapped at my clothes a couple of times, and spent a minute coughing. Then I ran water in the sink, washed my face and hands, dried them on some paper towels. I still looked like I'd just climbed out of a ruin, but at least I was clean enough to get by.

With Ted behind me, I left the room.

A second later I remembered something and went back. After hunting around the room for a minute, I found Ginny's purse. I fished out the keys to the Olds and took the purse with me.

After all the confusion, things in the hospital were starting to get back to normal. Cops poured in, but at the nurses' station some people had already resumed doing paperwork. I told them where I was going, and asked them to get word to me as soon as Ginny came out of surgery. Then I took Ted down to the cafeteria and bought us both supper.

Not because either of us was hungry. I had as much trouble as he did choking down whatever it was the hospital called food. But we had a long night ahead of us, and we couldn't afford to collapse. A long night—and the only part of it I was sure of was the part where I intended to knock heads with Detective-Lieutenant Acton. So I chewed away at some kind of cardboard-and-sawdust sandwich until it disintegrated in my mouth, and whenever Ted pushed his plate away I pushed it back in front of him. And all the time I couldn't help thinking that the two of us together made a pretty poor replacement for Ginny Fistoulari.

If we had any alternatives, I couldn't figure them out.

I was in the middle of repeating my threat to force-feed Ted when a man the size of a small tank appeared in the doorway, and in a voice like a bulldozer with the cutout open said, "Axbrewder."

Acton. When he saw me looking at him, he beckoned for me with two middle fingers of his right hand. "I want you."

Ted glanced back and forth between Acton and me with something like nausea in his face, but I didn't give him a chance to ask any questions. "Stick with me," I whispered. Then I got up and left the cafeteria.

Acton was waiting in the hall. As I came through the doors, he started to say something, but when he saw Ted following me, he changed it. "This is private, Axbrewder."

I stopped in front of him, looked at the dull glare in his eyes, at the way his jaws were clamped together. "No way," I said. "I need a witness who can tell the judge you hit me first."

His fists came out like pistons, caught hold of my jacket, rammed me against the wall. "Listen, Mick," he growled, "I'm the law, remember? I can have you locked up so fast it'll make you piss yourself. I said this is private."

I didn't struggle. I didn't even want to. I just stared him

straight in the face. When he started to feel hesitant because I wasn't resisting, I said, "My partner got her hand blown off. My niece is in a coma. Do you really expect me to just walk away from it?"

He held me for another ten seconds. Then he took a deep breath through his teeth and backed up.

"All right," he said. Still deciding what to do with me. "Tell me something. I was in the medical superintendent's office a little while ago, and this goddamn sonofabitch Stretto came in. He damn near accused me of setting that bomb myself. According to him, I'm implicated in what's happened to all these girls. Now where did he get an idea like that?"

I shrugged. Trying to stay calm. But all of a sudden my heart started to pound. Without transition I felt sure that I could get something I needed out of Acton.

"Stretto almost got killed," I said as evenly as I could. "Now he wants to blame somebody. You're as good a scapegoat as any."

"How do you figure that?" He sounded like he needed a lump of granite to chew on.

"The bastard who set the bomb knew Alathea was here. Who could've told him? Five people. You, me, Stretto, Ginny, and Lona. And you're the only one who wasn't there."

I had him now. That was the kind of argument he understood. He chewed his lip for a while. When he said, "I didn't even know what room she was in. Who did you tell?" he wasn't challenging me anymore. He was working on the case.

I said, "Nobody," and waited.

He chewed for another moment, then spat, "Damn it, I did. I didn't talk to Stretto at all. He wasn't in when I called. I left a message for him with one of his secretaries."

"Which one?"

When he finally met my eyes, he looked like he was actually angry at himself. And just like that I knew what was going on with him. He was such a belligerent cop because he didn't have any other way to let out his frustration. For almost two years now, he'd been trying to figure out what happened to these missing girls, and all he'd got was nowhere. Their deaths—and the manner of their deaths—made him sick with rage, but he hadn't accomplished a thing. So he took it out on people who made him look bad to himself. When he said, "I didn't get her name," I wasn't even disappointed. I was relieved. Because now I knew he would answer my questions.

"Never mind," I said. "We already knew it has to be somebody who works for the school board."

His anger jumped into focus on me. "How the hell do you know *that*?"

I took out the piece of paper that Ginny had taken from Martha Scurvey's office and handed it to him. While he checked it out, I told him where it came from.

That made a difference to him. "Now maybe we've got something." He put the paper away in his pocket. "All those other sheets. We've had them analyzed. We can prove they were all made by the same company—but we already knew that from the watermark. We haven't been able to prove they came from the same ream. Too many minute variations in the composition of the paper. Except for the last two. The lab boys are ready to swear they came from the same sheet. Fiber-tear, composition, everything matches.

"If this piece comes from the same ream, we'll have some proof we can use."

I could almost see the wheels turning in his head. Get a warrant, search the school board offices, track down the source of the paper. Embarrass Stretto as much as possible in the process. It was a good system. It might even work.

But it would take time—and I didn't have time. Mittie didn't have time. So I took hold of myself and asked, "Acton, why did you have to scare people like the Christies? You didn't think they were pimping or pushing for their own daughters. What were you trying to do?"

He didn't look at me. But he answered.

"Ah, screw it. I was trying to make something happen. Push here, and hope the wall cracks over there. I wanted to keep it all out of the papers. Send a message to whoever was responsible. If I kept a lid on sensational stuff like that, the people who knew what was going on would know I was still after them. I wanted to make the bastards nervous."

I almost asked him why he thought that was a good enough reason to make miserable parents feel even worse, but I was afraid he'd stop talking. Instead I said, "It was worth a try. Tell me how you found Alathea."

He still didn't look at me, but now it was for a different reason. "I didn't tell Mrs. Axbrewder the whole truth about that. Some guy saw her out on Canyon Road and called in. I told Mrs. Axbrewder she looked sick. The fact is, she was wandering down the middle of the road buck naked. And bleeding. The guy who called said he thought she was trying to hitch a ride. When the doctor saw the cuts and scrapes on her, he said it looked like she'd crawled through a broken window or something."

I was staring at Acton, but I didn't really see him. I was thinking, Naked. Crawled. Something I'd been trying to figure out earlier came back to me. The timing. Every one of those kidnapped girls had been missing for two or three months before turning up dead. Except Alathea. She'd only been gone for ten days. Why?

Now I knew why. Because she'd escaped. They didn't fill her up with junk and then leave her to die like the other seven. She escaped. For a while, she managed to fight off the junk. She broke a window where they were keeping her, and crawled out, and went down Canyon Road, trying to hitch a ride until it was too much for her and she passed out.

Which put her in a coma.

She'd tried to do something that nobody could do. Alone she'd struggled to climb out of a hell she hadn't chosen and couldn't refuse. Just thinking about it made me want to scream. But I didn't. Instead I said, "This time you'd better put a guard on her room."

"Believe it," Acton growled. "Anybody who wants to get at her now will have to fight off half the department."

I said, "Good."

Then I asked Ted to tell Acton everything he knew about Sven Last.

Acton had already heard that the bomb was planted by some clown pretending to be a doctor, but he didn't have the details. I made Ted spill them all. He hated doing it— hated having to say such things out loud—but I didn't leave him any choice. I wanted to cover every bet I could think of.

When Ted was done, Acton went one way to put out an APB, and I went the other. Ted followed me as if he were being sucked along in my wake.

I didn't have a very clear idea of where I was going. First I wanted to see Ginny. After that I'd try to figure out what came next.

I got lucky. I caught up with her while she was being wheeled from surgery to recovery. The aides objected, but I made them stop long enough to let me take a good look at her.

She was still unconscious—dead to the world, pale, breathing gracelessly through her mouth. The stump of her left forearm had been strapped in tight white bandages, and the rest of the arm wore a cast to keep the bones from shifting. Helpless as a kid.

I could've kissed her and she never would've known the difference.

I let her go. I was too tense to stand there. Once I'd put her purse beside her so that she'd have her .357 handy when she woke up, I found out from the aides what room she'd be in when she came out of recovery. Then I let them take her away.

With Ted still trailing behind me, I left the hospital, feeling like a murderer who just hadn't managed to find the right victim yet.

16

The sun was setting in a bloodlike red wash as I drove the Olds out of the parking lot, and while Ted and I cruised down Paseo Grande toward the Murchison Building, darkness slowly thickened in the air. It was night when we parked in the basement garage and rode the elevator up to Ginny's office.

I'd taken her keys. I unlocked the door, snapped on some lights, and we went into the back room. The smell of very well-done coffee reminded me that I'd left the pot plugged in. I offered Ted a cup, then poured myself one and sat down at Ginny's desk to drink it. It tasted like burnt sweat-sock squeezings and motor oil, but I sipped at it anyway as if it were liqueur.

For a couple of different reasons, I didn't want Ted to ask me any questions. He hadn't said anything since we'd left Acton, and I didn't want him to start now. For one thing, I didn't have any answers. And questions would just interfere with what I was trying to do.

Sitting in Ginny's office, at her desk, drinking her coffee, I struggled to think like she did. I didn't have any red-hot flashes of my own, and I knew I wouldn't get any if I tried to force them. So instead I tried to look at things her way.

Six hours ago, she'd been sitting right in this chair and she'd said. *Its right here in front of me, but I can't see it.*

She'd had all the pieces she needed, she just hadn't been able to put the puzzle together. Now she was in the hospital, doped up with scopolamine or sodium pentothol, and I had to do it for her.

Which wouldn't have made sense to Ted, even if he'd been in the mood to try—which he wasn't. He stood me as long as he could. Then he said in a strained little voice, "Let's go."

I drank some more coffee, almost gagged. "Exactly where?"

"After Last. He's our lead. Somebody can tell us how to find him."

"It's too early," I said. "Pimps don't even *think* about business until after ten."

"For God's sake!" he protested. "We've got to do something. They're doing it to her right now!"

He was probably right about that. Now would be a good time for them to shoot her up if they wanted her compliant later on—say between eleven and two. But reminding me about things like that only made it harder for me to stay calm. "Goddamn it, Ted!" I began "you think—?"

I stopped. An idea hit me—an obvious idea, something I shouldn't even have had to think about. Something Ginny would've done automatically. But for some reason it felt like more than that.

I grabbed the phone and called her answering service.

When the woman answered, I said, "This is Axbrewder. Ginny Fistoulari is out of circulation for a while. I need to know if there are any messages for her."

Ginny—bless her punctilious heart—had kept my name active with her answering service. In a bored voice, the woman said, "Some man's called four times in the last two hours. Didn't leave a name. He wants her to call him back."

She read off a phone number. I grabbed a pen, scrawled the number on Ginny's blotter. Thanked the woman and hung up.

"What is it?" Ted asked.

I was already dialing. "Do you believe in intuition?"

"Intuition?" he rasped. "What the hell are you talking about?"

"In that case, maybe what you ought to do is pray." The number rang. I shut Ted out of my mind, concentrated everything I had on the secrets hidden in that phone line.

Somebody picked up the phone. A burly male voice said, "Yeah?"

"I was told to call this number." I held the receiver against my head so hard it felt like it was bending.

"Who'd you want?"

"I don't know. They want me. All they left was this number."

"Your name?"

"Fistoulari."

The man covered the mouthpiece. I heard him shouting, but I couldn't tell what he said.

A minute later another man was at the phone. "Fistoulari?"

It wasn't much, but it was all I needed. "No. I'm her partner. My name's Axbrewder. I was with her when you pulled your little doctor act at the hospital."

There was a long silence. Then the voice snarled, "Well, aren't you the clever one? How did you know it was me?"

"I'm good at voices."

"Goodie for you." He paused. "Where's Fistoulari?"

"That little toy you left behind blew her in half." I wasn't about to tell him the truth. I didn't want him to go back and take another crack at her.

"Too bad it didn't get you, too."

"Too bad for you. Kidnapping, dealing, and prostitution aren't bad enough. Now you've got murder one. You're as good as dead, punk."

"Yeah, well—" His voice changed, became softer and greasier. "That's what I want to talk to you about. I heard rumors that bomb didn't do everything it was supposed to. I shouldn't have let him talk me into it in the first place. But that little whore can identify me. I want to deal."

"Deal, hell." I gripped the edge of the desk to keep myself from shouting. "You killed my partner. Why should I deal with you?"

Ted stood in the light across the desk from me. He was chewing on his mustache, and his hands made fists at his sides.

"Because," the voice said, all oil and lechery, "I can give you the man who's responsible for all this. I'm just the errand boy. He's the one who kidnaps the girls. He's the one who gets the junk and pumps it into them until they're ready to do anything. Anything, Axbrewder. He's the one."

I took Ginny's battered old letter opener in my free hand, bent it double, and threw it across the room hard. It took a sizable hunk out of the plaster. "Convince me."

"No problem. But I won't give you time to locate this number. I want to meet."

"That sounds like a great idea. Then you can just shoot me, and there won't be any witnesses left."

"Suit yourself," he snapped. "I'll be in that abandoned Ajax warehouse down at the end of Trujillo. About an hour from now. That's a good place for me, because I'll be able to tell if you bring anybody with you, like maybe the cops. If you do, you'll never find me."

The line went dead. I was left with what felt like a perfect set of my fingerprints indented in the handle of the receiver.

Ted hadn't moved a muscle. He stared at me, dumb with pain and urgency.

I didn't want to say anything, but I forced myself for his sake. "You got most of it. That was Last. He wants—he says he wants to deal. Trade us his boss for some kind of immunity. Either he's telling the truth, or he wants to set me up."

Ted struggled to find his voice. "What're you going to do?"

"What the hell can I do? I'm going to meet him."

"He'll kill you."

"No," I said evenly. "You're not going to let him."

While he absorbed that—or tried to, anyway—I dialed the answering service again. When I got the woman, I said to her, "Listen, this is an emergency. Call the police, get a message to Detective-Lieutenant Acton. That's A-c-t-o-n. Give him that number you just gave me. He can track it down, I can't. Tell him I just talked to Last. L-a-s-t." I hung up before she could think of a reason not to do what I told her.

"That's going to do a lot of good," Ted said acidly.

I shrugged. "It's worth a try." Got to my feet. "I can't tell Acton where we're going. Last says he can spot it if I don't go alone. If he sets me up—or gets away from us—maybe Acton can nail him by staking out that number."

Ted didn't answer. He looked bedraggled, as full of self-pity as wet poultry, but the dull glare in his eyes said as plain as words that Last wasn't going to get away from us.

"Come on," I said softly. "It'll take us a while to get down to that warehouse."

Ted just turned on his heel and walked out of the office.

I unplugged the coffeepot, snapped off the lights, locked the door, and followed him to the elevator.

While we rode down, I said. "It could be that he really does want to deal." I wanted to be sure that Ted wouldn't go off half-cocked. "He's not stupid. And he knew about Ginny and me. This partner of his must've told him we were prying. When he saw us at Alathea's room, he knew he had a chance to get us all.

"After he sets the bomb, he gets out fast. He doesn't want to take any chances."

The doors opened, and we headed into the basement toward the Olds.

"But then he can't find out what happened. So he starts trying to call Ginny. If somebody returns his call, he knows he's in trouble and he better find a way to get off the hook."

I unlocked the Olds. We climbed in.

"If nobody calls back, he can figure he's in the clear. No witnesses who can tie him to the kidnappings. He can go back to pimping for his partner, and his partner will never know the difference."

Ted paid no attention. Instead he stared out through the windshield into the night. Tears streamed down his face again. I locked my jaws to make myself shut up, and concentrated on just driving for a while.

But silence wasn't what he wanted, either. By the time we were down in the valley, working our way south along the river, he'd started to talk himself.

"She's all I have left, Brew." He was gnawing on his mustache the way a drowning man clutches at straws. "You probably don't know what happened to us. Things like that don't happen to hotshots like you." He was bitter—but not at me. "We were happy back then, she and her mother and me. Before Mittie was born, I was a cop, pounding a beat in the days before they switched to squad cars, and we had a little house over on Los Arboles, and we were happy, her mother and me.

"Except her mother didn't like me being a cop on the beat. She wanted me to be a detective. But in those days they had rules that said I was too short to be a detective. When Mittie was born, I quit the cops to work for myself. I wanted her to have a father she could be proud of.

"But it didn't work out like that. People don't hire you for what you can do. They don't know what you can do. They hire you for what you look like. You're built like a tree, and Ginny looks like a steel trap, and people just naturally go to you when they've got something important. They come to me when they've got something grubby.

"Domestic surveillance." His bitterness was so thick it practically fogged up the windows. "Prove that so-and-so is cheating on such-and-such. Then so-and-so can get a fat divorce settlement.

"You know something, Brew?" He chuckled sourly. "They almost put me out of business when they first invented no-fault divorce."

For a while he went back to staring out the window. I hoped that maybe he wasn't going to tell me any more. I was in no shape for it. But he wasn't finished. A couple of minutes later he continued.

"Her mother wasn't impressed. I wasn't doing what she thought detectives did. Solving murders, rescuing kidnapped babies, breaking up drug rings. When Mittie was three, her mother ran off with an insurance salesman." His tears kept running, but he had a curious kind of dignity about it. It didn't make him sob or lose control. His voice didn't even shake as he said, "I raised her myself. She's all there is."

It took me long enough, but I finally figured out why he was so desperate. He was terrified that the pimp we were after would feel the heat and decide to go out of business. Hide under a rock somewhere.

After destroying the evidence.

As long as Alathea remained in a coma, Mittie was all the evidence there was. If the pimp knew that Alathea was still alive, he might've already killed Mittie.

I took a tighter grip on the wheel, pushed down harder on the accelerator. Because there was nothing else I could do.

Even then it took us damn near an hour to get far enough down on Trujillo to reach the vicinity of the Ajax warehouse.

I didn't rush in. When we were still half a mile away, I pulled over to the curb and stopped.

Asked Ted if he had a gun.

He didn't.

I took out the .45 and handed it to him. While he checked it over, I flipped the switch so that the courtesy lights wouldn't come on when I opened my door. Then I said, "Here's what we're going to do. You're going to hide down under the dash. When I get to that warehouse, I'll park in the darkest place I can find. I'll get out, leave the door open. I'll go into the warehouse wherever I can find a door.

"Give me two minutes. Then sneak out and get around the back somehow. Come in looking for me. Keeping me alive is up to you. I won't be able to do much for myself. This is his turf."

Ted didn't say anything. He just slapped the clip back into the .45 and ducked down under the dash.

I put the Olds in gear and drove the rest of the way down Trujillo.

The city fathers don't spend much on streetlights down in that part of town. The whole place was black as a grave. But the sky still held enough light to silhouette the warehouse, and my headlights picked out the rest.

The building stood behind a steel mesh fence, but the gates were gone. That was the only way in—which was one good reason why Last had chosen it. But that wasn't the only reason. It was a three-story building. Battered steel siding covered the first two floors. The top floor was lined with windows on all sides. He'd probably been up there for the past half hour, watching. If he saw anything he didn't like, he could get out of there fast.

The moon wasn't up yet. Nothing offered me a particularly dark place to park. I coasted up to the front of the building, positioned the Olds so that Ted had a good straight run to the east corner, doused the headlights, and stopped.

"At least two minutes," I whispered. "I'll be moving slowly." Then I opened the door and got out.

I stood beside the car for a minute, letting Last see that I was alone. Then I moved toward the door beside the cargo entrance.

When I put my hand on the door and pushed, it squeaked bloody murder. Demonstrating my good faith, I made sure Last could hear me shut it behind me.

Inside I stood in darkness thick as stone. When I waved my hand in front of my face, I could barely sense its movement.

With the cargo entrance beside me, however, I figured that I stood in a pretty big open space. Holding my arms out just in case, I started forward. Slowly. Very slowly. My heels made an echoing sound on the concrete, but I didn't worry about it. I didn't want to surprise Last. I was counting on Ted for that.

And wishing like hell that I had Ginny covering me instead. I trusted Ted's determination, but I didn't know how much good sense he had left.

Oh, well. If he didn't have enough, that made two of us. Probably Ginny would've never let me get myself into this situation in the first place.

Then a voice barked, "That's far enough!"

I froze.

For about a minute while I stood still, I thought I heard faint scuffling noises in the distance.

After that a light snapped on.

It just about nailed me to the floor. I was right under a powerful bulb with a reflector that focused the beam into a circle on the floor maybe fifty feet across. With me in the center. Surrounded by a secret and dangerous darkness that my eyes couldn't penetrate.

Very neat. Last could've killed me with a slingshot.

But he didn't shoot. Apparently he had something else in mind. After a couple of minutes I heard heels on the concrete. By degrees Last materialized in front of me on the edge of the circle of light.

His right fist held an automatic with a caliber the size of a cannonball.

He came a few steps forward, no more. Not counting the automatic, his main advantage was that he could get out of the light a lot faster than I could.

I didn't even imagine moving. I didn't want to give him an excuse.

He knew how to hold a gun. It never wavered. He was grinning, and his voice sounded like margarine. "All of a sudden, you don't look so tough, Axbrewder. How come that bomb didn't get you? I bet you wet your pants when it went off."

Part of me wanted to just forget everything and take him. "I came to get convinced, punk," I said. "Convince me."

He glanced around. "You alone?"

"Can't you tell? I've got two cops in my pocket. I'll get them out if you want."

"All right." He got down to business. "What do you want to know?"

"Who's your partner?"

"Ah," he grinned. "I'm not going to tell you anything you can use. I want to deal. You get the DA to give me immunity, and then I'll give you his name."

"We'll find him without you."

"No, you won't." He sounded very sure of himself. "You're not even close."

"You still have to convince me. I need something I can take to the DA."

"That's why I'm here. What do you want to know?"

I took a deep breath. "I want to know why you used a goddamn bomb. Why didn't you just needle her to death? You've done it before."

"Not me, pal," Last said flatly. "He handles the junk. I never touch it. I don't even know where he stashes it."

That got me nowhere. I wasn't thinking straight. I should've asked a better question. *Come on, Axbrewder,* I snarled at myself. *Don't blow it now.*

"All right," I said. Holding onto myself hard. "How many girls have you kidnapped?"

"Nine," he said promptly. "But I didn't have anything to do with that either. Getting them was his job. Like doping them was his job."

"What was your job?"

"Well," he grinned, "the main thing was rounding up customers. Mostly I made myself available. When some john who liked his white meat young found me, I made the arrangements. Then I took him to the action.

"Other than that, I took care of them. Fed them. Got them the right kind of clothes. A lot of johns like to see a kid in fancy stuff—peek-a-boo bras, lace panties open at the cunt, stuff like that." He was grinning so hard I could barely look at him.

I said, "Keen. You're a nice man, Last. But I'm going to need something more solid. Tell me—"

Then I almost faltered, almost gave it away.

In the darkness behind Last, I saw a pale shadow, recognized Ted. Only the white of his face and hands showed.

He had the .45 in both fists, pointed straight at Last's back.

It was all I could do to go on. "You kept each of those girls for three or four months. Then you ditched them. Why?"

Last shrugged. "We had enough customers, but most of them are regulars, know what I mean? After a while they want fresh meat."

"Yeah," I growled. "And you didn't get rid of one girl until you'd had time to break in a new one. So how come you killed Carol Christie right after you picked up Alathea Axbrewder?"

"Axbrewder," he said. "She some relation of yours?"

"No."

"Yeah, well," he said, "that Christie chick was trouble from the word go. Something funny about her metabolism.

My partner had a hell of a time getting the dose right. Either she wasn't dopey enough or she was all the way out. It was just an accident she got killed when she did."

"An accident," I said. "I bet it broke your heart."

I could see Ted's finger trembling on the trigger. Easy, Ted, I thought at him as hard as I could. Take it easy.

"What made you decide to go for two kids this time?" I asked Last. "You never did that before."

"Just improving the quality of our service." Last's smirk hurt like a knife in my guts. I thought my nerves were going to snap. "Give the customer more variety. Some johns like blond; some like brunette. Some like a little two-on-one. And we wanted to make up for the trouble we had with Carol Christie.

I could hardly believe it, but he actually seemed to enjoy telling me all this.

"It was a good thing we had two," he went on. "That Axbrewder was a feisty little bitch. We were going to have to get rid of her anyway. Some of the johns were bleeding when they got done with her."

Well, by *God*, Alathea. Good for you!

"Hangst was another story." I hated his grin. Right then there was nothing in the world I hated as much as his grin. "She was just what we wanted, times two. Once she got the hang of things, she couldn't get enough.

"I'll tell you, Axbrewder." He lowered his voice—he was about to let me in on a secret. "Most of our johns don't like cherry meat. My partner and I used to take turns popping them. Kind of work them into shape, know what I mean? Hangst was my turn. God! she was a juicy little cunt."

Ted was moving.

I shouted, "No!" but I couldn't stop him.

He took one step into the light.

Fired.

The first shot hit Last like the kick of a mule. I saw the slug plow through the front of his chest.

Clenching the .45 in both hands, Ted kept pulling the trigger. I had to hit the floor. The slugs that missed Last ricocheted off the concrete and went screaming into the dark.

When I heard the slide rack empty, I raised my head, started to get up.

Ted stared at the gun. Trying to realize what he'd done.

I got my feet under me, went toward him.

Then it penetrated him. His face broke open. He dropped the .45. It landed with a clatter on the concrete.

Without a sound, he turned and ran into the darkness. Before I could even try to catch him, he was out of sight and gone.

17

I chased his footsteps for a few seconds, but once I left the light I was blind. Sooner than I expected, I ran into a sheet-metal wall that rattled like thunder when I hit it. After the din died down, I couldn't hear Ted anymore, anywhere.

Cursing uselessly, I went back to the corpse.

Ted had done a thorough job of it. Last was about as dead as he could get without actively being cut up into pieces. At least three rounds hit him—two in the chest—and there was a hole I could've put my fist through where his face used to be. It might've made me sick if I hadn't already been too furious to give a rusty damn. Let him rot in his own blood. I just wanted to get my hands on Ted.

I'd lost my only lead to Last's partner. The asshole who actually took the girls.

I wanted to tear Ted Hangst into little pieces.

Unfortunately Last dead was as much of a problem as Last alive. Maybe more. Now I had a body on my hands. A body that was killed with my .45. If the cops caught me, I'd have one hell of a time explaining all this.

And explaining it would be the easy part. Getting the cops to release me would be a lot tougher. I'd probably have to sit in jail until they identified Ted's fingerprints on the gun.

I wasn't about to take this particular rap for Hangst. And I wasn't about to let the cops lock me away, even for a few hours. That meant I couldn't afford to leave the evidence behind. So I dug out a handkerchief and used it to pick up the .45. Instead of wiping it off like I wanted to, I carried it by the barrel while I groped my way out of the warehouse.

Out in the night, it was a relief to be able to see again. And an even bigger relief to find the Olds where I left it. In my usual brilliant fashion, I'd left the keys in the ignition.

But Ted hadn't taken it. Apparently he hadn't been thinking about things like that. I was still mobile.

I still had a chance.

I got in, locked the .45 in the glove compartment, and drove out of the warehouse yard onto Trujillo without turning on my lights.

I didn't turn them on until I started to hit traffic, almost a mile back north in the direction of the city. But I still hadn't figured out where I was going.

Everything was too urgent. Mittie was in danger for her life, if she wasn't already dead. The cops would find Last's body pretty soon—I'd left the light on because I didn't know how to turn it off, and before long a patrol car would see the light and check it out. Ginny lay in the hospital with her hand blown off. Ted was running around completely bananas.

I couldn't relax, couldn't clear my head. I needed inspiration, and I as sure as hell wasn't getting it. After a while I caught myself pounding on the steering wheel with my fist.

Panting, I dropped my arm. All right, ace. You don't know what to do. What would Ginny do?

Good question. Concentration took so much effort that in five minutes the wheel was slick with sweat. Eventually, however, I dug deep enough to get hold of an idea. After which I spent a couple of miles looking for a phone booth— and wondering what I carried around in my skull instead of brains.

Last knew Alathea was in the hospital. His partner told him. How did his partner know? Through the school board somehow. Acton had called Stretto, left a message with one of the secretaries.

What *I* needed to know was basically simple. Which secretary? And who, exactly, did she tell? How many people got that particular piece of information?

Acton probably hadn't gotten that far yet. First he had to get a warrant, search the school board offices. Talk to Stretto. Maybe to Martha Scurvey. There was a good chance that I wouldn't run into him.

Finally I spotted a phone booth and pulled over. I used the directory to get Julian Kirke's address, then headed the Olds in that direction. Out toward the east side of town.

It seemed to take forever to get there, but actually it wasn't more than forty-five minutes. He lived in one of those fancy singles' apartment complexes that sits on a lot about four blocks long and has tennis courts and swimming pools as well as a "recreation center" for dancing and other predatory activities. This particular complex was called Encantada Square, and the apartments all had terraces and balconies with wrought-iron railings, arched entryways, redwood doors. Inside they probably had mirrors on the ceilings of the bedrooms. But the place didn't look all that expensive. The "swinging singles" usually aren't rich.

After a little trouble, I located Kirke's apartment. It had a modest little card that said J. KIRKE in a slot above the doorbell.

When I rang the bell, I was trembling. I didn't think I could handle it if Kirke wasn't in. I needed to talk to him. If I missed him—The way I was feeling, I'd probably sit down on the floor inside his nice arched entryway and start to cry.

At the moment I had absolutely no idea how I'd managed to function at all back in the days before I met Ginny. I missed her so much I was in danger of blubbering.

Then the door opened, and Kirke stood in front of me. He kept one hand on the doorknob. In the other, he held a drink, which I identified instantaneously as scotch on the rocks. He wasn't wearing a shirt. I could see that he was a lot stronger than he looked with all his clothes on. He had the kind of muscles you get from lifting weights.

I could also see the bruises I'd made on his upper arm.

Two or three different varieties of surprise and anger twitched across his face as he looked at me. I took advantage of them by brushing past him and walking into his apartment.

His living room was designed to look nicer than it really was. Sunken floor two steps down. Soft, supposedly seductive colors. A thick cheap carpet, plastic potted plants here and there. A picture window with a clear view of the next-door neighbor's picture window. And not much in the way of furniture. Just one recliner, a stool, and a sofa big enough to sleep three or four swingers at the same time.

I paused in the center of the room for a minute and tried to figure out how to handle Kirke. I had too many priorities—protect Alathea, get information, stay out of jail, find Mittie alive. And nothing but terrible consequences in all directions if I failed. I was looking for some really devastating way to curse my lack of inspiration when Kirke broke the silence.

"Mr. Axbrewder," he said. "What an unexpected pleasure." He sounded like a beaker of sulfuric acid that he intended to throw in my face. But he hadn't done it yet. Civility and sarcasm were doing some kind of balancing act.

"Yeah." I turned to face him.

He stood at the top of the steps, which gave him a chance to look down on me. His hand cradled his drink as if he knew what it could do to me. He'd regained his self-control—his anger and surprise were gone. He was master of the situation.

"That's the story of my life," I said. "One unexpected pleasure after another."

He studied me for a moment. Then he said, "You've had a rough day. You need a drink." He started toward a side-board bar behind the sofa.

"I don't need a drink," I snapped. My nerves were in worse shape than I thought. "I need some answers."

He waved his glass at me. "You sure?"

"I don't drink while I'm working."

He shrugged and sat down sidesaddle on the back of the sofa. The perfect host, showing me he didn't need to look down on me.

He sipped his scotch.

I waited.

By then you would've thought I was ready for anything, but he still managed to catch me off guard.

"I heard what happened to your partner," he said. "Too bad. It must be tough for you."

"My partner?" I asked stupidly. I had the horrible feeling that I was completely out of my depth.

"Getting her hand shattered like that." He looked thoughtfully into his glass. "Messy.

"But it shows one thing, Axbrewder. You're smarter than I thought. Most of the big tall he-men I know have an irresistible compulsion to protect helpless little women. You don't have that problem. I admire that. Let them take their chances, like anybody else.

"Of course"—his civility slipped a notch—"your partner isn't much of a woman." He took another swallow of scotch. "She should've been born a man."

I must've been staring at him like a lunatic, because the next thing he said was, "Are you sure you're all right?"

"No. Ginny is the brains of this team." Why was I telling him that? "Without her, I'm in lousy shape."

I practically had to clap my hands over my mouth to make myself shut up. It was like trying to cork a bottle you're holding upside down.

"What can I do to help?" he asked.

He sounded civil again, but the sneer on his face would've turned butter rancid at fifty paces.

Suddenly everything went cold inside me, and I was calm again. Still mad enough to knock down walls with my forehead—but calm. The muscles of my face and shoulders relaxed. "Answer a few questions," I said evenly.

"If I can." He was looking me straight in the eye.

"How did you know about Ginny?"

"Chairman Stretto called me this evening. He told me all about it. He wanted to brag to somebody. But bragging isn't good politics, so he used your partner as an excuse to mention his display of courage. I suspect that by now he's called most of the school board, the mayor, and half the city council."

I groaned dishonestly. "Wonderful. With help like that, I'm going to need a fucking Ouija board to crack this case."

"Why? What's the problem?" he asked. Mildly interested.

"Oh, hell," I said. "Why not?" I didn't look at him. I was afraid that my expression might warn him. "This is an 'information' case, Kirke. It all comes down to who knows what when. And how they found out. Like, how did Stretto know that Alathea was in the hospital in the first place?"

"That's easy. A cop called our office, a Detective Acton."

"Did Stretto talk to him?"

"No, he wasn't in. Acton left a message with one of the secretaries."

"Which one?"

He grinned maliciously. "Sondra." He liked hurting her.

Sondra. The innocent one. "And she gave the message to Stretto?"

"No. She gave it to me. I run that office."

"Were you alone?"

"Are you kidding?" He snorted. "Nobody is ever alone in there. Half the office heard her."

"Like who?"

"Let me see," he mused. "Mabel and Joan. Connie. I'm sure of them. There may've been a few others."

"And what did you do with the message?"

Keep it going, Axbrewder. Don't give him time to think.

"I gave it to Chairman Stretto, of course."

"As soon as he came back in?"

"Sure."

"Was he alone?"

"No. Astin Greenling was with him."

"Who did they tell?"

Kirke paused for a moment, stared at me. Then he said, "How the hell should *I* know?"

Apparently he didn't need time to think. He must've been as innocent as skim milk. Or else he was too smart for me.

I sighed. "Yeah. Well, you see my problem. Someone on the school board is leaking information to the bastard who set that bomb. But finding out exactly who is starting to look impossible."

He asked, "Are you sure it's the school board?"

I went on looking out the window. The man in the next-door apartment sprawled on his sofa reading his book.

"I am," I said. "The cops aren't."

He considered that for a minute. "I know what your trouble is, Axbrewder," he said finally. "You're too tense. You need to relax, get your mind off it for a while."

I turned around. "How am I supposed to do that?"

He got to his feet. "Change your mind. Have a drink. I have some scotch here that's to die for. It will make you kiss all your troubles good-bye."

I glared at him. He sounded like he was making fun of me. "I told you—" But if he knew about my drinking problem, he didn't show it. He sounded almost sincere. I made an effort to swallow my anger. "The problem is, I'm an alcoholic. I have a hard enough time staying sober as it is."

His jaw dropped. "You're kidding."

"No."

"Oh, come on. A man like you? I don't believe it."

Now I had the distinct impression that he was sneering at me.

"Believe it," I growled. I was in no mood to put up with his scorn. Abruptly I started for the door.

He caught my arm. Something in his face looked too earnest to be a sneer. Too earnest—or too urgent. "Come on. That woman you call a partner has been putting you through the wringer. Now she's convinced you that you can't even have a few drinks. You're no alcoholic. She just tells you that to keep you in line.

"Stick around. We'll put our feet up, have a few drinks, tell each other secrets. I know some things about the school board that will give you hives."

He was making me sick. I said, "No, thanks." For some reason, I didn't break his hand. Instead I stepped past him toward the door.

Right then, all the decisions that I hadn't been able to make were made for me. Something in my head shifted, and I knew what I had to do.

When I reached the door, I turned to face Kirke.

He was still watching me. He held his hand out, offering me his glass. He was trying to smile.

I said, "I had a talk with a guy named Last tonight."

He didn't even blink. The way he said, "Oh, yes?" you would've thought we were discussing the weather.

"He's the guy who set the bomb. Unfortunately he got shot before he could tell me anything useful."

That made Kirke look curious. "Did you shoot him?"

"No. But I wish I had."

Then I left his apartment. Got out of there before my anger made me shake hard enough to stutter. When I reached the Olds, I had to lean against it and hold my head in my hands to steady my heart.

I'd done what I could for Mittie. I'd planted the information that Last was dead. If Kirke talked to anyone on the school board, anyone at all, word might get around. Then the bastard I was after might think that he didn't need to kill Ted's daughter. At least not right away.

That was the easy part. A quick gamble that might improve Mittie's chances. It wasn't why I'd started to shake.

I had the shakes because I was afraid.

Because now I knew what I had to do.

I had to talk to el Señor.

18

The idea would never have crossed my mind if old Manolo hadn't suggested it. When he'd first given me his advice, his breath smelling of anisette and secrets he couldn't or wouldn't reveal, I'd thought he was just politely telling me to go to hell. But now I knew better. Old Manolo understood things better than I did. He'd known what this case might cost me in the end.

The bare idea turned my guts to water. El Señor could sink a drunk like me without so much as making ripples. He didn't like Anglos, and he didn't like private *chotas*. All he had to do was raise one aristocratic eyebrow, and I'd find myself holding cement together in the foundation of some new building. Or bits and handfuls of Axbrewder-burger would fertilize apples up in the North Valley.

Oh, el Señor was a gentleman—sort of. He didn't bother people who didn't bother him. But offhand I'd say the easiest way to commit suicide in Puerta del Sol is to go ask el Señor questions about his business. Some of the cops who tried it haven't been found yet.

Of course, I didn't have anything as threatening and maybe pointless as "law enforcement" in mind. All I wanted was to protect Alathea. Do something for Lona and Ted. Rescue Mittie. Nail the sonofabitch who was responsible.

But I was an Anglo and a private investigator. I was scared. El Señor had more reasons to kill me than talk to me.

And I was alone. That was the real crusher. I've done worse things with Ginny either backing me up or leading the way, and they weren't this bad. Because she was there. Now she wasn't. And the bastard who crippled her was going to try one of two things to protect himself—destroy the evidence, or kill the people on his trail. I was the only one left who could even take a crack at stopping him. If el Señor decided to stir me into a ton of concrete or feed me to the apples, then somebody else would die tonight, too. Somebody I cared about.

But the things that had me so scared were the same things that made me put the Olds in gear and drive away from Encantada Square. For a while, I doddered along down the road, driving like an old man—but I drove. And after a few blocks the cold air and the night helped me pull myself together. Night was something I understood. At night people did things for reasons that made sense to me. I didn't rush the drive—I needed time to recover—but I went where I had to go.

El Señor's headquarters is an old movie theater not far from where I live. Or it used to be before he had it completely rebuilt inside. All he left was the façade, the marquee, and the ticket window. Now the place fronts as a nightclub called El Machismo. It's one of those places where people go—mostly Anglos, but certain kinds of Chicanos and Indians show up, too—when they have too much money and not enough sense to know that the man who feeds them their kicks has nothing but contempt for them.

Considering that el Señor mostly makes himself rich off the pains and weaknesses of his own people, you might think his headquarters would be down in the old part of town, an area that would help shield him from things like the law. But his location suits him. From his converted theater he can go fishing for rich Anglos as easily as he can run numbers, extort loans, sell drugs or bodies for his own people. Puerta del Sol is full of society dudes and broads, money-punks of all flavors, who think going to El Machismo at night is "exciting" but who wouldn't be caught dead going into the center of town.

I parked the Olds in the lot across the street, gave the attendant a couple of bucks so that he wouldn't lose my keys, then spent a minute standing on the sidewalk. Hesitating. The marquee was lit, proclaiming "El Machismo" in big letters the color of cheap lipstick. On a good night, going in there was like meeting an old whore. This time I felt like I was on my way to arrange for me and a few other people to become cadavers.

But I did it anyway. Crossed the street. Paid my cover charge at the ticket window. Pulled open the blackout doors and went in.

After wading a few yards along a carpet as deep and rich as lava, I reached the club host. He looked like a matador in a tuxedo. His eyes flicked over me, and he pigeonholed me somewhere down around not-worth-the-trouble. When he asked, "Table for one?" he sounded so bored he was almost snoring.

"No, thanks," I said. "I don't want food. I want action."

He lifted one eyebrow. "Action?"

He was part of the screening process. He was supposed to distinguish between people who just wanted dinner and entertainment and people who were after something spicier. And he had to be able to spot *chotas*. Either way, I didn't look good to him.

But I was in no mood to argue the point. I glared down at him and said, "I want to see el Señor."

At that, he actually blinked. Both eyes. "El Señor?" he asked evenly. "Who is el Señor?"

I grimaced. "Call the manager. I'll talk to him."

He couldn't hold back a grin. "As you wish." He picked up the phone on his desk, dialed. When he got an answer, he spoke Spanish, thinking I wouldn't understand. "With me," he said, "I have an Anglo who wishes to speak with el Señor. Possibly he is from the police. I think you wish to learn about him a little before you throw him out."

He listened briefly, then hung up and turned back to me. "One moment," he said in English.

A moment was all it took. Then a door beyond him opened, and a man came out.

From my point of view, he wasn't tall. But he was built like an armored car. His arms were so heavy they made his sleeves look like sausage casings, and he couldn't have buttoned his jacket across that chest with a steam winch. He didn't even make an effort to hide the gun tucked into his waistband. Under his nose, he had a hairline mustache, and his eyes bulged like a frog's.

I recognized him by reputation. Muy Estobal. Rumor had it that he was el Señor's bodyguard.

He looked toward me. "Will you accompany me, Señor?" He sounded like a piranha inviting me to lunch.

I shrugged and followed him.

We went through the door he'd come out of, and he led me down a long hall to a small office with a door so heavy I half expected to see a combination lock on it. When he closed it behind us, it made a permanent-sounding little *thunk*. It wasn't the only entrance to the room, but that didn't make me feel much better.

Muy Estobal didn't sit down. Didn't offer me a seat. Moving so fast that I couldn't stop him, he spun around and hit me in the stomach.

I doubled over, reeled back against the wall. For a long minute I couldn't breathe. Little suns danced around the air in front of me. My guts felt like I'd been shot with a howitzer.

While I was helpless, he checked my empty shoulder holster.

"Now, he said, "you will tell me your name."

With a gasp, I got my lungs working again. "Axbrewder," I panted. Staying doubled over.

"What are you?"

"Private. Investigator."

"What do you wish with el Señor?"

"None of your business."

His right fist jumped at my head like a cannonball. But this time I was ready.

I slipped his fist past my left ear and straightened up hard. With all the strength of my legs and back and shoulder, I hit him an uppercut that flipped him over the desk behind him.

I vaulted after him, landed practically the same time he did. Before he could move, I clamped one foot down on the back of his neck. I held him that way while I helped myself to his gun, a snub-nosed Smith & Wesson .38. Then I let him up.

When he reached his feet, glaring as if he couldn't decide how to kill me first, I said, "Now it's my turn, *pendejo*. I want to talk to el Señor. Ask him a couple of questions. I'm not here to cause trouble. No hassle, *comprende*, Estobal? I have a problem of my own, and I think he might give me a little help. One or two answers. If I don't get to talk to him, *then* I'm going to cause trouble.

"For a start, I'll break your neck." He didn't so much as swallow. "Are you listening, *pendejo*?"

He spat. "Yes."

"Good." I took a deep breath, but I couldn't hold it. My stomach hurt too bad. I broke open his .38, took out the cylinder and dropped it in my pocket. Then I put the gun down on the desk. "Take me to el Señor."

Giving up the gun probably helped convince him that I didn't want to cause trouble. He picked up his .38 without taking his eyes off me, shoved it back into his waistband. Then he opened the other door to the office and stalked out.

I followed him. Close enough so that he couldn't break away, far enough back so that he couldn't turn and hit me again.

But he didn't try any tricks. He led me down another hall and out into a large room where the people approved by the host did their gambling. The air was thick with smoke, the steady clash of coins and chips, and the noises people make when they're throwing their money down a drain and calling it a good time, Roulette, craps, blackjack—all illegal as hell in this state, and every one of them nothing but a cheap shot disguised as magic, a chance to make something out of nothing.

There were house players scattered around the room— hookers, really—handsome studs and luscious broads daring the customers to believe the obvious fact that el Señor wouldn't be in this kind of business if he could ever lose. But most of these fine folks couldn't see the dare. The magic already had them by the throat. If you told them that putting their money in the toilet was gambling, you wouldn't have been able to stop them from emptying their pockets and flushing the stuff away themselves.

But that wasn't the only thing going on. Estobal moved quickly across the room, but I still had time to spot at least one man and two women who didn't have the vaguest idea that they were tossing away every cent they had. They were so stoned that you could've hit them over the head with a brick and they wouldn't have known the difference.

The really screwy thing about it all was that if you'd taken a poll in the room, most of those suckers would've told you they were more *alive* right then than under any other circumstances.

But it was none of my business, and I didn't have time to get up on my white horse about it. Estobal was holding a door open for me. When he closed it, we were in a short little hallway, maybe ten feet between doors, and there were two other goons with us. They didn't look at me, didn't wave guns, didn't even talk to Estobal. They didn't have to. We all knew what they were there for.

Estobal opened the next door, and I followed him with the two goons on my heels. Into an office that made Ginny's look like a phone booth. It sported a full bar complete with bartender, a couple of Olympic-size sofas, and a desk you could've played tennis on. The carpet was like a trampoline. I half expected to see potted sequoias in the corners.

Aside from the bartender, the only man in the room sat behind the desk. From his manicured fingertips to the ends of his vandyke beard and mustache, he was the perfect dapper grandee. He couldn't have been more than five six. That desk should've made him look like a dwarf, but it didn't. Instead it reinforced his commanding presence, his air of possession. Somehow he fit in that office. It was his, and he liked it the way it was.

El Señor.

Estobal marched up to the desk. Without speaking, he took his gun out of his pants and put it down on the blotter so el Señor could see that the cylinder was missing.

In Spanish el Señor asked, "What is the explanation of this?"

I answered for him. "I am the explanation. I am named Axbrewder. I do the work of a private investigator. I wish to speak with el Señor."

I was hardly finished when I heard pistol hammers cocking. I didn't need mirrors to know that the goons behind me were ready to blow me in half.

"Chota!" Estobal spat.

Trying not to sound desperate—or even in a hurry—I said, "I wish to speak with Héctor Jesús Fría de la Sancha."

El Señor's eyes narrowed. For a moment he studied me. Then he leaned back in his chair. "Please to be seated, Señor Axbrewder."

His fingers made a delicate gesture at the goons, and suddenly they were standing back against the wall. As I sat down, Estobal stamped out of the room.

After half a minute, el Señor asked quietly, "How does it transpire that you know my name, Señor Axbrewder?"

I answered him in English. Trying to shore up my position by exerting at least that much control over the conversation. "What difference does it make? The people who told me don't have anything against you. And I don't want to give you any trouble. I'm here for myself. Leave it at that."

He steepled his fingers, gazed closely at the way the pink tips touched each other. "Already you have given me trouble. You have humiliated my Estobal. Now he will be unsure of himself. Also he will be very angry. His value has been made less."

"He'll recover," I muttered.

"Nevertheless." El Señor was not accustomed to being contradicted. His English had a mechanical precision more threatening than any amount of rage or screaming. "Your presence casts doubt upon my Estobal. It casts doubt upon my personal safety. Now you say that you are here for yourself. You presume a great deal upon my benevolence, Señor Axbrewder."

I said, "No." At that point I didn't really care whether I contradicted him or not. "I'm already too familiar with your reputation for 'benevolence.' What I'm counting on is your reputation for honor."

He considered me closely, then said, "I think I do not like the tone in which you address me."

"Señor Fría——" I hunched forward in my chair, half protecting my sore guts and half pleading with him. "Let me tell you why I'm here. Then you'll understand my tone."

He unsteepled his fingers, rested his arms on the arms of his chair. "Very well. Begin."

Begin, hell. It wasn't that easy. There were so many things I had to explain before I could get to the point. I felt a sharp urge to stand up and start pacing around the room, try to relieve the tension. But I didn't. I didn't want to make the goons nervous. For a minute I just sat there racking my brains. Then I said, "I'll tell you what happened to my niece."

Carefully I told him Alathea's story—her disappearance, the note, Lona's concern, her decision to hire Ginny and me, Alathea's reappearance, her condition, the bomb in the hospital. And all the time I watched el Señor's face, studying it for any kind of surprise or sympathy that would tell me where I stood with him.

But his smooth neat features didn't show a thing. When I stopped, he said, "Some word of this bombing in the hospital has come to me. A very bad thing. What has it to do with me?"

"I told you. She's in a heroin coma. At thirteen she's been forced to become a junky and a whore, and she's in a coma."

Abruptly he leaned forward, placed his hands flat on the desktop. "Señor Axbrewder," he said softly, "I do not sell heroin to young girls."

"I know that." I did my best to make him believe it. My life depended on whether or not I could make him believe it.

He didn't move a muscle. "Continue."

"Señor Fría," I said, "seven young girls Alathea's age have been kidnapped in the past two years. They disappear. Their parents get phony notes. Then somehow they get hooked on heroin, and they turn into whores. And three or six months later, they end up dead. My brother's daughter was number eight. Number nine is still missing."

"Again I ask, what has it to do with me?"

"Heroin." I wasn't afraid anymore. I was past that. My voice was as soft as his. "Every nickel bag in this state has somebody's name on it, and you know all the names. The man who kidnaps and rapes and dopes these girls gets his junk from somewhere. You know who he is.

"I want you to tell me who he is."

"Go to the police. Let them find him."

"They will," I rasped. "But not tonight. They're not that fast. And he knows they're getting close. Tonight he's going to kill number nine and get rid of the body. Destroy the evidence."

"I see." Again he leaned back in his chair, considered me from a distance. Then he said, "Perhaps I know the man. It is possible. Tell me, Señor. Why should I deliver him to you?"

Praying that old Manolo hadn't betrayed me, I answered, "You're a man of honor. What he's doing is terrible."

"He is Anglo. The girls are Anglo. Honor means nothing among Anglos."

"Anglo, Chicano, it doesn't make any difference. *They're only thirteen.* Some of them are twelve."

"You also are Anglo. You are a *chota.*"

Through my teeth, I said, "Señor Fría, I'm her father's brother."

Something about that reached him. He was silent for a long minute, looking at the ceiling. When he spoke again, his tone was softer. "I myself have two daughters. If I were dead or in prison, and some evil were done to them, my own brother would pay any price to punish that evil."

With one hand, he gestured at the bar, and two seconds later the bartender set a bottle of tequila down on the blotter. With two glasses.

"We will drink together," el Señor said. "Then I will give thought to this thing you ask."

Right there, it all collapsed. I stared at the bottle while everything inside me went numb. Stared while he poured hefty jolts into both glasses. Took one himself. Pushed the other across the desk to me.

I didn't touch it.

"Drink, Señor," he said softly.

My hand tried to move, but I didn't let it. I just sat there and stared at the glass and didn't touch it.

"Señor Axbrewder." Soft and ugly. "I give nothing without price. You are known to me. You are what the Anglos call 'alcoholic.' Also you are Anglo, and a *chota*. You have intruded upon myself and humiliated my Estobal. This is the price."

I didn't touch it.

"Do not insult me," he said. Soft and ugly and fatal.

I wanted to say something, appeal to him somehow, make him understand. But I didn't have any words for it. There weren't any words. If I took a drink, the name he was offering me wouldn't do me any good. Once I started to drink, I wouldn't be able to do anything. About anything.

I got to my feet. "Sorry I bothered you," I muttered. "I should've known better."

El Señor made a cutting gesture with the edge of his hand. His goons hit me before I could step away from the chair. Maybe I could've taken them if they'd given me a second to move, but they didn't.

They caught my arms, jerked me back down into the chair. One of them knotted a fist in my hair, hauled my head back. It all happened too fast. I was gasping and couldn't help myself.

El Señor came around the desk, picked up the bottle, and started pouring tequila down my throat.

Then I went blind with tears while the stuff burned its way into my guts.

19

The goons turned me over to Muy Estobal, and Estobal turned me out of El Machismo.

He was methodical about it. First he half carried me down a couple of back halls until we reached a door that took us out into a dark alley behind the place. Then he searched my pockets until he found the cylinder to his .38. Then he pounded on me.

Grinning like a barracuda.

One hit split my lips so badly that I sputtered blood every time I breathed. Another almost cracked my jaw. A couple more continued the job he'd already started on my ribs. Eventually he had to hold me up with one hand so that he could go on punching me with the other.

I suppose I should've made some effort to defend myself. I wasn't all that drunk. But everything had fallen apart on me. It was all hopeless, and I couldn't think of a good reason to exert myself. So I didn't. If Estobal wanted to beat me to death, that was his business. My brain was numb.

Numbness is a wonderful thing. I really didn't feel his fists much. Half the time I couldn't even see him.

Nevertheless I could hear him fine. He panted like a locomotive, working himself up into a terrible lather. Every time he swung, he grunted like a small explosion, a lesser bomb. After each blow came a penetrating thud, muffled and profound.

Then I heard something else. A voice—a woman's voice. It sounded dimly familiar.

It said, "Release him." In Spanish.

Estobal stared down the alley for a second. He braced himself to hit me again.

"I do not jest, Estobal," the woman snapped. "This man

is known to me. I am in his debt. For his sake I will risk many things to punish you. The police will be grateful for any reason to seal you in their prison."

Estobal pushed me away. I bounced against the wall and fell on my face. "Do not make threats to me, girl," he rasped. "El Señor will be displeased."

"Then permit him to be displeased. If he seeks to harm me, all Puerta del Sol will laugh at the man who revenges himself upon a woman."

Estobal muttered some kind of retort, but I couldn't make it out. Then he was gone. I heard the door slam behind him.

A minute later, the woman was kneeling beside me. "Ay, Señor Axbrewder," she said in English. "Are you severely hurt?"

With her help, I rolled over onto one side. My chest and face were starting to hurt, and I had to hunt a long way through pain and alcohol to find her name. "Señorita San-guillán," I said. At least that's what I tried to say. "What're you doing here?"

I heard a tearing noise. Then she began dabbing my chin and mouth with something. It felt soft, like a piece of her slip. While she tried to clean me up, she answered my question.

"I wished to speak with you. Señor Sevilla, who is known to you"—old Manolo—"is the father of the man who married the daughter of my mother's brother. When I revealed to him my wish, he informed me that you had a great matter in your heart which compelled you to seek words with el Señor." She kept wiping at my face while she spoke, and it hurt off and on, but I was too fuzzy to care. "Therefore I came to this place and inquired of you. I was informed that you had been admitted to speak with Muy Estobal." Suppressed fury rasped in the way she said his name. "I chose to await you."

Under her breath, she muttered, *"Pendejo."* I knew she didn't mean me.

Groaning, I tried to crank myself into a sitting position. It wasn't easy. I wasn't absolutely sure which way was up. But she got her arms around my shoulders and helped me.

With her face close to mine, she studied me anxiously.

"Is it possible for you to rise?"

I said, "Teresa." My mouth felt like it was full of broken glass. I could hardly mumble. "Why did you want to talk to me?"

She hesitated, then said, "If you rise, I will inform you."

I shook my head. "Just tell me."

She sighed. "Very well, Señor Axbrewder. But you must not think ill of me."

I wanted to tell her not to worry, but I didn't have the strength. Or maybe what I didn't have was the moral substance.

Facing me squarely, she said, "I have taken back the charges against the man who sought to harm me. I do not wish you to speak against him."

That was the last straw. It was all too much for me—nothing mattered anymore. I let myself fall back against the cement and closed my eyes.

"Señor!" She shook me, but she didn't weigh enough to move me much. "You must understand. Because of this Captain Cason, I have lost my employment in the Heights. He spoke, and I was sent away without reference. He is too strong for me. He desired me to take back the charges, and I agreed so that he would permit me to find some other place of work."

I didn't move. Why should I move? The only thing she could've offered me that would've meant anything was a bottle—and that never occurred to her. After a while she quit tugging at me. I didn't even hear her leave.

I must've blacked out. The next thing I knew, she was back. With help. Two young men—old Manolo's sons, if I understood her right. They propped their shoulders under my arms, heaved me up, and lugged me off.

I dragged along between them for a couple of minutes. But the strain hurt my chest too much, and I had to pick up some of my weight to ease the pain. Eventually old habits took over. By the time we reached her destination, I was practically walking by myself.

Her place was a ramshackle old adobe tenement maybe

five blocks from El Machismo. The walls had once been painted, but now they were so chipped and weathered that the building looked diseased. Stricken by terminal futility. The young men levered me up a flight of rickety wooden stairs, and then she was home.

The one room she shared with her mother and two sisters was never going to look clean no matter how often they scrubbed it. Ordinary soap and muscle can't keep up with rats.

She sat me down in the middle of the room in the only chair. Her mother heated some water on a stinking oil stove while her sisters watched me from their blankets with frightened animal eyes. When the water was ready, the young men held my arms while Teresa scalded the cuts on my face.

The pain blinded me again. It wasn't until after my eyes cleared that I realized somebody else had come into the room.

Old Manolo.

He regarded me with a face full of sadness. But I didn't pay any attention to that. I had something else in mind.

He had a bottle of anisette in his coat pocket.

It was almost full.

As soon as his sons let go of my arms, I lunged at Manolo and got my hands on his bottle.

Putting my mouth around the mouth of the bottle tore my cuts, and the alcohol burned them like the lick of a whip. I stood it long enough to get three or four good swallows. I've never liked the taste of anisette, but right then I didn't give a shit. All I wanted was to get drunk. Drunker. Drunk enough to pass out.

I put the cap back on the bottle, stuffed it away in one of the pockets of my jacket. Then I looked old Manolo in the face. "I took your advice," I muttered stiff-lipped. "Went to see el Señor. Now here I am. If you've got anything else to tell me, you'd better say it now. While I'm drunk enough to stand it."

His old brown gaze never wavered. "Ah, Señor Axbrewder," he sighed, "this night I have heard many sad tales. The daughter of your brother's widow has been found without

her mind. A bomb has taken the hand of your partner. The
setter of the bomb is dead, and you have come no nearer to
the author of these evils. It is a deep regret to me that el
Señor saw fit to withhold the knowledge you seek. Never
again will I give such counsel as I gave you. I am an old
man, and old men are foolish."

His eyes held me until I couldn't stand it anymore—I had
to look down. I didn't want him feeling sorry for me. I was
in bad enough shape without that.

"Señor Axbrewder," he asked gently, "what will you do?"

That was a good question. Since I didn't have an answer,
I took another slug of anisette. It was starting to get to me.
Some of the numbness I needed crept into my nerves.

"Will you not go to the Fistoulari woman? She has the
name of a strong and clear-sighted person. Surely she will
wish to know what has befallen you."

Ginny. Just thinking about her made my heart hurt. But
Manolo was a cunning old bastard, and he knew what he
was doing. It was a sneaky way to give me advice, but it
worked.

Ginny.

That was it, of course. Things weren't bad enough yet.
They wouldn't be bad enough until I went and told Ginny
that I'd screwed everything up. Then I'd be free to drink as
much as I wanted. It wouldn't be my problem anymore.

Everything has to be paid for. Even freedom. Humiliation
is the price you pay for alcohol, one way or another.

I got to my feet, wincing at the way my ribs ground together. Shaking off the hands that tried to hold me, I went
past old Manolo to the door.

I was on my way out when I recovered enough decency
to turn around. Holding myself up on the door frame, I said
as clearly as I could in Spanish, "Teresa María Sanguillán
y García, I give you thanks. I think no ill of you, but only
good. When a burden is too great to be borne, it must be
set aside." Then I left.

I stumbled a couple of times on the stairs, but the railing
held me somehow.

After that things got harder. Walking made my chest hurt.

Also my balance wasn't good, and every time I stopped myself from falling I jarred my ribs. But I had to do it, and I did. Went back to El Machismo's parking lot to recover the Olds.

Then I was driving. I concentrated on it hard. The last thing I needed in the world was a DWI bust. But I couldn't help making mistakes. Once I had the distinct impression I was going the wrong way down a one-way street.

I hung on to the wheel with both fists and kept moving. A couple of times when things got fuzzy, I stopped and took a swig from my bottle. Not much—just enough to hold me together. After a long time I reached University Hospital.

It didn't occur to me that there would be a problem getting in to see Ginny until after I'd parked the Olds and taken a look around. Most of the windows were dark, which reminded me of the time. Naturally the security guards and night-duty nurses weren't going to want me wandering around their hospital at this hour of the night.

But I was too drunk to let that stop me. In spite of the alcohol, I still remembered Ginny's room number.

I went into Emergency. But instead of stopping at the nurses' station, I walked straight to the waiting room as if I had some perfectly good reason for being there. Then I sneaked over to the stairwell.

The door to the stairs had a big sign on it saying, "Emergency Exit Only." I went in fast. Once I got past the door, the only thing I had to worry about for a while was meeting someone on the stairs.

I didn't meet anyone. If I had, I probably would've gone to pieces.

When I found the floor I wanted, I looked out through the little window in the stairwell door. I didn't see anybody. Ginny's room was just two doors down from me on the opposite side of the hall. Getting in to see her would be easy.

Too easy.

I cracked open the stairwell door a couple of inches, made extra sure that the hall was empty. Then I went across to Ginny's door. And stopped.

I didn't want to just barge in. She had strong feelings about her right to privacy. And I knew how fast she could be with her .357.

Instead of just pushing the door open and going in, I knocked.

Waited. Knocked again.

No answer.

I took the time for one more quick drink. Then I let myself into her room.

It was a semiprivate room like Alathea's. The reading light over the head of Ginny's bed was on. The curtain separating the two beds had been pulled almost all the way across the room. No light came from the far side. Everything past the curtain was dark.

Ginny was sitting up in bed. The head of her bed hadn't been cranked up, and she didn't have any pillows behind her. She just sat there as if she were getting ready to answer my knock. But there was an IV hanging from a pole over her head, its tube plugged into her right arm. Which pretty well immobilized her. She couldn't have come to the door.

She looked at me.

Stared at me. Her eyes on either side of her broken nose were dark as bruises, as if she'd been mugged. Her face held a look of horror.

I didn't move. I couldn't. She paralyzed me.

Her voice cut through me like the flame of a blowtorch. "You're drunk!"

That staggered me. Rocked me back on my heels.

"You sonofabitch!" she snarled. "How dare you?"

I blinked at her like an idiot. Ginny? She didn't understand. She didn't know what had happened to me. I hadn't expected her to react like this. I wanted to explain.

She didn't give me a chance. "Get out of here, Mick." The tone of her voice made my ribs grind together. "I don't want to have anything more to do with you. Get out of my life.

"Do you hear me, *Mick*?"

She spat that *Mick* at me as if it were the worst thing she could possibly do to me without actually shooting me.

Mick. She called me Mick. Nobody calls me that. Nobody. Not since Richard—Not since I killed Richard. Rick and Mick. Nobody. I nearly cried out.

"All right." My voice shook. I couldn't control it. "If that's the way you want it."

Nobody! It would've been better if she'd shot me. No simple little hunk of lead would hurt like this.

But when I turned for the door, I caught a glimpse of her purse out of the corner of my eye. It lay on the floor a few feet away from her nightstand.

Shot me, I thought. With her .357. Which she kept in her purse.

What was it doing on the floor?

If she'd accidentally pushed it off the stand, it wouldn't have fallen that far away.

All of a sudden my skin began to crawl with intuition. A burning sensation mounted in the back of my head. Something was trying to get through to me. Reach past the stuff in my blood, make sense to me.

I struggled for it. Something—

I wanted to beat my head on the wall. I was too drunk. I couldn't think.

I had to think.

She'd called me Mick?

The pain was killing me. I couldn't stop it. I had to stop it. Had to think.

Ginny got her hand blown off because she didn't want anything to happen to me.

Think!

Her purse was too far away from the nightstand. It couldn't have fallen there accidentally. Someone must've knocked it or shoved it aside.

Why?

Think.

She needed me. I had to be sober!

But I wasn't sober. I was standing there like a lush, with a bottle of anisette in my pocket and my hands clenched in front of my face. Seconds slipped away from me, and I couldn't bring them back.

Hands clenched.

Clenched the way I'd clenched them around Kirke's arm a couple of days ago.

Why had I done that?

Because Kirke said Alathea was a little whore.

I almost screamed—

—and everything came into focus.

We hadn't told Kirke that this case had anything to do with sex. We hadn't said a word about that to the school board.

How had he known?

Kirke!

That's why he'd tried so hard to persuade me to drink with him. He knew I was getting close. He wanted to keep me with him until he figured out some way to kill me.

Then a horror of my own landed on me so hard I almost dropped to my knees.

Kirke knew that Ginny was in the hospital. Stretto had told him what happened to her. He knew she was here.

I had no idea what to do. My intuition didn't stretch that far. I'd left the .45 in the Olds. And I was too far away—

Against the wall beside the door stood a steel armchair with a green vinyl seat. I put my hand on it to hold myself up.

Then it all came together at once—intuition, rage, fear, love. I snatched up the chair, and with one sweep of my arm I threw it at the curtain near the head of her bed.

It hit something behind the curtain. I heard a muffled curse. A gun went off. The slug plowed into the ceiling.

Ginny and I moved simultaneously. She flipped out of bed and sprawled flat on the floor, reaching for her purse. I jumped over her, dove headlong across the bed into the curtain.

The chair had torn the curtain. It came down under my weight. I landed half on the chair, half on a struggling body. It twisted frantically under me, trying to get up.

The curtain hid him. I didn't know if he still had his gun. But I didn't care. I just hammered at his veiled shape with my fists. The third time I hit something hard that must've been his head. He slumped under me, stopped moving.

I didn't stop. I heard Ginny shouting, "Don't kill him! He knows where Mittie is!" But the pressure was too strong, and I couldn't stop.

I pounded at him with everything I had until another gunshot crashed through the room.

Unsteadily I rolled off him. Got up.

Ginny stood beside her bed with her .357 pointed at the ceiling. The IV tube had been ripped out of her arm. Blood dripped slowly from her elbow.

There was nobody in the other bed.

I swallowed hard, managed to ask, "Kirke?" I hurt everywhere. My knees felt like mush, and my head floated sideways. I had to hold onto the bed frame.

Ginny nodded. Then she put her gun down on the nightstand. For a second she looked like she might faint. But she fought it off. "Oh, God, Brew," she breathed. "I thought he was going to kill you."

Slowly I came back under control. Reaching down, I pulled away the curtain. Just making sure I hadn't hit him too hard.

I'd battered him pretty good, but Kirke was still breathing.

The whole room stank of anisette. One side of my jacket was soaked, and I had a pocket full of broken glass.

20

Acton got an address out of Kirke. I don't know how, and I don't want to know. All I cared about was that Acton took me—and about eight other cops—with him when he went to check out that address.

It was a long way up Canyon Road toward the mountains. But Acton drove like a bat. We must've set a record getting there. The sky was turning pale, but the sun hadn't yet climbed over the mountains when we reached the house.

It sat in a little valley between two hills, completely out of sight of its neighbors. It was a rich man's place, a sprawling ranch-style house complete with everything except its own airstrip. But right then none of us felt much like admiring it. Acton broke the door down, and all ten of us went charging in.

We found Mittie alive. Hungry, strung-out, and frantic—but alive. One of the cops took her back into town to the hospital while the rest of them searched the house.

I didn't do any searching. Once I knew that Mittie was safe despite all the stupid things I'd done in the past twelve hours, a lot of the tension inside me snapped, and I had to sit down.

After a while Acton came and stood in front of me with his hands in his pockets. His fingers jiggled keys or coins or something.

I said, "You weren't surprised to see who it was." Which was true. When he'd reached the hospital and seen Kirke, he'd looked like he'd known it all along.

He said, "Naw. I spent half the night talking to the school board. Scurvey and Greenling both said they got their note paper from him. He's the board secretary. He's supposed to provide things like note paper. Tearing sheets in half is an old habit of his. Didn't prove nothing, but it sure as hell made me suspicious."

I nodded tiredly. Then I said, "You'll have to find her father."

"Naw," he growled again. "He turned himself in around two thirty this morning. He babbled something about killing the man who set that bomb. I wanted to talk to him, but right about then we got this call"—he grinned sourly—"about a shoot-out at the hospital. He's still sitting in the cage."

"He used my gun," I said. "He didn't carry one. It's in the glove compartment of the Olds." Then I said the only thing I could think of to help Ted Hangst. "He was covering me. Last had a gun on me, and Ted was trying to keep me from being blown away."

Acton nodded. I could see that he was going to accept my story without worrying about it. Another piece of tension faded, and for a few minutes there I almost went to sleep.

But then the cops started finding things. The note paper didn't give them any trouble. The desk in the den held a stack of neatly torn half sheets. Same watermark as all the runaway notes. That and the fingerprints in the house gave the cops the kind of evidence courts love. Nine counts of kidnapping and seven of murder.

And after some more diligent searching that made the house look like it'd been used as a test site for high explosives, Acton's team found the heroin and the money. Not a particularly big cache of junk. Kirke probably had to drive down to Mexico every three or four months to stock up. But it was enough. The money came out to over a hundred thousand dollars. It was all Kirke had left after paying for housing, junk, food, clothes, and Sven Last. Obviously he kept it in cash so that it wouldn't show up in his financial records. Which explained why Smithsonian thought he was clean.

Acton rubbed his hands together. "This bastard's going to get the gas chamber."

A couple of cops stayed behind to keep an eye on things until the print-and-picture boys arrived. The rest of us piled into the cars and went back to Puerta del Sol.

Acton dropped me off at the hospital. The sun was up now, and all that crisp morning light made me squint. But for once in my life I was glad to see it. Nights like that last one I could do without.

It was nominally too early for visiting hours, but the hospital staff didn't make me wait. By then Ginny and I were celebrities—if that's the right word for it. The head nurse made an exception for me and took me up to Ginny's new room.

This time when she saw me Ginny smiled. It lit up her whole face.

I sat down in one of the chairs against the wall, and for a minute or two we didn't say anything. We just smiled at each other.

I didn't want to do anything else. But after a while I started to feel like I was in danger of making a fool of myself. "All right," I said. My voice was so husky it almost made me laugh. "All right. I can't stand the suspense. After what I've been through, I want to know how you figured out this case."

She looked beautiful to me. Even her broken nose was beautiful. "What makes you think I figured anything out?"

"You were right on the edge of it." That was something I knew for sure. "At the time you were too tight to get it. But I'll bet you had the answer when you woke up after surgery. You probably tried to call me, but you couldn't track me down."

She nodded. I was right, of course. Intuition didn't have anything to do with it. I just knew Ginny.

"I missed something obvious," I went on. "I'm going to go crazy unless you tell me what it was."

She leaned back against her pillows, looked up at the ceiling. Fistoulari thinking. "I missed it, too," she said after a moment. "It wasn't Stretto or Scurvey. We were pretty sure of that. And you were sure it wasn't Greenling. I was willing to believe you. So it had to be Kirke or one of the secretaries.

"Finally it all came down to the way Kirke ran that office. Each of those girls was kidnapped during the day. At different times during the day. By somebody with the authority to make the girls go with him. Somebody who could supply a good excuse for himself if he got stopped. That excluded any fiancées or husbands. It had to be somebody who actually worked for the board.

"But each one of those little kidnapping operations must've taken a fair amount of time. Drive from the office to the school. Pick up the girl. Take her out to that house on Canyon Road. Run back to the office. That's what we missed.

"Kirke was the only one who could arrange so much time away from the office during the day. If one of his secretaries had disappeared for that length of time, he would've nailed her to the wall. The way he ran that place, he was the only one who could get away."

Well, I was right about that too. I'd missed something obvious. Axbrewder the genius. Some days I'm amazed to find that I've put my clothes on straight.

Ginny was looking at me hard. I didn't understand it until she started to say, "I'm sorry I called—"

I interrupted her. "Forget it. I was in a fog. You had to get through to me somehow." Then I grinned. "And you knew Kirke didn't know my first name."

For a minute she blinked back tears, and I couldn't think of anything to say.

There was a knock at the door. Ginny nodded, and I said, "Come in."

It was Lona.

She wore a vaguely startled look, as if she couldn't quite believe what had happened. At first she had trouble finding her voice. Then she said, "I wanted to tell you. I just talked to the doctor. He said"—she swallowed convulsively—"he said Alathea is getting stronger. Her vital signs are stronger. And steadier. He said that probably means she's going to come out of it. Maybe soon. He thinks she might be all right."

After that I couldn't see for a while. My eyes ran, and everything blurred.

Ginny said, "I'm glad. She's a wonderful girl."

Lona said, "You didn't find her. You didn't save her."

When Ginny didn't answer, I knew Lona was talking to me. Blindly I said, "I know. She saved herself."

For a moment Lona remained silent. Then she said, "You caught the man who was responsible. That's what Richard would have wanted you to do."

I had to cover my face with my hands. When I got myself back under control, Lona was gone.

Ginny smiled at me like the sun.

I got to my feet. She'd had a rough eighteen hours—she needed rest. And Ted would need me to tell the cops my side of the story. He might even need me to post bail.

But before I left there was one thing I had to do.

I walked over to Ginny and bent down. Deliberately I gave her the best kiss I had in me.

It hurt my cut mouth, but I didn't care because she wrapped her arms around my neck and kissed me back. Hard.

When we stopped, I was grinning like a crazy man. I practically floated as I turned away, started for the door.

Her voice stopped me. "What're you going to do now?" she asked. "Go have a drink?" She didn't sound angry or accusative. There was none of that in her tone. Just pain.

"No." I faced her again so that she could see I was telling her the truth. No big promises or predictions, just the truth about how I felt. "I'm going to put that off for a while."

Look for

THE MAN
WHO RISKED
HIS PARTNER

by

Stephen R. Donaldson

Available in November 2003
from Forge Books

Turn the page for a preview

1

Six months after that bomb took Ginny's left hand off, she still hadn't gotten over it. I didn't need a degree in psychology or a message from God to figure out what was going on. I lived with her—I could see it.

And I was living with her for all the wrong reasons. Not because she liked having me around. Not because she thought I was a particularly nice person to share a bed with. And certainly not because I was so all-fired tidy that I made the mess in her apartment stand up and salute.

No, I was living with her because she couldn't live by herself anymore. She only had one hand. She needed somebody to take care of her.

If I'd said that to people who knew her, they would've laughed out loud. Sure, Axbrewder. She needs you. Tell us another one. She was Ginny Fistoulari, the boss and brains of Fistoulari Investigations. With her keen gray eyes and her attractive face and blond hair and the way her tall lean body moved in her clothes, she could've been a society doll, the wife of some big snort who owned a country club or two, or maybe just half the first-born children in Puerta del Sol. But her nose had been broken once when some clown had clipped her with a crowbar—to which she'd replied by shooting the sucker in the face. And she'd lost her hand by holding a bomb out the window of a hospital so that it wouldn't blow up in the building or on the people below. When things got tough, she had a way of looking like her features were molded over iron instead of bone.

As for me—at six foot five and too heavy, I was big enough that most people wouldn't ordinarily laugh at the idea I was needed. But I was only temporarily sober. I was known to be totally fubar, "fucked up beyond all repair," even before that wonderful day—the highlight of my life—when in a fit of civic righteousness and alcohol I'd tried to apprehend a purse-snatcher and ended up shooting my brother instead. Like they say, anybody who can't aim a .45 better than that ought to have his brains recalled for production defects. And I was never going to get my license back. The commission watched Ginny like a hawk because she insisted on hiring me when I didn't have a license.

Sure, Axbrewder. She needs you. Tell us another one.

Well, in this particular case, "temporarily sober" had been going on for six months. Almost every night, I dreamed about the special amber peace you can only find somewhere near the bottom of a bottle, and woke up grinding my teeth. Almost every day, when I wasn't braced for it, my throat ached for the lovely burn of whiskey. I still had withdrawal flashes that made me sweat and tremble and hold my head like a junkie. The simple smell of Scotch was enough to turn my guts inside out.

On bad days, when I got out of bed, I said to myself, *Maybe today's the day.* The day I get to take a drink. Just one. Or maybe two. Two drinks can't hurt me. I've earned two drinks.

But I didn't do it.

For a drunk like me, sobriety is like trying to push a brick wall down with your nose. Six months of it gets to be pretty painful. But I hadn't had a drink yesterday, or last week, or last month, and I wasn't going to have one today.

Because Ginny really did need me.

She wasn't actually helpless. In practice, she could've done just about anything she wanted. With her purse on a strap over her right shoulder, she could get what she needed out of it almost as fast as usual. And the doctors had fitted her with a prosthetic device—"the claw," she called it—that looked pretty handy to me. Sure, it was made of stainless steel, which isn't exactly one of the primary flesh tones. But it strapped over her stump and worked off the muscles of her forearm, so that she could open and close the pair of hooks just by acting like she still had fingers. Down at the base, they had sharp edges that came together like scissors—

which I thought was a nice touch. And they were strong enough to punch in the tops of beer cans.

She refused to wear the damn thing.

It made her feel worse.

The problem was simple. She was Ginny Fistoulari, hot-shot private investigator, smart, tough, give-me-a-running-start-and-I-can-do-anything. And she was maimed. Without her hand, she felt like a cripple, ugly, undesirable, and bitter. The claw made her hate herself.

I knew exactly how she felt. I was Mick Axbrewder, the drunk who killed his own brother. She never would've lost her hand if I'd had the brains God gave a spaniel—if for example I'd thought of using my belt to hold that bomb.

So I took care of her.

Yes sir, we were quite a pair. Leaning on each other because neither one of us had the bare guts to stand up alone. Me, I was used to it. But I hadn't expected it to happen to her. If I hadn't been so busy being dogged and useful, I would've gone out and become a drunk again just to forget the constant misery burning like a low-grade fever in her eyes. Those eyes used to be as sharp and alive as a hunter's. Now they just hurt.

Somebody should've locked the two of us away in a nursing home somewhere so we wouldn't get into any more trouble. But maybe that wouldn't have solved the problem. And maybe trouble comes to those who need it. We sure as hell needed something.

Monday morning we slept in later than usual because we were between cases and didn't have anything better to do. I got out of bed first, used the bathroom, and went to make the coffee. While the pot was perking, I cleaned up the mess she'd made in the apartment the night before.

Her apartment was in Turtleshell, a complex near what used to be the business center of town, before the banks moved. The building was at least middle-aged, but it was designed and furnished in the American Impersonal absence of style. She could've been living in Indianapolis. She stood it the same way she stood the clutter.

Which wasn't all that bad—her coat on the floor, clothes

dropped wherever she happened to be when she took them off, coffee cups everywhere, case and tax records tossed down on the table so hard that a lot of them had splashed onto the carpet. And anyway I couldn't really object to it. I knew why she did it. It was as close as she could come to expressing her resentment.

Before she lost her hand, of course, she'd been messy out of ordinary absent-mindedness. Too many other things to think about. But now she cluttered the apartment because she knew that I was going to clean it up. She resented being dependent—so she resented me for helping her, for being the one she was dependent on—so she did little things to make my job harder.

We had a lot in common that way. I kept cleaning up after her for exactly the same reason.

In fact, we were spending more and more time playing that kind of game. When the coffee was ready, I took her a cup. But instead of drinking it, she let it get cold while she was in the shower. Then she had me pour her a fresh cup. Meanwhile I fixed her a breakfast she didn't want and could hardly choke down. If I'd been anybody else, I couldn't have made her eat breakfast by holding a gun to her head. By preference she lived on vitamin pills and coffee until at least noon.

It was a rotten way to live. If something didn't change soon, one of us was going to go off the deep end.

So after we slogged our way through another breakfast, I helped her get dressed. I buttoned her blouse—which should've been a whole lot more fun than it was—buckled her shoes, got her coat over her shoulders. I stuffed the papers she wanted into her briefcase. Then I held the door open for her, and we went out into Puerta del Sol's winter.

We hadn't had anything to say to each other for going on sixteen hours.

Puerta del Sol is far enough south so that we only get snow in alternate years. But the terrain around the city is high desert. The mountains east of us go up to 10,000 feet, which is only 5,000 higher than the Flat Valley, where Puerta del Sol sprawls on either side of the river. So the winters are about as cold as I can stand—at least when the sun isn't shining. And the sun today had a bleached-out look, like it was overworked. But Ginny and I still could've talked to each other while we walked to her office. We just didn't. Instead I huddled into my jacket, looking ridiculous the way somebody my size always does when he feels sorry for himself. And Ginny puffed at the cold while her broken nose turned red.

Her office is in the Murchison Building, on Paseo Grande. It's one of the three structures in Puerta del Sol that stand more than five stories tall, but that turned out to be misplaced optimism on the part of the developers when all the banks moved three miles farther down Paseo Grande, away from what the real estate speculators call "Chicano creep." As a result, space in the Murchison Building isn't as expensive as you'd expect. That suited me. It helped Ginny stay in business. But I wouldn't go to any doctor or insurance agent who had an office there.

Unfortunately the heat wasn't working, and Fistoulari Investigations was on the wrong side for the morning sun. You could've stored cadavers in there. I picked up the mail and newspapers from the empty waiting room and carried them into the actual office. I put the mail on Ginny's desk and dropped the newspapers on the sofa I used for a chair. Then I started up the electric coffeepot. We had to have something warm to keep us going until the sun reached the picture window looking out toward the flat Valley.

Booze would've been warmer, but I tried not to think about that.

While Ginny scanned the mail and threw it into the wastebasket, I glanced around at the only things she had hanging on her walls—her diplomas and the display copy of her license. In this state, the commission wants private investigators to be "professional," like doctors and lawyers. So Ginny decorates her walls with the sort of stuff that makes the commission feel good. And she has a waiting room for all the people who never come to see her. As a rule, the clients who come to see a private investigator are the ones you don't want—divorce cases and loonies. Good clients call. They expect you to go see them.

After the mail, she pulled one of the phones closer to her and started dialing. To keep myself from watching her, I picked up the papers. When I heard her ask for the manager of the Murchison Building—she was calling to complain about the heat—I stopped listening.

Amazing what you can learn from newspapers. Monday morning's edition was on top, and the headline said:

GANGSTER SLAIN
BODY FOUND IN RIVER

Under that:

Murder Mob Related, Police Say

Do tell, I said. My, my.

At 11:09 last night, according to the story, the body of Roscoe Chavez was fished out of the Flat River, down in the south part of town where the warehouses and *barrios* are. He'd been shot six times in the chest. His pockets had been filled with rolls of pennies for weight, but the body bloated up enough to float.

Somewhere in the fourth paragraph, the Puerta del Sol *Herald's* keen-eyed and incisive reporter finally got around to using the word "alleged." Roscoe "Bambino" Chavez was "alleged" to have ties to organized crime. He was "alleged" to be responsible for illegal numbers gambling in our fair city. The cops didn't have any particular theory about why he was killed. They were just glad he was gone.

I gave this flash the respect it deserved. Actually until this minute I hadn't believed that our fine and upstanding guardians of the law were even aware of the connection between the Bambino and Puerta del Sol's thriving numbers racket. As for why he was killed—I could've answered that with my eyes closed. He'd been killed for doing something el Señor didn't like.

Being a good citizen myself, I applauded the demise of

brother Chavez. But I still wished that he'd gotten away with whatever it was el Señor didn't like. I had a small grudge against the man the *Herald's* reporter would've called Puerta del Sol's "crime czar"—if the cops had ever admitted that such a man existed, or if the reporter had been smart enough to figure it out. I was glad to hear that some-body had the guts to cross him.

On the other hand, there was nothing I could do to el Señor myself. He was too strong for me to mess with. And I'd never had anything to do with the Bambino. Ginny'd finished complaining about the heat. Now she was talking to her answering service. I looked to see what else was in the paper.

Near the back of the city section, an item caught my eye. I don't know why—I could just as easily have missed it. But when I started reading it, it didn't have any trouble holding my attention.

Ginny went on using the phone. Part of my mind heard her explain we didn't do that kind of work, but I wasn't really listening. I was concentrating on this news item about Pablo Santiago.

He wasn't anybody special—not like Roscoe Chavez. Just a ten-year-old kid I happened to know. Ginny and I worked for his family a couple of years ago on a protection-racket case. The Santiagos ran a grungy little *tiendita* down in the old part of town—one of those places where toothless grandmothers bought beans and tortillas at prices that were actually reasonable, and kids stocked up on Coke and lic-orice—until some of the local *muchachos* decided to finance their hobbies by extorting "insurance" from small busi-nesses. Since the *muchachos* were freelance, the Santiagos could have turned to el Señor for help. But then they would've ended up paying *him* protection money. That they didn't want, partly because they were honest, and partly be-cause they valued their independence. So they hired Fistou-lari Investigations.

Which was how I met Pablo Santiago.

According to the paper, he'd been missing since Saturday night.

I opened my mouth to say something to Ginny, but she was already in the middle of another phone call. I don't know what hit me hardest, the fact that a kid I knew was missing—another kid! Or that a Chicano kid who'd been gone for less than forty-eight hours was suddenly considered news—which wasn't exactly normal behavior for the *Herald*. Or the sheer coincidence of it.

The combination felt like a gutful of rubbing alcohol. The last time I saw Pablo, he was running numbers. He was one of the errand boys who collected people's bets and distributed winnings.

I didn't bother telling myself that it wasn't any of my business. I have a thing about kids in trouble. And I didn't have to guess very hard to figure out why somebody as insignificant—or at least Chicano—as Pablo made the news. Because the cops were looking for him and wanted help. Because of Roscoe Chavez. On top of that, the Santiagos were good people. They deserved better than they were going to get.

I dropped the papers back on the sofa, hauled myself to my feet, and started for the door.

Before I got there, Ginny hung up the phone and demanded, "Where do you think you're going?"

"Grocery shopping," I muttered. Reflexive counter-punch. I didn't like her tone. When I looked at her, I saw that her resentment had moved right up to the front of her face. Not very nicely, I added, "I'm getting tired of sitting on my hands."

A masterstroke of tact. She loved it when I reminded her about her hand. But this time something more complicated was going on. She resented me for the same reason that she didn't snap back. Almost politely, she said, "That can wait. This is more important."

Always fast on my feet. I stared at her and wondered how she knew about Pablo.

But she didn't know about Pablo. "There's a man up in the Heights," she said. "A Mr. Haskell. I just talked to him. He wants to hire us. We need to go see him."

If she hadn't been Ginny Fistoulari—and if I hadn't understood why she resented me—I would've said, *Tell him to stuff it*. But she was, and I did, so I didn't. Instead I stood there and waited for her to finish.

Her eyes wandered away while she tried to get a handle on something that looked suspiciously like panic. "He says he needs protection. He says somebody's trying to kill him."

Well, at least we were talking to each other.